And Then They Were Doomed

Also available by Elizabeth Kane Buzzelli

LITTLE LIBRARY MYSTERIES

In Want of a Knife

She Stopped for Death

A Most Curious Murder

And Then They Were Doomed

A Little Library Mystery

Elizabeth Kane Buzzelli

CROOKED
LANE

NEW YORK

Copyright © 2019 by Elizabeth Kane Buzzelli

Published in the United States by Crooked Lane Books, an imprint of The Quick Brown Fox & Company LLC.

Crooked Lane Books and its logo are trademarks of The Quick Brown Fox & Company LLC.

Library of Congress Catalog-in-Publication data available upon request.

ISBN (hardcover): 978-1-64385-000-9
ISBN (ePub): 978-1-64385-001-6
ISBN (ePDF): 978-1-64385-002-3

Cover illustration by Irina Garmashova-Cawton
Cover design by Lori Palmer
Book design by Jennifer Canzone

Printed in the United States.

www.crookedlanebooks.com

Crooked Lane Books
34 West 27th St., 10th Floor
New York, NY 10001

First Edition: August 2019

10 9 8 7 6 5 4 3 2 1

For Joshua Mullin, who always steps in and puts me on the right path.

For the crew at Arby's in Kalkaska: Tera, Gina, Casandra, Sam (well, not really), Scott, and everybody else. They let me work there for hours on end and give me nothing but smiles.

For Jessica Faust, Jenny Chen, and Jen Donovan for their kindness and caring during a difficult time in my life.

And, as always, for Tony.

A mother's love for her child is like nothing else in the world. It knows no law, no pity. It dares all things and crushes down remorselessly all that stands in its path.

—Agatha Christie, *The Last Séance*

Prologue

It was November, the month of death on the Great Lakes. Men and women, wrapped in heavy wool coats and jackets, huddled near the edge of a decaying pier jutting out above the river that curved north in wild, tumbling splashes toward Lake Superior.

The people bowed into the cold wind, heads down, each reaching out a shaking hand as a woman passed among them with blue-capped vials. She whispered, "Bless you" as each took a vial of ashes and slipped it into a pocket to save.

A man standing under the pier, just out of the reach of the turbulent water, waited for the word that she'd finished handing out the vials, and when it came he waded up to his knees into the river, waves breaking around him, each new wave trying harder to knock him over. His clothes were soaked, his hands and face turned raw with cold as he hung on to the wreath of white roses he carried, holding it high, keeping it above his head until she was ready.

When the woman joined him in the water they held the wreath together. The people above watched but made no sound. No hymns were sung as the couple lifted the wreath as high as they could reach, then let it go to sail straight out until the wind caught it and it started to fall, then caught another current of air and sailed off, at first above the waves, and then down into the river, where it became a bobbing circle, slowly caught on the crest of a wave flinging itself out to where the river turned.

"It won't be long now," the man called up to the others above the roar of the water.

"An eye for an eye," the woman said to her husband.

Part 1

The Invitation

Chapter 1

Zoe Zola knew somebody was dead.

Somebody was always dead when one of these black-edged envelopes arrived.

But not in such a long time.

None since that last one killed Evelyn Zola, and Zoe moved north, to Bear Falls, up near the top of Michigan's mitten, where she thought she was safe.

* * *

"Sorry, Miz Zola," Mr. Cavendish, Bear Falls' bent-over mailman, said when he placed the ominous envelope into her tiny hands. "Hate to do this to you. Found it in the bottom of my bag. Must've missed it yesterday."

Zoe smiled a weak smile up at the tall man, then looked at the black-edged envelope she held and worried about touching evil. Real evil. The kind that came in silently—left in the mailbox back when she lived with her mother in Detroit. The kind that was hidden in the bottom drawer of her mother's dresser, until that last envelope left Evelyn bent and sobbing, weakening fast until she was dead.

"Nobody likes to get things like that," Mr. Cavendish mumbled and tipped his official hat.

Mr. Cavendish had been a postman in Bear Falls for a long time, long before this little person, Zoe Zola, moved to town. He'd delivered things like this envelope a few times to others. Not much anymore, but enough to make him dread the deliveries that brought no happiness to people he liked—especially people like little Miss Zola, a favorite of his, whom he tried not to make unhappy and, but for this letter, usually didn't.

Whoever was dead must have meant a lot to poor Miz Zola. Her face went blank white when she looked down at the thing in her hand. Kind of knocked her off her feet. She'd turned away to take a deep breath while that crusty little dog of hers, which he didn't trust completely, stood back, and eyed him.

* * *

Zoe shut the door after Mr. Cavendish hunched his bag over his shoulder and walked back down her curved walk through the little gardens of June blooms and gatherings of fairy statues.

The envelope still lay in Zoe's hands, square and bulky but made of fine, white cotton paper. Her name and address were written in black ink, done in calligraphy with fancy, twisted curlicues, perfect spacing between the letters, all of them the same height. Someone had taken time over this. Someone had a very personal reason for perfection. Only an address in Calumet, Michigan, on the back. No name. It was the same as all the others sent over the years. Like poisoned darts they'd arrived one by one until that last, when Evelyn muttered, "My mother's gone," and bent her tired head over the envelope and cried until she was gone too.

Zoe took the letter to her kitchen and set it on the oak table, leaning it against the vase of flowers she'd set at the very center. They were poison flag from her garden, from the flower bed where her favorite fairy, Liliana, stood watch. Purple poison flag set among white forget-me-nots—the favorite flower of her mother, Evelyn Zola.

She stared at the envelope from where she sat—a chair she had to climb up the rungs to sit on so she could lean on her elbows, then rest her head in her hands, and keep watch so the envelope didn't move or change.

Fida sat at attention beside her on the floor. Fida, Zoe's one-eyed, feminist dog (she liked women more than she liked men) always pretended to be looking elsewhere when there was trouble, but would roll her eye toward Zoe, ready to shoulder her share of the burden—or at least that's what Zoe liked to think.

There was black ink—like all of the letters. There were curlicues at the ends of the *Z*'s, plump *E*'s in Elderberry Street, a bloated *B* in Bear Falls, a mountainous *M* in Michigan. The return address was simply a box number in Calumet, Michigan.

Sitting uncomfortably, with stinky Fida, who needed a bath, in her lap, she let a thought drift a minute, ignoring the black trim.

A wedding invitation. Someone wanting her to be happy for them. It could have meant a gathering of Bear Falls neighbors, an afternoon or evening of celebration. A loud DJ. They would talk for weeks before about what they would wear. Jenny would grouse about having to wear white, swearing everybody would know she didn't deserve it. Dora would be adamant that her daughter's big day should be perfect. Tony would expect it.

Zoe got madder as she thought how this could have been a happy sign that all was well with her next-door neighbors: Jenny Weston and her mom, Dora.

Jenny could drive anybody crazy. Did not know what she wanted. First to marry Tony, then to stay single. *"I need time. My first marriage was awful."*

Tony didn't know how to give Jenny enough space of her own—that was part of it.

But it was Dora, Jenny's mother, who loved both of them and suffered the most when they broke up—over and over again. Right now, Jenny was in the middle of one of her snits. Tony was pushing marriage.

The damned thing on her table should have been their happy announcement that the war was over: they were getting married.

Instead, it was this 'thing' trimmed in black, a kind of grave with hard, dark edges. And inside would be: Mrs. So and So is dead. Mrs. So and So won't be knocking at your door—ever. Mr. and Mrs. So and So, your loving relatives, want you to know that another loved one is lost to all time. Everybody in the world around them must join in the mourning. *Attention must be paid.*

And with each envelope, Evelyn Zola, who had no right to the name Zola and wasn't wanted by her own family, the Jokelas, was to die a little more of her shame.

* * *

Zoe slid down from her chair to do more important things. She bent to lift Fida under her arm and take her back to the room where they did their literary detective work, searching into writers' lives, into their writing, for who they really were, for what had been hidden. Now they were doing Agatha Christie—she and Fida. A woman well written about but still a figure of mystery.

She nuzzled Fida's head. Muse and guard and nudge and friend—everything Zoe needed wrapped up in dirty white hair that hung into the dog's bright eyes—one of them no help at all in getting around fairy houses in the garden.

Chapter 2

Next door, Dora Weston was going through her mail—ads for hearing aids, which she thankfully didn't need yet—and an electric bill.

She left the mail on the dining room table. Jenny liked to go through it when she got up, though there was rarely anything for her, which made Jenny mad and, lately, took her dark mood deeper. Dora suspected it was fear that her life was changing while she sat it out.

Dressed and ready for the day while Jenny was still asleep, Dora made herself a third cup of tea and sat down to take pleasure in the quiet, before whatever she was feeling was upon them.

It had to be a happy day ahead. Lisa'd called. She was in the Upper Peninsula, working on a documentary about poor women fighting to keep their way of life. She was always excited when Lisa called—this daughter who wanted to change the world one documentary at a time.

* * *

"Finnish women, Mom. They stayed with their families when the copper mines up here closed. They live an old life. They're poor but so proud. Think differently about everything we take for granted. They've got their own standards and beliefs. Some you won't believe. Strict. I mean a way of living the world hasn't seen for years."

"And when will you come home?"

"Soon, Mom. When I'm finished. Or you and Jenny can come up. I'd like you to see what I'm doing. Maybe then you'd understand and—"

"I understand, Lisa. You're just like your father. But I worry. I mean, do you make enough money to take care of yourself?"

"Oh, Mom. I can't worry about that."

"I can, Lisa. I can worry about that a lot."

"Oh, Mom. Money's not the only thing in the world to think about."

"I know, Lisa. Not the only thing. Unless you like to eat and have a roof over your head."

Chapter 3

For the next two hours, Zoe stayed away from the kitchen. She worked on her book, *Inside the Murderous Mind of Agatha Christie*, losing herself to the devious interior of Agatha's head and not her own.

She was at a good place in Agatha's life story, tracing Christie's alter ego: Ariadne Oliver, a character, and a writer in *A Pale Horse*. If Ariadne was truly meant to stand for Agatha, Zoe had to watch her closely. Christie could be devious. She could dart and switch, be in her story, then out of it, on to creating something real and tragic in her own life, like her disappearance on Friday, the third of December, 1926. Her car had run down into a swamp and been left with the lights on and the driver gone, nowhere to be found for many long and frustrating days, a case that became the biggest news in the United Kingdom.

In her books were hints of what had happened, hints of a woman scorned, a woman cruelly betrayed by her husband. Afterward there were claims of amnesia, but Zoe didn't believe it. She smelled revenge. She smelled a woman's retribution for not being loved.

Zoe tried to stay inside her work, but she was tired by lunch, and Fida was whining to go out.

In the kitchen, she put Fida out to pee in one of her favorite fairy gardens—still a matter of dispute between them—and climbed on a chair to stare again at the envelope as if it might announce the message at any minute.

"My turn?" Zoe asked the envelope. She smiled at the inked address, the fancy handwriting.

Shadows moved in her brain where shadows shouldn't be allowed to live so long.

*   *   *

They lived in Detroit, on Beaubien Street, in a tiny house that hadn't seen a paintbrush since Evelyn Zola was abandoned by the man she loved: Alfred Zola, who said he couldn't stand babies and was long gone, leaving Evelyn behind with her too-tiny daughter and no wedding ring. Even so, Evelyn claimed the name, raising her little Zoe as Zoe Zola rather than Zoe Jokela, Evelyn's maiden name, which didn't have a lilt to it, and because the Jokelas didn't want her either.

This one thing—a purloined name because Alfred would never marry her, claiming he not only didn't believe in babies but also didn't believe in the married state—was all she had left of him, and Evelyn treasured it as one good thing she had done for Zoe. Her people, the Jokelas, led by her grandmother, Anas Jokela, found sin wherever they looked and set themselves up to seek it out and destroy all evil—beginning with Evelyn.

One day Alfred had left their Detroit house to go out for a pack of cigarettes and had never come back. Evidently, Alfred also didn't believe in obligations any more than he believed in the 'married state' or babies, as he never sent Evelyn money for his little girl, who would need a doctor's care and a lot of love for the rest of her life.

Evelyn became an expert at getting welfare and a little bit of disability from the hotel where she used to work before she fell down a flight of stairs and broke her right leg in many places.

They stayed inside the house with the shades drawn most days because Evelyn didn't trust the neighbors on Beaubien not to look in their windows.

"Everybody wants to see who we are," Evelyn would lean down and whisper to Zoe. "We don't want them to know things about us, do we, Zoe?"

"We've been here a long time, Mom. Nobody cares."

Evelyn only made a noise and kept the shades firmly pulled to the sill.

* * *

When Zoe went to school, she found books and a teacher, Miss Hunt, who slipped her at least one new book a week. She kept her nose in that book (as Evelyn said) most of every day and ignored the other children, who weren't very nice and grew way above her as the years passed.

In books, Zoe found that people didn't necessarily live the way she and Evelyn lived—hidden away as if it was a terrible shame they were alive at all.

Other people lived in big houses—or little houses—that were clean and in order. Other people had family that came to dinner— or family like Tiny Tim's, who loved him and celebrated with a big turkey on Christmas, which Zoe didn't even understand. Not what Christmas meant, nor all the fuss about giving presents and pretending to be happy.

When Zoe turned sixteen, she realized the life they lived wasn't normal, and she began to clean their four-room house and, in summer, get the grass at the front cut by a boy from down the street in exchange for chocolate chip cookies she bought at the corner store. Trimming the grassy edges on her knees was fun. Summer sunshine made her body feel better, her arms stronger.

She noticed flowers in her neighbor's yards on her walks to the Roy Jones Hardware Store and back. She looked up different flowers in an old encyclopedia and then found racks of flower seeds at the hardware store. Roy Jones pretended not to see her, because her head barely came to counter height. He would call toward the door: *"Somebody there? Think I hear a voice, but I can't see you."*

That was Mr. Jones's joke. He liked it and said it every time she came to the store. But soon he answered her questions: *"Did this flower grow in Michigan? Is that flower tall or short? When can I plant seeds?"*

Mr. Jones was impressed with her love for flowers, unlike that of most of his customers, who only wanted a washer for a faucet or a gallon of paint. He offered her tips, like digging in manure before planting. He told her which fertilizers to give the Peace rose she bought to go dead center in front of the house. Then, because she didn't have enough money for all of those things, and she couldn't have carried them home anyway, he gave her broken bags of composted manure; torn bags of fertilizer; and his son, Malcolm, to carry them for her.

Malcolm was the only boyfriend she'd ever had. They both liked flowers and they both liked talking about the universe and all those stars. But Malcolm went to California to live with his mother and never came back to Detroit.

When the flower bed was finished and growing, filled with white forget-me-nots and zinnias and sunflowers along the back and the peace rose was in bloom, she coaxed her mother out to the porch, to see what Zoe had created.

Only that one time. Evelyn never came out of the house again, despite the forget-me-nots. That day, too, one of the dreaded letters trimmed in black was in their mailbox, and Evelyn grabbed it from Zoe's hands, clutched it to her breast, and began to cry.

For those last few years, when her mother was bedridden most of the time and on a lot of medication, Zoe didn't let her see the black-trimmed envelopes because they weren't only letters about another dead person; they were letters Zoe was sure were meant to kill.

By this time Evelyn was afraid for Zoe to go out the door alone. To go out after dark. To go out in rain or snow or heat. Most of all, afraid of what people would say. They had that much power to hurt her. "Be careful out there, Zoe. Don't look at people; they'll only make you sad, the way they treat you. The way they call you names."

In Evelyn's last year, Zoe threw out the black-trimmed envelopes that arrived, though there were only two that year. She was sure the people who sent them didn't mean her mother and her any good.

Zoe shook her head as Evelyn one day sighed and said she wondered whatever happened to her sister, Susan. "She's the only one I care about. I loved Susan. I think she loved me.

"At least she was always kind to me." Evelyn leaned over the side of her bed, clutching her faded robe, with one hand, at the neck. The thought of Susan made her happy for a little while.

Zoe didn't know if this Aunt Susan was dead or alive and didn't care. Zoe enrolled at Wayne State, studying English literature, and was doing very well by the time the last envelope arrived. Since Zoe was at school that day, Evelyn answered the door to the mailman.

She took the letter and held it close to her heart all day. When Zoe got home, Evelyn cried and told her that her mother, Anas, was dead. The notice came from her sister, Susan.

"But not another word. I'd always thought when Anas died, Susan and I would be friends again. But not a word. Not another word."

She went into her room and rarely came out.

Zoe was eighteen by then. She worked at the hardware store on weekends. She had her schoolwork. She wasn't the same frightened girl she'd been throughout all the other arrivals of black-edged envelopes.

That night she went into Evelyn's room and pulled a chair to the side of the bed. She refused to leave until Evelyn told her about the letters: who those people were and why they wanted to hurt her.

It didn't happen that first time. Zoe sat there talking and talk-ing until Evelyn pretended to be asleep. But pretend sleep didn't stop Zoe from asking. Nor did clenched eyelids. Nor a short hunger strike after that.

Every spare minute she had, Zoe sat in the musty and darkened room and asked over and over, "Who sends those letters, Mama? Why do they make you so sad?"

One day, after the visiting nurse left, shaking her head sadly at Zoe, Evelyn called from her room, "Zoe? Zoe? I have to talk to you."

And Zoe went back into the room, pulled the unpainted wooden chair to her mother's bedside, climbed up, and listened as her mother told her about her years-long shame—that she'd run off with Alfred Zola, but never married him. So, he wasn't really Zoe's father—not legally. And her name wasn't Zola—not legally.

It was Jokela. Which Zoe didn't like at all.

At first, Evelyn told her, she'd gone back home when Zoe was just a baby, because she was abandoned with no place to go. Her mother, Anas, hadn't wanted her to stay, but Susan, with a baby of her own, named Mary, begged to keep Evelyn and Zoe Zola with them. Anas muttered again and again, when they were in the same room, that corruption could be caught, just like other sins.

Anas kept Susan from having anything to do with Evelyn and didn't want the little cousins to grow up together. *Contamination* was the word Evelyn said she remembered.

The rest of the family took a vote and agreed Evelyn's sin had tainted all of them, and now there was her little dwarf. They would have to go. Then came talk in their church, some parishioners even wondering if *any* of the family should be allowed to attend Sunday mornings. And there were people asking in very low voices if Susan's daughter, Mary, might be an outcast too, because of the stain of sin around Evelyn and the little girl with a fuzzy head of blonde curls and big, round, staring blue eyes that made some people uncomfortable.

Evelyn had to leave Cheboygan and return to Detroit. It was an excommunication. They cut her off until all Evelyn ever heard from them were the death notices—letting Evelyn know that one more of the family was gone. One more she would never hear from nor see again because of her loose ways. One more who could never forgive her.

That evening Evelyn pulled a stack of the letters, wrapped in a black cloth, from the bottom drawer of her dresser and told Zoe these were the dead people.

"What they do is awful." Zoe handed the letters back to Evelyn. "Why don't they just leave us alone?"

Evelyn smiled and put her hand out to touch Zoe's cheek. "They missed out on knowing you, didn't they? My mother lost. My father lost. My sister, Susan, lost. Now her daughter, Mary."

"Let 'em burn in hell, Mom."

"One good thing did come from what happened between me and Alfred. His mother, Rosalie Zola, was kind for a while. She wrote us letters at the beginning. That was nice."

Evelyn, exhausted, closed her eyes and fell back against the pillow, the cloth-covered letters next to her.

"Are any of them alive?" Zoe demanded. "Will we keep getting these things?"

"It'll never end. There are cousins and second cousins. People we don't even know might come after us. You have to be careful. You are the last one they have to punish."

"I won't be careful, Mom. I'm not afraid of them."

Evelyn took Zoe's hand and held it. She closed her eyes for the last time.

* * *

After the funeral, with only Zoe and the funeral director there as he read out scripture about the end of days, Zoe came home and took the covered stack of envelopes out of her mother's dresser, along with a box of yellowed photographs of people she didn't know.

From the back of each envelope, she made a list of the addresses and the few names she could decipher, then went to a local print shop and spent a lot of money on the thickest card stock and best white envelopes she could find. There were eighteen cards and eighteen envelopes trimmed in black, printed to alert people that Evelyn Jokela Zola had left this world and was with her Lord and Savior in Heaven, to the eternal unhappiness of all those who loved her.

Zoe brought the box of death notices home and addressed them, one by one.

She did her best at calligraphy. She wrote her name and address on the back and mailed them off. As she stuck them, one by one, through the slot at the post office, she wondered if any of the people would write her back.

She wondered if any of these people ever loved Evelyn.

There wasn't even one answer to her funeral notice.

When Zoe moved from the house on Beaubien Street to a room in a house near Wayne State, she took the box of black-trimmed envelopes with her but threw the box of photographs in the garbage bin.

A few years later an official letter from a Detroit law firm came, announcing that Rosalie Zola, Zoe's unofficial grandmother, was dead, and Zoe was the beneficiary of a house in the small Northern Michigan town of Bear Falls. When she drove up there, not expecting much because the house had been a rental for years—that's what she found: nothing much. A little house with white peeling paint and a weed-filled yard. Inside, the walls hadn't been painted in years, and the kitchen floor was covered with cracked and torn linoleum. There wasn't a stick of furniture left in the place. Even necessary things were gone—window shades and the toilet tissue holder from the bathroom.

The realtor who handled the transfer of the house to her name said he thought a bunch of people came from somewhere and carried off everything that moved, but it was like hearing about ghosts. It was almost funny—that the other side of the family punished her too. They stripped their grandmother's house so Zoe couldn't have anything. Not a single thing—except the walls.

* * *

The day Zoe moved in, a woman from the house next door saw her as she struggled from her car with a load of sheets and towels. The woman waved. A pretty smile and solid body, like a woman who faced her years directly, in jeans and a sweatshirt that read "Garden or Die" on the front. The neighbor walked over to greet Zoe. She'd heard a relative of the last owner was moving into the house and welcomed her to Bear Falls.

Zoe Zola made her first real friend, other than Malcolm, whom she never forgot.

The woman, Dora Weston, had looked down into Zoe's wary face and smiled. She told Zoe she'd lived in Bear Falls since her girls, Lisa and Jenny, were small. She asked if Zoe needed anything and invited her in for a cup of coffee, and they began to talk about the garden Zoe could plant. It wasn't until much later, when they were good friends, that she mentioned the frenzy of wild-looking relatives who'd come to cart off furniture and everything else they could move from Zoe's house. She'd seen one carry a toilet out to an SUV. And—she was sure of it—even the screens from the windows went into the back of one of the cars.

Later that day, when Zoe was alone again, she walked through *her* house of completely empty rooms. In the kitchen there was a black square on the floor where a refrigerator had stood; a greasy

17

black square where there'd been a stove; and bare pipes next to the stove, where a sink had been.

She opened and closed every cupboard, feeling lucky that they'd left the few that were there. She pulled each drawer open. Empty, but dirty. One drawer stuck. When she peered along the side of the drawer, she could see something was blocking it from closing. Inch by inch, she pulled out the paper wedged there. When she looked at the photograph in her hand, Evelyn smiled up at her. A very young Evelyn, in a pretty dress, holding a large round hat in her hands.

On the back was written in blue ink:

"Nobody loved her."

Chapter 4

She sat in her wonderfully redone house into the evening, until the kitchen grew very dark. She watched the envelope until she couldn't think anymore. She finally went to bed.

That night Evelyn Zola sat in a rocker close to Zoe's bed. She sat lightly, as though she might float away.

The rocker was behind Zoe's eyelids.

She didn't want to open her eyes and have Evelyn disappear.

If she could only find a way . . .

Eyes still closed, Zoe felt along the side of her hip, for Fida, who leaned up to lick Zoe's hand and then fall back to sleep. A woman had to take her love where she could get it.

"Mom," she whispered, letting Evelyn know she got the message, and she was feeling now what Evelyn must have felt all those years: despair, something like hatred, fear, and a deep chunk of shame.

Evelyn rocked and looked off into space—or out of a window that wasn't there. It was the absent look women got when there was no place left to go.

Zoe squeezed her eyes tighter. This was grief—yes. But something else.

An invitation from shadowy people. They must know she was a writer. Maybe knew she was writing about Agatha Christie. They knew where she lived. Maybe they'd read her books or followed her career. They had a plan in place. Not to kill. They wouldn't kill so easily. Better to torture.

Some kind of contest then. Her against all of them—all those Jokelas and whatever else they were called. A kind of vendetta handed down—she was the last.

Zoe covered her eyes hard with the heels of her hands then opened them. Evelyn was gone.

Chapter 5

The next morning the backdoor opened and Dora Weston stuck her head in—tri-color blonde hair mussed and stuck through with twigs from cutting lilacs. Dora's appearance made Fida bark, as usual, and growl a couple of times the way she always did, then lick Dora's hand, a ritual Fida had come up with by herself.

"Thought you'd be working hard, not sitting here in your pajamas. Do you know what time it is?" Dora complained, sensing something very wrong in Zoe's house.

She pointed to the metal, moon-shaped clock high up on Zoe's kitchen wall. The clock said nine.

Dora set a film-covered dish that smelled like cinnamon rolls on the counter, then pulled out a chair at the table and sat down, sighing, and shaking her head. She looked at the envelope, propped against the poison flag, but her mind was on other things.

"Got good news. Lisa's in the Upper Peninsula, doing a documentary. Guess there's a group of Finnish people who live up there, away from everything. They decided—sounds like mostly women—to stay after the copper mines closed, kept their life—the way it was in Finland. That's what Lisa said. I'm hoping she'll come stay awhile when she's done. I miss her. My eldest child."

"I'd love to see her too. Lisa's fun."

Dora nodded, then thought hard. "There's something else. I just can't help coming out with it. I'm so unhappy."

Zoe saw her kind face wrinkle. Dora was usually happy. She served as Bear Falls' unofficial librarian, choosing to bring books to her neighbors through the Little Library boxes in front of her house: one for children, one for adults. She said the books made her happy, and so did talking about books with all the new readers in town.

"You can choose to be happy, you know," Zoe said. Dora said the same thing every time Zoe showed the least sign of depression.

But Dora wasn't happy now. "Can't hold it in. I've got to tell somebody. I'm bursting."

Zoe waited.

"A man from Troy Enterprises was with Tony last night. They were talking a deal to sell Little Library boxes on their website—millions of followers. Worldwide! Can you imagine? Tony's excited. He already told Jenny to quit her job at the law firm and work with him."

She pulled in a deep breath. "I think he's hoping they can get married finally. But . . ." She rolled her eyes. "Jenny's saying she's not ready. Though when she will be, God only knows. Now she's mad at me because last night I got tired of listening to all her 'poor me, poor me,' mealy-mouthed business about how she wasn't ready, how she's finally got a job she likes. I told her—came right out and told her—she can't keep pulling poor Tony around in circles. She's got to decide—one way or the other. Marry the poor man—he loves her very much—or set him free.

"Maybe I shouldn't have—" Dora stopped herself.

"Had to get out of there this morning. Hate to face Jenny again. Usually I keep my thoughts to myself."

She glanced at Zoe, her pale eyes red-rimmed. "I don't know what to do or say anymore. She's going to wait too long. I'm afraid for her. She could end up alone for the rest of her—"

"You're describing me, and I'm happy just the way I am." Zoe didn't want to hurt her friend but there were times when words got too loud to keep silent.

Dora shook her head. "But Jenny's not you. Ten years from now she'll be wailing how she should have married Tony. She'll be unhappy all over again, just like she was when she divorced that phony Chicago creep and—"

"He ran away with another woman. That hurt for sure."

Embarrassed, biting at her lower lip, Dora said, "It's just that I'm her mother. I know her better than—"

"Maybe you should back off. Give her some thinking time. Of course, she's gun-shy. A bad divorce can do that."

Dora sighed. "So much all at once. I don't know what to worry about first. Did you hear what's happening to Little Libraries across the country? Just when so many people here in town are donating books and taking books they want to read. One after another, they stop by to tell me how grateful they are to have a library in Bear Falls—no matter what the size."

Zoe shook her head. "No, I haven't heard, but I can't imagine anybody not appreciating—"

"I just read an article in *The Atlantic*. It could ruin everything."

Zoe, unable to bring her brain around from her own trouble and Jenny's trouble, said nothing.

"Guess what the government wants to do?"

Zoe waited.

"They want to shut down Little Libraries. Can you imagine? Leawood City, Kansas. A nine-year-old boy put up a Little Free Library, and two of his neighbors didn't like it. They went to the city council, called it an 'illegal detached structure,' and told the boy he'd be fined if he didn't remove it. Then, Los Angeles; then, Shreveport, Louisiana. They're making criminals of us. People are refusing to take down the library boxes. Fighting back. And I will, too, if anybody tries something here in Bear Falls. Can you imagine? For spreading literacy and neighborliness, they're turning us into criminals!"

"Have you talked to Keith Robbins? He's the city manager, he'll know if anybody's been complaining."

Zoe didn't have her heart in Dora's problem, but Dora was the kind of woman everybody wanted to help, no matter the misery in their own life at the moment—like an unwanted letter.

Zoe got up to brew tea to go with the cinnamon rolls Dora'd brought. Behind her back, while she stood on her stool, putting a kettle of water on the stove, she heard Dora say, "What's this letter, Zoe? Haven't seen one of these in years."

*   *   *

By the time Jenny walked in, they were quietly sipping tea and biting at cinnamon rolls, heads almost touching as they stared at the black-rimmed envelope together.

"What's going on?" Jenny hoped it wasn't more drama. The pot of tea on the counter and the cinnamon rolls looked good. Jenny'd missed breakfast, hoping not to run into her mother first thing in the morning after their argument.

She opened the dishwasher to take out a clean cup. She looked the rolls over, going for the one with the most swirled chocolate and cinnamon, then joined the two women staring at the envelope propped in front of them.

"What's that?" Jenny motioned toward the odd envelope. Nobody answered.

She chewed and drank. If they stayed quiet, all the better.

If Dora brought up last night, she planned to say she was happy for Tony. Money to supplement his police pension. A real business going for him. Everything happening was a good thing.

He was coming over later with papers to sign. She would be a partner. He'd planned it all along.

Jenny didn't look forward to seeing him, for the sadness she was giving him, for the sadness she was feeling. For the misery she was creating—though she couldn't help herself.

She stared at the envelope along with the other two. A daughter should be able to tell her own mother how she felt. She loved that she was making her own money again, not living off her ex-husband, Ronald Korman. She loved having real things to think about and new friends to think about them with.

Tony kept talking about getting married, right down to the flowers in the church. "Fall," he'd say. "Mums, don't you think?"

Then he talked—again and again—about the new company he would put in both their names. He talked about her handling the business end and him handling the design and manufacturing. He kept talking.

Not once did he stop to ask what she wanted.

Jenny bit into her roll, then brushed crumbs from the corners of her mouth.

"You hear Lisa's in the U.P.?" she finally asked Zoe, who nodded. "I'd love to go see her."

No one spoke.

"I've been thinking about maybe going away. Taking some personal days at the law firm."

Neither woman said a word.

She gave up and nodded toward the envelope. "So, what is that thing? Black around the edges. What's that mean?" She reached out and picked up the envelope, turning it back and forth in her hands.

"Looks like a wedding invitation—except for all that black." She turned the envelope again. "Who do you know up in Calumet, Zoe? And how come you didn't open it?"

She raised her eyebrows at Zoe.

"Came yesterday."

"And you haven't opened it? Aren't you curious?"

Zoe shook her head.

"Is this like a death notice? Is that what the black trim means?"

Zoe made a face.

Jenny turned the envelope in her hands again, picked at the sealed flap with one chipped fingernail, then tore the envelope open before Zoe could stop her. She pulled out the card and read it to herself.

Jenny pulled her dark hair away from her eyes, holding it back with one hand as she read the enclosed card again. She frowned across the table at Zoe.

"Want to know what it says?"

Zoe shook her head.

"I do." Dora said.

"It's an invitation."

Zoe made a face. "To what? A funeral?"

"Something about Agatha Christie. Hmm. This place. Netherworld Lodge. It's in the Upper Peninsula. The Northern Michigan Agatha Christie Society." She looked at Zoe, astonished. "They're planning a meeting of Christie experts. Important webinar where you'll all discuss her work. No wonder they want you. You're writing a book on Christie. How does word get out?"

By now she was frowning. "I mean, well, Christie must still be important."

"Let me see that." Zoe snapped the card away from Jenny. "I've done webinars before. I don't mind doing them. People watch you on their devices and get to ask questions. There's a charge, like any seminar, but they don't get to catch you in a corner and demand answers. The audience can be anywhere in the world they can access the internet."

An invitation to take part in an important work of Agatha Christie. *But why the black edging?*

Zoe didn't believe for a minute her envelope was nothing more than this, an invitation to an Agatha Christie event.

When she looked up, her cheeks were burning. "Scam. I don't believe it."

She read the invitation again, then waved it at Dora.

"Listen to this. Two weeks! It's in two weeks! It says a group of American experts. I'd like to know . . ."

She stopped talking to bite at her lower lip and wave the invitation in front of her face over and over.

"Imagine. It's from an Emily Brent." Zoe leaned back, her eyes huge. "You know who Emily Brent is?"

Both women said no.

"She's a character in a Christie book. I should know. I'm reading all of them for the third time. Terrible character. Sanctimonious. Judgmental—led to the death of a poor woman pregnant out of wedlock."

Leaning back in her chair, she held her breath.

"It's aimed at me. Because my mother was—" She stopped herself.

Zoe looked hard at her friends. She told them about the pious relatives who had tortured Evelyn Jokela Zola.

"Whatever 'wedlock' is," Zoe finished while the two women sat quietly, listening to the story of a cruel exile for a young woman and her pint-sized baby.

Chapter 6

Tony was waiting in Dora's kitchen when they got back. He slapped a sheaf of legal papers on the table when they walked in; his rugged face was all smiles. "There," he said. "It's all set. All you have to do is sign."

He grinned up at Jenny as he pushed the papers across the table toward her. She stood with her arms crossed, leaning on the sink for support, her eyes fixed on him.

"We're in this together, Jen. Right? A whole new adventure. Time to get married, I'd say. What do you think? This fall? Like I said, mum time. Right, Dora?"

"Mums smell bad." Dora kept her back turned. "You don't want pots of them, especially indoors."

Tony waited while Dora finished wiping off the counter that had been wiped earlier. He watched her and then turned back to Jenny, who stood with her head down, not saying anything.

Dora gave a long sigh. "Maybe I should leave the two of you alone to talk about this."

She put down the sponge she'd grabbed to have something to do while the tension settled in the room.

"No! We're all in this together." Tony turned from Dora back to Jenny. "Just need the papers signed, and we're in business. I've got new designs. Wait until you see the boxes I drew up. Think you'll be pleased."

He grew quiet, looking hard at the women, who didn't look at him.

Dora left the kitchen.

"You're happy, aren't you, Jen?" He laid one hand on the papers in front of him. "All you have to do is sign these damn things, and we're in business. Remember? You said it was a great idea."

Jenny nodded. "I did. But I didn't know you expected everything to change like this. I mean, so fast."

He shook his head, leaned back, and let out a deep breath. "So, what's wrong? What's going to change?"

"You never asked me. You told me I had to leave my job. A job, by the way, I had to fight to get. I'm making pretty good money. I've been . . . free . . . for the first time."

"Free? You mean free of me?"

She shook her head. "No, not at all. Maybe *'independent'* is a better word."

He rubbed his hands together. "So, this is about your job?"

When he looked at her, his eyes narrowed. There was an old darkness there.

"I just need time to learn to breathe again."

"You've been divorced a couple of years. That guy's out of your life. We're engaged, remember? Usually, that means we get married. Is that off too?"

Jenny rubbed at her forehead. "Nothing's off, Tony. Nothing. I want to help you in your business."

"*Our* business."

"But not right now. I can do your books at night."

"What about the phones? What about meetings? What about dealing with customers? And the wedding? Not right now?"

She didn't answer.

Tony Ralenti got up, taking time to rub at the leg where he'd been shot, back when he was a detective on the Detroit Police Department, back when he thought nothing could be harder than being a cop. Until now.

That was all before he'd found Bear Falls, a quiet small town near the top of Michigan's Lower Peninsula, and he no longer carried a gun. He made things with his scarred hands and took pleasure in new shapes and angles and colors instead of dead bodies and the ugliest parts of human beings.

He wasn't usually a man of many words and didn't find any now.

He gathered the papers from the table and took a long time rolling them into a cylinder. He stuck the cylinder under his arm and went to the door, his limp a little worse than usual.

"Maybe I should wait until you call me, okay?" He turned back from the open door. "I'm going ahead with this."

He pointed to the papers. "And I'll find somebody for the office. Don't worry about that part. I just need to know . . . if you love me or not."

His dark eyes were wet when he glanced up at her, then quickly away. "I need to know that, Jenny."

When he closed the door behind him, Jenny felt empty. She sat down at the table and put her hands to her head, not thinking about what had just happened, only feeling things she couldn't put a name to.

*　*　*

Dora was back when she heard the door shut behind Tony. What she'd like to do was follow him through the door, assure him that her daughter was complicated, that the divorce from Ronald Korman had hurt her a lot, that she was still fragile.

She didn't. A mother had to stay out of such things and keep her mouth shut. This was Jenny's life to fix or mess up.

And people did mess up their lives.

Poor Zoe and what her family did to her and to her mother. Zoe'd gotten smaller as she told the story of those relatives who took pleasure in punishing a woman who didn't deserve punishment of any kind, only maybe a little love.

Death by a thousand cuts.

Better for her to keep her nose out of everybody's business.

If she could.

She hadn't done too well with Zoe.

"Terrible for both of you." Dora had tried to make things better after Zoe's bitter confession.

Jenny had only shaken her head.

Zoe's bottom lip had begun to bleed from where she'd bitten down on it.

She'd looked from Dora to Jenny, round eyes fixed into blue marbles.

A decision had been made right at that moment, but only Zoe knew. She was going to this writer's event at Netherworld Lodge, in the wild Upper Peninsula, outside a city called Calumet, because she knew it wasn't a writer's event at all. It came from Jokela country, where those people lived. She felt it in her soul. The bastards were coming after her. They wanted to put an end, once and for all, to Evelyn's little mistake.

Chapter 7

Jenny said nothing when Dora came back into the kitchen, standing beside her, watching as Jenny slipped her engagement ring from her finger and set it on the counter.

"You can give it to Tony. I think I'm . . . going away. Take a few personal days . . ."

Dora watched her daughter's engagement ring being pushed behind the sugar canister.

"I've got to get back to Zoe's," she said, pretending she hadn't heard Jenny. "I'll bet she's going to that thing. I'm afraid she's making an awful mistake."

Dora busied herself with a platter that belonged on a top shelf and then with a drawer that wasn't completely shut. When she turned to look at her daughter, she opened her mouth. She closed her mouth. This wasn't a time for a mother to say a word—other than maybe put her arms around her child and tell her how sorry she was that things had gotten so bad . . . *because the girl was stubborn and flighty and didn't know what was good for her.*

A mother couldn't say things like that to a daughter, *even one as pig-headed . . . as determined to mess up her life all over again.*

Just like she did with that awful Ronald Korman.

Dora said nothing out loud, just looked at Jenny directly.

*And I told her that time too. Don't marry the man. He condescends
to me every time he walks into my house. "Oh, Mrs. Weston, what a
quaint little place. I have a decorator friend in Chicago who would just
love to see this. And she says cottage style is out."*

*Never liked the man. Knew from the beginning it was going to end
badly, but did she listen? No. And now this. A chance to be happy, and
she dumps him.*

* * *

Jenny knew there was a lot of chattering going on in Dora's head, a
lot of motherly advice not given because it would make Jenny mad.

She frowned hard, willing Dora to keep still.

Dora was the first to look away. "I better go," she said. "You
don't have to come."

She walked to the door, her hand up to stop Jenny. "I won't be
home to make lunch. Guess you'll have to do that for yourself. Guess
you'll have to get used to doing a lot of things for yourself."

She held on to her last sentence, watching Jenny—with her bare
feet up on the chair, though she knew Dora didn't like that. Bare
feet sweaty footprints on her nicely polished chairs.

Dora made a slight noise as she went out the door.

On the back porch she stood still, holding her sides hard with her
elbows. She got madder as she thought of the grandchildren she would
never have—both her girls too wrapped up in themselves to think
about *that*. Lisa, in the U.P. with a group of Finnish women doing a
documentary on their lives. So devoted to her career. Hard to sell her
work to Netflix or Showtime—or straight to TV—"*but don't worry,
Mom.*" Hard to make money—don't worry, Mom. Just like Jim. He
thought life wasn't worth living if he wasn't helping someone.

Jenny, thirty-eight. Lisa, forty. Teetering on the edge of meno-
pause. Well, close enough.

Dora walked through the thick pines between the houses but turned back. The last thing she wanted was to bring Zoe—with troubles of her own—into this latest mess with Jenny. She headed instead down to the street and her car. Then over to Myrtle's Restaurant to see who was there to take her mind off Zoe and Jenny. A dose of a quiet neighbor, or even Minnie Moon, who never kept a single thought too long in her head, would be a blessing right then.

Chapter 8

Demimonde, demiworld, half-world, underbelly, underworld.

Synonyms for netherworld.

Who would have named the place? A bunch of hunters? Really?

Zoe searched the internet for Netherworld Lodge, Calumet, Michigan.

The photo she found was of a long, dark building lost among young pine trees. Across the front was a covered porch, low windows, then a second story, more low windows. Not a cozy or welcoming sight—more utilitarian. Perfect for a tribe of hunters.

Built in the 1930s, by the CCC, it read—Civilian Conservation Corps, organized to make work for people during the Depression.

Probably smelled of mold.

The lodge, the citation went on, was first used as a hunting lodge for the movers and shakers of Calumet. Converted to a denominational fellowship meeting hall in the 1970s. Recently used by local universities and literary groups for meetings, study sessions, and programs.

Not much else. But it looked legitimate, though she was still skeptical of anything calling itself "The Northern Michigan Agatha Christie Society." Especially in the remote Upper Peninsula. She still couldn't get her head around it. How convenient for them: The Northern Michigan Agatha Christie Society. The black trim on the invitation. Was that to add mystery to their event? Or was that what she was supposed to believe?

Zoe closed her computer and picked up her cell. She called the number she'd jotted down for the Netherworld Lodge.

Six rings before a voice answered.

"Netherworld Lodge. Emily Brent speaking."

That the place and the name were real took Zoe's breath away for a minute. She'd almost convinced herself none of it existed.

"Who is this?" The woman was immediately impatient. "Netherworld Lodge. Can I help you? Hello?

"This is Zoe Zola."

A long pause from the other end.

"Oh, Miss Zola. Bless your heart. You're calling about our planned event—the big Christie webinar with all you experts here at the same time. Me and Mary Reid are very excited and hope you're coming. Especially since you are currently writing about our Agatha."

"The invitation was a little out of the blue. I hadn't heard—"

"A kind benefactor gave us the money after the idea was floated. Then we got more money from what's called a crowdfunding site."

"May I have his name? This benefactor?"

Pause. "He wants to remain anonymous. Afraid everyone will come to him with requests."

Another pause. "I hope the remuneration is ample. Five thousand. That's a thousand dollars a day, you know. I've checked with other webinars, and that's—"

"No. No. That's generous."

"And you will be our last speaker. That will be on Thursday morning. What we'd like is for you to sum up our five days together. A kind of wrap-up of the daily topics: the points you've all made, disagreements—if any, new findings. We already have hundreds of subscribers from all over the world. Very successful. Mary Reid was right: Agatha Christie sells."

"Actually, there's nothing in here about what I'm to talk about." Zoe held the invitation in front of her.

"Now, that's not true. I helped send out the invitations. I know for a fact Mary Reid included an information sheet in every one of the letters."

"Not in mine."

"Oh, dear. Well, sorry."

"Who else is coming?"

"A wide array of Christie scholars. All from the United States. Let me see. Professor Leon Armstrong from Ralston College. Dr. Louise Joiner, Amherst College. Anthony Gliese—he's an editor with Conway Books. Dr. Nigel Pileser, Colorado Reserve. Betty Bertram—she's a graduate student from McGill. That's Canada, you know.

"Eh, we have Gewel Sharp, a recent graduate in the master's program at Michigan State. Oh, here's Mary Reid—she's a member. Owns a very fine bookstore in Houghton. Anna Tow. Well, Anna's got a small press. Only published her own book on Agatha so far—oh, and a book of Mary's. Anna's hoping to get something more from this event. Oh, and Professor Aaron Kennedy. Comes from California. That's it. And you, of course."

Zoe scribbled down the names as the woman rambled.

"May I ask about your name, Miss Brent?" She set the notepad aside.

"My name? What about it?"

"Emily Brent. Have you taken the name just for this event?"

"*What?*" The woman sounded angry.

"Emily Brent was a character in one of Christie's books."

"You don't say? Well, isn't that a coincidence. Which book?"

"*And Then There Were None.* A very religious woman responsible for the death of an unmarried, pregnant woman. She didn't approve."

"Oh dear. Well, that's nothing like me. Terrible. Guess I haven't read that one yet."

"Oh, and the black edging."

"What black edging?"

"The invitation was trimmed in black, like a funeral notice."

"Nothing of the kind. I don't know what you're talking about." She sounded incredulous.

"But—"

"I guess we'll be seeing you on that Saturday, then," Emily hurried on. "The others will be thrilled. This is going to be the biggest event we've ever given. God bless you, Miss Zola. Have a safe journey up here. You know it's been raining for over a week now. The roads are wet. Oh, and we have a plank bridge on your way into the lodge. There's water over the planks right now, but not to worry. Very safe. Very safe. And the rain's due to stop any day now."

Zoe had no more questions. Nothing that would tell her anything she didn't know: *a woman in charge named Emily Brent; a woman who hadn't read* And Then There Were None, *one of Christie's most famous books. And a woman who didn't know one of the invitations was trimmed in black.*

"God bless you too, Emily Brent," Zoe whispered to herself. "I'll be seeing you soon."

* * *

She waited until after lunch to call Christopher Morley. He usually didn't get into his office at the publishing house until afternoon.

She asked what he knew about the event in Upper Michigan.

"Not a lot." His voice warmed when he recognized who was calling. "Sounded solid. Good credit for you—could call it a keynoter. Get you more reviews when the new book comes out. Did I do something wrong?"

A good friend. A tall, thin man with long, gray hair that touched his collar. Gentle—for an editor. Understanding—when Zoe called him in a snit because she regretted ever starting this "damn book about the dullest of writers," which she did on almost every one of her books.

He asked if she wanted him to call up there and get more information, but there was no reason to get him trapped in the middle of this very personal thing she was facing.

"Just spoke to Emily Brent. She's the chair, I think. Recognize the name?"

"Of course, I do. Is this some kind of a costume thing?"

"If it is, I wasn't told. There's something odd about the whole thing."

"Don't do it if it doesn't feel right."

"It doesn't feel right, Christopher. It feels so wrong. But I'm going. If I didn't, I'd never know for sure."

"Now, Zoe—"

She put the phone down.

Chapter 9

It didn't take Jenny long to get out of the house after Dora left. She couldn't go to Zoe's. Not if her mom was there. Anyway, taking her problems to Zoe seemed like a form of treachery. Dora and Zoe had been friends since Zoe moved to Bear Falls. One woman didn't take over another woman's friend just because she couldn't think of anywhere else to go.

And after that morning, with Zoe's sad confession, she wasn't sure she had any of the right words to help anybody.

* * *

Traverse City was only twenty miles or so from Bear Falls. There were fine restaurants. There was the State Theatre. She hadn't been to a show in ages—so much of her life taken up with Tony and Mom and even Zoe. She could easily move into Traverse City, find a nice little condo—maybe facing the lake. Could be fun. New friends. No one demanding things she couldn't give.

She thought about Lisa, her older sister, close enough to visit for a change. *"Come on up, Jenny. Bring mom. Or that guy you're going to marry. I'd like you to see what I'm doing and meet the women especially. I'm always talking about you to Janne, my cameraman and man-of-all-things film. Say, he'd be a good guy for you to—oops, you've already got one. Anyway, it's not fancy—how I'm living—but it always feels . . . important."*

Lisa was a possibility. She might go up there—just to get away and think. Nothing but trees and bear and moose and wolves . . . and Lisa.

* * *

In Traverse, Jenny bought a latte and a three-cheese sandwich at The Brew, sitting at the front counter to eat.

As soon as her sandwich came, a man moved to the stool next to hers.

There was a tap on her arm. No way not to look around. He probably wanted the salt passed or a napkin from the holder. She could have groaned but smiled instead.

"You're Jenny Weston." The man was almost good-looking. Maybe the smirk wasn't pleasant. But his face was tanned, though it was only June. He had a set of very bright white teeth, and a big smile. His eyes were the kind of blue that make a woman think of a warm beach—maybe in Barbados, a couple of swaying palms, a big conch shell, and her looking absolutely beautiful in a teeny-tiny bikini.

All of this happened in the minute it took to frown at him, trying to place the face and the body and the smile.

"Matthew Foster. Remember? We were in the same English class in high school."

"Matt!" The word popped out of her—too loud.

He laughed. "That's me. Been awhile."

"Forever!" She settled herself better on the stool, moving around to partially face him. "What are you doing back in T.C.?"

"Designing a building." He smiled a wide smile that could move her in ways she shouldn't be moving.

41

"Are you back to stay?" She had the urge to reach out and brush a stray lock of his black hair from his forehead.

"Morley's hired me to design their new building. I'm drawing up plans. Thought I'd spend the whole afternoon working on it, but now . . ."

He tipped his head closer to hers, still smiling. "Want to take a walk?"

It wasn't Barbados. She still wore a pair of old jeans and a sweatshirt that said "Woman Power," but she walked to Open Space on the lakefront with Matt. The whole of West Bay was next to them as they talked about the people they'd seen from school and how they were doing.

They sat on the seawall and talked some more.

Well, mostly Matthew talked while she listened.

"Yes, I was ready for this divorce," he was saying. "Seems like after a while we both got bored. But you must know the feeling. I heard you're back in Bear Falls. My mom still lives there. Guess you had a bad breakup, eh? My mom said the guy was cheating on you. That right?"

He reached over to take her hand in his. "Happens. Like I said, after a while you just get bored."

"That wasn't it at all," she began to say and inched her hand back to her lap.

"I just got my papers." He stopped as a pair of teenage girls rode by on their bikes. He watched their rear-ends hike one way and then the other; watched for a long time and then brought himself back to her. "So, I'm free, I guess. And looking forward to it. How about you?"

"It's been quite a while now and I—"

"Not remarried, though, I hear."

She shook her head and wiped her hand unconsciously on her jeans.

"You have kids?" she asked, giving him her brightest smile.

He made a face, ran a hand slowly over his hair, and nodded. "Two girls. They're with their mom."

"You mean your wife?"

"Not anymore." He threw his arms out toward the lake and laughed. "I hear you never had any. Kids, I mean."

"Your mom tell you?"

He nodded and laughed. "Mom keeps me up on my old friends, whether I want to know or not. Most of them are . . . you know, kind of dreary. Can you imagine Katy Dunn with five kids? Remember how her dogs were always getting hit by cars? Poor kids."

She looked out at Power Island, down the coast, and thought about a day when she and Lisa had gone there with their father, when he'd had his powerboat. They'd swum off the little island. Her father had worn a patch over his eye, made out of a handkerchief. He was the pirate captain.

A good man, her father. A man who would never be snide about a woman with five children.

"Maybe we could get together." The look he gave her made her skin crawl, gave her the urge to jump from the wall into the lake and swim away from everything and everybody. Maybe as far as Power Island.

"I think we could have a lot of fun, Jenny Weston. You never knew it, but I had this thing for you in high school." His eyes watered slightly. "I've got a suite over at the—"

She coughed and pointed to her throat as she slid off the wall. "Think I'm going to be sick," she choked out and ran as fast as she could back out to Front Street. She turned to make sure he wasn't behind her. He still sat on the wall. Humpty Dumpty came to mind.

She found her car—with a parking ticket because she'd been gone too long. She snapped the ticket off the windshield.

"When life starts handing you a barrel full of shit"—she whispered the words just under her breath—"better get out of the outhouse."

* * *

Her cell kept ringing on the way back to Bear Falls. Twice it was Tony. Three times it was Dora. She didn't answer either of them. There was nothing to say. She'd just had a glimpse of what her life could be like and it scared her all over again. Losing Tony was the other end of this mess she'd made for herself. But marrying him wasn't fair to anybody. She didn't want to become the kind of person she'd already divorced. And not a lonely old lady with ten cats either.

* * *

Jenny turned down Elderberry Street and pulled up Zoe's drive, stepping out among the flower beds of peonies and budding roses, with foot-high fairies watching from beneath some of the bushes.

Zoe lived in her own world, like Lisa did. She lived in a world of books—where she made up her own truth.

Lisa lived in a world of indignation.

Both of them busy in their lives. If she went up there, to Lisa, maybe Zoe would go too, and the two of them would leave her alone to walk in the woods and think and straighten out a life she couldn't seem to untangle.

Maybe, with enough time, Dora would forgive her.

Maybe, with enough time, she'd learn to make good choices.

Part 2

Saturday in Netherworld

Chapter 10

"What did Dora say?" Zoe asked from her side of Jenny's car, looking at the morning dark, the black trees beside the road, and the rain on the windshield falling faster than the wipers could clear.

"Not much."

"What about Tony?"

Jenny shook her head. "I didn't talk to him. The ring is still on the counter. Dora can give it to him."

Zoe shivered. "A ghost from a life that never was—"

"Stop it!" Jenny ordered. "I don't want to hear about this for four hundred miles."

"Me either. So, what should we talk about for four hundred miles?"

"Let's talk about you. This Emily Brent knows you're coming, right?"

"She told God to bless me." Zoe made a noise in her throat.

"What's wrong with that? She could have wished you worse things."

"'God bless you.' Just what that awful character in Agatha's novel would have said. She told me she was happy I'd decided to come to Netherworld. I just bet she is—whatever they've got planned for me. Maybe the whole lousy family will wipe me off their crap list. Maybe it will be something like the Salem witch trials."

"You checked out the academics. They're legit?"

Zoe nodded. "I think they're all involved with Christie somehow. They teach where it says they do and have published work on her novels."

"So? I don't get what you're worried about. All sounds okay to me. Who are these people?"

"Which people?"

"You know, the people taking part."

"Anthony Gliese? I didn't bother. Too many editors. Too many publishing houses."

"Think you should've."

"Betty Bertram—nothing on her. A graduate of McGill. And somebody called Gewel Sharp. Michigan State University. Let's see. Oh, Mary Reid, owner of the Ulysses Bookstore in Houghton. I didn't call, though. And Anna Tow. Looks like Tollance Press is a two-book press, so I don't know about her.

"Then there is Louise Trainer. Professor. Teaches at Amherst. Looks solid."

She thought a while. "Aaron Kennedy from USC. A Nigel Pileser. Leon Armstrong. There are exactly ten of us."

She sat quietly for a while.

"It isn't these people I'm worried about. It's that black trim thing that started it. Nobody else knows what the Jokelas did to my mother. Nobody. The first time I told anybody anything about that life was when I told you and Dora."

"And that's all you've got?"

"What do you mean?"

"One thing—a black-trimmed envelope. Maybe somebody with that Christie group, at the last minute, thought it might be mysterious to add the black."

"And not mention it to the woman in charge? You really think that's the way these literary things go? Everybody winging it?"

Jenny shrugged, then stomped hard on the brake as a deer leaped across in front of them.

After a while, when she could take a deep breath again, Zoe said, "You know I'm the 'stain' on that family. My mom warned me they might turn on me next. Her whole life—without knowing it was coming—then they'd rub it in: another family member who should have loved us, dead. No forgiveness for our sins. My mother lived with a man without marriage. She had a baby. God smote her with a dwarf. I think they'll come after me. I don't know when, but I sure as hell think it might start with a letter trimmed in black."

Overhead, in front of them, lightning flashed across the sky, showing the deep woods on either side of the road. The rain fell as if a faucet opened overhead. Jenny could hardly see to drive. She slowed and put the wipers on as fast as they could go. For a while, she crept along under forty; then, when she could see again, she pulled over to wait out the rain.

They sat there, not a word between them, until the rain slowed and Jenny dared to get back on the road, slower this time, watching for places covered with deep water.

For the next fifty miles, the rain was slow and steady. There were few cars to worry about, but somehow that sudden downpour had quieted them both, as if they'd been shown a sign.

It was miles more before Zoe, as if she'd been thinking all the time, said, "What about Emily Brent?"

It took Jenny a couple of seconds to connect what Zoe was saying with what they'd been talking about so many miles back. "So what?"

"Convenient having a woman in charge who has an Agatha Christie name like Emily Brent. And—think about this—the novel she is in: *And Then There Were None*. Have you read it?"

"I suppose so."

"It takes place on an island. A group of people are invited to a party—for all sorts of believable reasons. Sound familiar? Only, once they all get there, people begin to die, one by one, until no one is left but the murderer, and then the reason for the murders comes out."

Jenny ran a hand up one arm. "Wow. Weird. I see what you mean. Like, there's something else going on."

"The Jokela family is all I can think of. People completely crazy enough to pull a stunt like this."

"You should've told them to go straight to hell and take their webinar with them. Now you're driving all this way to the middle of nowhere. You probably won't get any publicity out of it."

"I will if I'm dead."

"You know what I mean. There's nothing for your upcoming book. You'll spend all of your time hunting for murderers who don't exist. All because of a letter trimmed in black. That's probably what this whole thing is about—to screw with your head. We can still turn around, you know."

The look Zoe gave Jenny was long. "What about you? Five days with Lisa. You two fight like caged squirrels."

"We're not alike, but we get along—really. She's just not practical—all these docs of hers."

"She's won awards."

Jenny shrugged. "Her work's important to her. She'll understand me. She's forty—well almost—and doesn't worry about getting married."

"You shouldn't either! Just be honest about it."

Jenny said nothing. "Yeah, honesty. That's something we both have trouble with, isn't it?"

Chapter 11

It was hours later, after the sky had lightened as they crossed the Mackinaw Bridge, and then more hours later, as they drove the metal bridge over Portage Lake between Houghton and Hancock, that the dirty sky opened again.

This time Jenny ignored the rain. It was. Nothing to do but ignore it and drive straight north, dead center up the wild Keweenaw Peninsula, on a two-lane road, through old villages of mostly abandoned houses and businesses. And then bright banners and "Open" signs where somebody tried yet again.

With her head resting back against the seat, Zoe watch the wipers for a while, then closed her eyes to imagine Evelyn and herself living up here. She couldn't. And having family here? A family that would do the things to Evelyn that they did? Anas, a mother so vindictive she punished her own daughter, and a granddaughter, eternally. For what? A past based on not a mistake, but love.

She wondered when it was ever okay to chase a daughter away, and then when women began punishing each other for sex, and not the men. And then when women turned on one another, greater punishers, vying with each other to see who could be the cruelest.

Evelyn had once lived in Cheboygan—tip of the mitt—in her childhood, and then when she tried to go back with Zoe. No one

51

had welcomed her. She had been driven away. Though Zoe didn't remember being there exactly, she remembered a little girl. They had played together. It seemed Zoe remembered something like happiness connected to the child.

Would something in her recognize that woman if she saw her again? Zoe wondered. *Would some blood thing answer gene to gene?*

*   *   *

After a while, the rain isolated them from each other. Jenny tried not to think too much. She was still unhappy about the mess she'd left behind her. Some of her own making, but that couldn't be helped. She needed time to think without someone telling her what to think. She needed space to feel in a way she hadn't felt in months. Maybe the person she needed was really Lisa.

Lisa, with her eyes wide open but seeing only what she wanted to see. Lisa—excited that the amazing Zoe Zola was coming with her to an Agatha Christie event at a place called Netherworld Lodge.

Jenny called her but got no answer. A few miles farther along the road, her phone rang. Lisa, out of breath. "I had to run into Copper Harbor to call you. Not much service in the woods."

And then she leaped on. "Zoe's going to Netherworld Lodge? I've heard of the place. History and nature. A wonderful opportunity. Wonderful!

"And Jenny, you'll get to meet my amazing women. Women making their way up here all these years. Very few men. A lot of babies—which I don't quite understand. 'As good here as anywhere,' they keep telling me. A different breed of woman. Oh, just think, and I'll get to see Zoe Zola."

"She might be busy with this event."

"If she can't come here, I'll go there. What the heck—on Sunday Janne's taking the day off for a concert in Marquette. He won't be here. The cinematographer isn't coming for weeks. No editors. Nobody but me. My favorite time on every one of my films. Tell her, okay? See if that works. What a genius! And you too."

"Not a genius."

"Well, almost. Can't wait to see you, Sis. Wish Mom could have come up, but I'll be down before winter."

When Lisa stopped for breath, Jenny got muddled directions to where her trailer was parked back in the woods, where she and Janne were getting establishing shots, learning the terrain, and getting to know the women and their stories. All of it told in Lisa's breathless way of talking.

Jenny was certain Lisa followed roads inside her head as she described the trip through the woods, being precise with some things and wildly off with others.

"A left into the woods before Copper Harbor, then about twenty miles. Hmmm, a right down a narrow road with a green arrow at the end or near the end, another right—about eight miles, and then a long drive on a dirt driveway with the name 'Martine' on the sign. Really wild. You'll probably see bears, but don't stop—they don't like people much. Keep going until you see two small trailers under a tall stand of maple trees."

Zoe woke as Jenny talked: "Lisa's off tomorrow. She wants to see you,"

Zoe yawned. "First day there. There might be events."

"Then we won't come. Call us."

"What time?"

"How should I know?"

"I want to see Lisa. I'll work it out."

* * *

They drove through town after town of old mine houses and small businesses trying to make a go of it, most not surviving—badly weathered signs and weeds, the opposite of a welcome.

"I hope you're going to be okay up here," Jenny said after a while. "Can't imagine a more remote place to hold an academic event. After all, your Agatha's an English writer."

"Supposed to be experts, the lot of us," Zoe said. "We won't agree on anything. Every one of us will be there to be crowned the ultimate Christie critic. The webinar will be wrecked. People will get into fistfights. Everyone will be embarrassed—worldwide." She laughed. "Actually, I'm kind of looking forward to all the mumbling and disagreeing—if that's what this turns into. Five days of wrangling and flipping pages of articles under each other's nose. Or we'll agree on everything and be bored to death. Maybe we'll have a splendid time together in Michigan's great North Woods, where we'll be chased by moose and go home with tall tales of harrowing exploits."

Her face said how possible she thought that was.

"I hope they're not all like your Emily Brent. Harridans."

"*Harridans.*" Zoe leaned against the seat and sighed. "*Harridans.* Actually, the word comes down to Hairy Dan, doesn't it? Not right in this situation. Don't you wonder who thought it up? That word? What does it really mean—at its heart? Which language? Can't you just see it? Two arguing women, say in the Middle Ages, going at it over . . . oh, say, a fish."

"Then the word would be *fishwife.*"

"But, instead, they're fighting over a very hairy Daniel, who is the enemy of the barber in town."

"Stop it! I'm serious. I'm not sure I should drop you off at that place where you've never been, to be with people you don't know. I'm really, really serious, Zoe. You have to call me if you catch even a tiny whiff of trouble."

"Might turn out to be fun."

Jenny looked around at her. "You really mean that?"

Zoe made a face. "No. Somebody wants me up here. Somebody knows about me and Evelyn. Somebody's out to settle an old score. Maybe not everybody up here will know about it, but I will."

She looked out, through the rain, at a sign welcoming them to Calumet.

Chapter 12

The outer edge of the town was a half-circle of fast-food places, grocery stores, and tourist stops, seen through a film of rain. Beyond—from what Zoe could see when they stopped at a Burger King on US 41 for lunch—were tall red spires and the tops of blood-red cathedrals. Red Square was all she could think of.

"You know where Netherworld Lodge is?" Zoe asked the girl behind the counter as they ordered burgers. The girl frowned and chewed on a fingernail as she thought.

"Why?" the girl asked.

"Because we're going there?"

"What for? Old place. You won't like it."

"But do you know how to get there? Is it far?

The girl shrugged and narrowed her eyes at Zoe. "Never been. Swanky place for a while. Not my kind of thing."

Zoe gave up.

"How long's it been raining like this?" Jenny asked.

"Seems like a week. We were just saying we feel moldy." The girl smiled, took her finger out of her mouth, and changed her look to friendly. She turned to two people cooking in the back and asked for directions to Netherworld Lodge, which ended with an argument about which roads would get them there, and then a kid came out of the bathroom and told them to use their GPS.

"Only way of getting there that I know of. Way back in the woods. Better watch yerselves." The skinny kid warned.

After lunch, with the warning in mind, they drove into the city, passed red-brick abandoned mine buildings and empty, decaying warehouses, all on little side roads going toward nothing. There were few people on the sidewalks. A few bent under large black umbrellas.

There were businesses along the streets; almost no 'Open' signs.

"Like a movie set." Jenny shivered as she turned a corner. Zoe hunched down into herself. "I mean, not real, is it? More like an archeological dig."

*   *   *

On Sixth Street, Zoe pointed to a theater building she'd read about online, more imposing than she could have imagined, huge palladium windows on the second floor, portholes on the first. A large portico covered the entrance. Squinting through the car windows, they could see the theater was still operating. There were what looked like recent playbills pasted in the door windows.

"That's encouraging." Jenny nodded toward the theater. "People around somewhere. It's just the rain, I'll bet."

Jenny's GPS said thirty miles to Netherworld Lodge Road—out Veterans Highway and then twenty more miles to go. Every road they passed was gravel or dirt, or a puddle-dotted two-track leading off into the bush.

From time to time, they caught glimpses of Lake Superior through the heavy mist, and then the wide blue water would disappear, and there was nothing but dark trees, getting darker against the muddy sky.

Jenny missed the first turn—all the roads looked alike by now. Nothing seemed important enough to be a turn. She had to go back—slowly—to a dirt road that didn't have a sign. She turned in, though water ran over the road—from ditch to ditch—in places.

The GPS said they had eight miles to go.

Chapter 13

Very few houses. A rundown horse ranch and then no houses at all. A dark, reed-filled swamp ran along the left side of the road shaded over by tall Jack pines. Spruce grew thick and lacy where the land curved up into the sandy hills. This was no manicured forest. Nothing parklike about it.

Netherworld Lodge was in there somewhere.

Zoe watched through the rain, beginning to realize what they'd come to. And what she'd taken on.

Jenny stopped at every opening in the woods to look for a sign. The GPS took them in a straight line while the road they were on turned and twisted.

They came on Crest Lake Road, a narrow dirt road leading into deeper woods. Another hard ride. Many overflowing puddles, and Jenny swearing that her car would never make it.

"How far do you think it is yet?" Jenny slowed, sliding through puddles.

"I don't know."

"Who would have a conference this far from civilization? I mean, people do have to get there."

More miles than there should have been. A single wild lake where geese flew up and over the car. Then a larger lake and a sign they almost missed, hanging crookedly on a wire and post fence: "Netherworld Lodge. Guests Only."

Jenny turned slowly up the muddy two-track. Around curves and turns through ancient trees, leading to a place where tire tracks disappeared, and water washed across a low-lying wooden plank bridge leading over a bloated creek.

Jenny stopped abruptly and got out to see how deep the water was, before she dared to drive through.

"What do you think?" she asked when Zoe stood beside her. "Maybe you should call."

Zoe looked hard at the swollen creek. She shook her head.

"Then give me the number and I'll call her."

"No bars." Zoe held her phone in the air. "I remember she said something about a low bridge. Something about rain. Water over the planks, but not to worry about it. 'Very safe,' she said."

"That's very safe?" Jenny pointed to where water rippled slowly across the planks, their shapes distorted by the water. "She's nuts."

"Let me walk it, see how deep it is."

"A six-inch wave will wash you away. I say we wait right here until someone comes along."

"Could be hours. I'm not waiting. I'm here now."

Zoe sat on the ground, feet in the air in front of her, and pulled off her sneakers. She rolled up her slacks, and before Jenny could stop her, she was in the water, walking carefully, slacks pulled to her knees. The water came to just above her ankles.

"See?" she said over her bent shoulder as she made her way to the other side of the creek then turned around. "It's not deep. It's solid underneath."

She came back across the sunken bridge, carefully making her way to Jenny.

"Things that start bad . . ." Zoe looked up to begin the quote. She was almost giddy now that they were here. And not to be stopped from making it to this mysterious lodge.

"Only get worse," Jenny said, finishing Zoe's quote as she edged into the water.

So close now. Zoe was happy she hadn't been afraid to come. She was learning things about herself.

They were back in the car, soon making small waves through the water and back on the trail, going uphill and around more curves until the road stopped abruptly. Just as Jenny'd begun to think there was no lodge this far back in the woods, on this ever-narrowing dirt road, a dark building, only a shadow of a building, appeared there, at the end of the road.

Chapter 14

The logs were painted a dark green, making the building a mossy thing that went on and on, getting lost at the far end in a stand of shaggy pines.

There was the covered porch Zoe'd seen in the photo, logs sinking into the earth like a building that had been there forever.

All of it was dark; no sun got through the trees. There was no grassy area, no flowers—nothing looked cared for. Just sand and spindly trees and another drizzle to greet them.

Zoe caught her breath. A camp. Maybe once a summer camp. But if her family came here, it wasn't with her. She was the hidden dwarf. The little person who shamed them. And doubly shamed by the dwarf's mother: pregnant out of wedlock. The man hadn't wanted her, nor the odd baby. Like something medieval followed them. Zoe felt Evelyn close by. Maybe that was why she'd come to her in the night. Maybe why the rocking chair. A sense of calm before what might be a terrible storm ahead.

She sat straight and stiff as Jenny pulled into an area of gravel with an arrow designating parking. She turned off the car and turned to Zoe.

"Well," Jenny said. "Here you are. I'll just drop you and get going. I . . ."

A tear ran down Zoe's flushed and angry face.

"You will not leave me." Zoe was serious. She looked at the building from the corners of her eyes. "You're coming in or I don't get out of the car."

"You wanted to come. Here you are. You want to know what's going on—if all of this is really about Agatha Christie, or it's your family coming after you. And I'm late. Lisa's waiting."

"I don't know who's in that place." She gestured toward the building. "They'll know me right away. I stand out wherever I go. If you leave, I'll be trapped."

"I don't think that's what this is about. Trapping you."

"Then what?"

"I think it's about Agatha Christie and a chance for you to puff up your ego."

"Take a look around you. Does this look like a place for academic events? Does it look like the halls of learning?"

Jenny shrugged. "They can be strange people, academics. I don't think they care where they are. As long as they get to talk endlessly on a favorite subject."

"Wouldn't that be nice if that's all I had to worry about—people bickering over Agatha Christie?" Zoe shook her head. "Instead, I have to wonder who is related to me and who had something to do with my mother's exile. And wonder why they're after me now. And if . . ."

She stared out the front window. The 'ifs' overtook her.

"Okay." Jenny wriggled behind the wheel. "Then forget this. Come with me to where Lisa's staying. I guess her place is small, but we'll find you a room. Maybe with one of her Finnish women."

"They would know I ran—this whole group." She motioned toward the lodge. "They'd think they won. This little person must be afraid of them. Putting my tail between my legs and heading for cover. Like hell!"

"Or maybe you go in there and keep smiling until you figure out what's going on. Honestly, Zoe. What do you care about any of them? If they are your family and after you for some perverted religious reason, why would you give those monstrous women the time of day?"

Zoe sighed. "Maybe I'm Evelyn. I'm the part of my mom that should have been strong but wasn't allowed to be. Maybe I'm what she could have been—at last. I'm not going to betray that. I'm not going to betray my mother."

Jenny sighed and opened the door. "Okay, I'll go in with you. If you don't like what you see or hear. Or feel. We'll leave."

Zoe looked around the parking area as she popped her umbrella up and slid out of the car. "Still nobody else here. What if it's canceled, this whole thing, and they couldn't get a hold of me?"

Jenny shrugged as she pushed her door open, into a dirty mist. She grabbed Zoe's suitcase from the back and handed Zoe a large brown paper bag and her computer to carry.

"Guess you'll find out."

They hurried up a path thick with the medicinal smell of wet pine. Jenny whispered over her shoulder. "You're here 'til Thursday. Better be alive when I come back."

Zoe hooted at her. "Sometimes you are a miserable person, Jenny Weston. Just a miserable person."

When they put their feet on the canted, unpainted steps, the heavy front door opened. A woman waited, half shadowed, beyond the rusted screen. She wore a flowered dress with a narrow black belt that gave her the look of being cinched tight in the middle. It was the look of someone from a long time ago.

The woman said nothing. She continued to stand behind the closed screen door and watch as Jenny and Zoe walked across the wooden porch toward her.

"Wipe your feet." The voice was nasal. Commanding. Less than welcoming as she held the door open for them. "All this rain and mud going to be tramped in hour after hour. I warned Bella we were gonna have a mess on our hands. Warned her. Try so hard, but this place is old, hard to keep up."

"You must be Emily Brent." Zoe's voice mimicked the woman's, with a quarrel buried behind every word.

Emily Brent stood back as they entered a large reception room lit with soft light from lamps on many end tables. There were over-stuffed chairs gathered in front of a low, burning fireplace and sofas and more chairs set in conversation groupings around the room. On all the walls, floor to ceiling, were bookshelves. The room was paneled in oak, each panel reflecting the lighted lamps and ceiling chandelier. Colorful Indian rugs covered the floor. An unexpectedly warm room despite the many stuffed deer and bear and moose heads on the walls.

Jenny set Zoe's suitcase down.

"I take it you're not Zoe Zola." The woman raised her eyebrows as she glanced at Jenny. "I was told to expect a very short person."

Jenny steeled herself for sparks to fly between these two soon. The woman couldn't seem to keep herself from being rude.

"This is Zoe Zola, the Agatha Christie expert." Jenny felt obliged to point Zoe's way, as if there were a choice of others in the room.

The screen door slammed behind Emily Brent. Her mouth opened and closed a few times as she looked Zoe over from head to toe, her eyes suspicious.

"You're a little one, aren't you? Pretty, though. I guess you'll fit in well enough with the others. Academics are always kind of weird. Some here already. Some coming later. All to celebrate Christie with this fine webinar. Lots of excitement. Too bad about the rain. Not going to stop. That's what we hear. Pity. We'll just ignore it and have an illuminating time." She grinned at Jenny and ignored Zoe as she came farther into the room. Standing with her hands folded across her stomach, getting a good look at her guests.

"Yes, illuminating," Zoe mocked.

Emily Brent looked back around. "Yup, you sure are a little one. Hope you can hold your own with the important experts we've got coming. Going to be a fascinating week. Yes, ma'am. A fascinating week."

Emily Brent pushed Zoe's suitcase across the room, leaving it in the archway to a hall.

A small stick fire crackled on the hearth. Zoe went to stand in front of it and rub her cold hands together, but the fire didn't give out much warmth.

"Will someone take me to my room soon?" Zoe turned to Emily, who stood nearby, arms pressed over her breasts, watching. "Jenny's got to go, and I'm tired."

"Certainly. In a few minutes. Bella's finishing with the upstairs rooms. Give her a minute. You're going to find we don't run around like chickens with our heads cut off up here at Netherworld. All have our place, and we keep to it. Have a seat." She wiggled a finger toward the loveseat before the fire. "She'll be back to get you."

"Not Bella Webb?" Zoe couldn't help smiling. Another character out of Christie's work: *The Pale Horse.*

Emily nodded. "A friend from our church. She's doing the cooking for the week. Doing most of the cleaning. Don't know what we'd do without her."

"And you're . . . what? Director? Leader?"

"Well, you could say that. Director, I guess. Me and Mary, together. We've got others who'll lead the sessions and help you all: what to do and when. Schedule of the duration of the event right over there beside the desk." She pointed to a plainly made desk off to the side of the room, with a board beside it where papers were thumbtacked.

"So, you're Emily Brent, and we have a Bella Webb. I didn't get the notice we were supposed to come as a character from one of the novels."

"What do you mean?" Emily Brent's face was wrinkled, her lips shut and pushed out.

"I mean that Emily Brent and Bella Webb are in Christie books."

Her mouth dropped open. "You said that before but it can't be true. I'll have to find a copy of those books. It would be just too strange."

She gave her version of a smile.

*　*　*

Jenny slipped down into the sofa beside Zoe when Emily left the room. "She's something. You think she's one of your relatives?"

"Emily Brent." Zoe jumped as hot coals fell among the burning embers. "I don't look like her, do I? Hope not."

"Maybe around the eyes."

"Mine are blue. Hers are lumps of dirt."

"Then it's the body shape."

"Okay. Maybe a little. Do I talk the way she talks?

Jenny shook her head. "Your nose isn't lumpy like hers. You don't talk the way she talks. And she's a lot taller than you."

"Oh, that's funny. What kind of help are you?"

"None. So, I'm going to go." Jenny got up and headed toward the door. "I'll call you in the morning. See what time you want us to come over."

Zoe wiggled her phone in the air. "No service."

"Oh, then we'll be here later in the day."

Zoe shrugged. "I don't know anything that's planned for us. I don't know what they do about meals. Awful . . ."

"Later. Seems right."

"If they tell you I left, don't believe them. I'll be dead and buried out in the woods, and the whole bunch of them will be dancing on my grave."

"That's what I'll look for then. A bunch of academics dancing on a very small grave."

Emily was back before Jenny could get away. She stood in front of Jenny, eyebrows pulled together, hands clasped, toes pointed out. A woman with something in mind.

"I hope you didn't come to stay." She was blunt. "We're filled, you know. Not a room left."

"According to who?" Zoe demanded, determined to question every word this person said.

The woman clucked. "Don't you mean 'whom'? There's going to be people here who really watch their p's and q's, you know. Me? I'm tolerant of everybody, but I just wanted to warn you. I imagine the competition's going to be stiff for top dog."

"Don't you mean 'there are' going to be people?" Zoe's voice was cool.

Jenny put a hand over her mouth.

"No. *People* is a collective noun. I'm right."

"*People* is a plural noun, not collective."

"Pish tosh. Plural. Collective. I know I'm right. You've heard, I suppose, that the purest mind is the most untroubled. Now, can I get you two anything? I mean, before your friend here leaves."

""Really? Hospitality?" Jenny couldn't help herself and thought of a glass of Pinot Grigio.

The woman rocked back on her heels. "I can make you a sandwich, if you want it. You hungry?"

Jenny shook her head.

"We ate in Calumet." Zoe's words came out like little bits of haughty dialog.

"So, where's everybody?" Zoe looked around the empty room. "My letter said to be here before two o'clock."

"You know you can't depend on people these days. So many without a secure sense of responsibility. To say nothing of morality.

What can we do, Miz Zola, except sound the warning bell? Though people in our group keep telling me I should keep my mouth shut this week. I mean, no pointing out to the women that they'll soon have to take a number to get into hell, unless they go back to the old ways of being."

Jenny put a fist to her mouth and turned away, afraid to look directly at Zoe.

"You are something, Emily Brent," Zoe said, her eyes wide and disbelieving. "And good, I think, at what you're doing. Looks like this might be fun after all. This Agatha Christie event that doesn't seem to be much about Agatha Christie. But while you're watching out for other people's souls, Agatha's Emily Brent was the fifth to die in *And Then There Were None*. Stung to death. Must've been bees. If I were you, I'd be damned careful serving honey."

Emily made a face. "We frown on vulgarity here at Netherworld Lodge."

Zoe and Jenny looked at each other and, unable to help themselves, began to laugh.

"I'm the one you come to if you want anything during the week." Emily took Jenny's arm, pulled her up from the sofa, and led her toward the door while talking over her shoulder to Zoe. "You can sign up for the bus to town if you really need to go anywhere. Or you might like to come to church with Bella and me while you're here. We're inclined that way, so we'll be glad to take you."

"There's a university involved in all of this, isn't there?" Zoe followed the two of them to the door.

"College of Forestry." Emily nodded.

"Forestry? What's that got to do with literature?" Zoe couldn't help her tone of voice.

"Well, you know." Emily Brent stretched her neck out. Her eyes slowly moved back to Zoe. "They like to give their students a well-rounded education, you see."

"Nobody said there would be students."

"No real students. Just this webinar thing. The students are helping us 'cause we don't know what we're doing when it comes to high tech. They've got the ads covered. I told you, lots of people signing up. A hundred dollars, and they get to ask questions at the end. An hour and a half a day. Never heard of such a thing myself, but I guess it's the way they're doing things now. Our Christie Society will get a lot of exposure. And you too—you can push your books if you want to."

"Didn't bring any. I'm not much of a peddler."

Emily shrugged off Zoe's indifference. "Webinar's going to do you a lot of good anyway. People hear about it, and learn you're here, they associate your name with Agatha Christie. Your book will do better. Could make you an important writer, you know.

"And money's been coming for our cause from something called a Patron site. So many excited about what we're doing up here and that's all we're after, giving the hard work of our members some exposure. And, of course, all of you—our experts." She turned away for a minute, then back.

"I'm told that a webinar is the modern way to promote your cause."

"And just what is the 'cause' here?"

"You could say promoting the woman we think is the best mystery writer who ever lived."

Zoe made a puckered face. "Really? And you've never read *And Then There Were None*?"

Emily Brent shrugged. "Guess I missed it. I'm a busy woman." She nodded again as she took Jenny by the arm and steered her toward the door.

"Have a good trip home." She ushered Jenny out without giving her time to give more than a wave back at Zoe.

* * *

With Jenny gone, Zoe stood in the open doorway, the sound of rain still loud. She wondered if she'd done the right thing, staying behind with Emily Brent and whoever else might be there.

Bella Webb . . .

"Now." Emily, behind her, wiped her hands down the sides of her dress. "I'll go find Bella before you get yourself worked up into a big snit over all these things worrying you."

Emily walked away, stopping to turn in the middle of the floor. The smile she gave wasn't pretty. "Probably a case of the jitters. I know I'm nervous. We're all in uncharted territory here—webinars, a bunch of experts, this historic place." She tried a different smile. No better. "I'll bet we end by being the best of friends. The two of us. I just bet we will."

Zoe looked at the poor woman and couldn't help herself. She lied. "You know you were right about that collective noun."

"Why did you argue with me?"

Zoe shrugged. "I don't know. Feeling mean, I think. By the way is Brent your married name?"

She nodded. "My husband, bless his soul, is departed."

"Not part of the Jokela family, are you?"

"Heard of them. Don't know any myself."

Emily Brent left the room. Zoe heard her heavy footsteps on a staircase off the hall and could have sworn she heard the word *bitch* trail after her.

She began again to wonder if they were related.

Chapter 15

Jenny started her car and backed around to head out the two-track and hope to find a main road again.

She looked over her shoulder at the lodge—only lights on in the reception room; the rest of the building dark, as if there was—in all that space—only one stage for players. As if only one story was about to happen, and maybe they weren't all evil people, the way Zoe thought. Or maybe Zoe was wrong, and evil was everywhere.

Back to the highway, heading north.

The directions to Lisa's trailer had as many twists and turns as Lisa's brain. A mile up one two-track, a mile back on another.

A left into the woods before Copper Harbor. *A left?* There were four roads to pick from. She chose the first and kept her fingers crossed. Then about twenty miles up one two-track and down another. Twenty-seven miles before she came to the green arrow she was supposed to look for.

Nothing in the directions about going straight down a slippery hill until she could get her brakes to catch. And nothing about a place where the road forked in two directions, and one ended at a deserted rock quarry, so she had to turn around and take the other, at times crashing straight through bushes that grew close to the road.

Eight miles, and then a long, bumpy ride on a dirt 'drive' with the name "Martine" on a corner sign. How was she supposed to know the difference between an overgrown two-track and a drive? Eight miles more, exactly, and she ended at a long swamp on one side of the road and an open field of burned stumps—a long-ago forest fire—on the other.

Knowing that Lisa had a tendency to underestimate, she drove on until she found it: fourteen miles down some pretty rough road. Two hump-backed trailers in a small clearing of wet weeds and dripping trees. There was a dim light in one. Then a skinny woman threw the door of a trailer open and jumped out in front of Jenny's car, waving her arms.

They hugged and laughed. Jenny bawled her out for her crappy directions, with Lisa, dark hair rolled into a knot on top of her head, pretty face drawn up in a smile she couldn't stop, scolding her sister for being late.

They hugged again and talked all the usual talk on the way to the little trailer: *Mom okay? How've you been? How long you staying?*

Jenny carried her suitcase into Lisa's small trailer and dropped it in what was either the living room or the dining room: a small round table, a couple of folding chairs, a card table with papers spread across it about four inches deep.

Two floor lamps stood at the edges of the work area. No sofa. Not a single comfortable-looking chair.

There was a tiny kitchen—big enough for half a person to cook in—a hot plate that could take one frying pan and maybe a coffeepot.

Lisa pointed out the highlights, laughing when she said the bathroom was so small you had to sit sideways on the toilet.

"Is there a bed?"

Lisa grinned. "Mine." She pulled down a closed trap door beyond the bathroom and pointed to blankets folded up inside.

"That's it? How do I fit in here?" Jenny poked at the blankets.

"Climb up. Won't be bad. We'll be sleeping together the way we used to."

Lisa grinned at her.

"I'll wake up black and blue—the way I used to."

"That's a lie, and you know it." Lisa swept her arm around the little place with pride, pointing to piles of scripts, her computer, equipment Jenny didn't recognize.

"Nobody can accuse you of not suffering for your art."

"This isn't suffering. Suffering will be if you still snore the way you used to."

"And I hope you grew out of farting. I hear one and I'll throw you right out of this trailer."

"My trailer. Throw yourself out."

"Well." Jenny looked around again. "I suppose it's not so bad. Hope you don't invite crowds very often. What do you do when you have people over? Entertain in the bathroom?"

"Toilet's my third chair."

"Where were you going to put Mom if she came with me?"

"A motel in Copper Harbor. She'd like that better, don't you think?"

Jenny nodded.

"Hey, if this is too . . . er . . . primitive for you, you can go to that motel."

"Not on your life. I'm staying wherever you stay. Sorry. I'm tired. Been worrying about Zoe all the way up here." She looked around, hoping there was a place to unpack but didn't dare ask now that she'd pissed off Lisa.

Lisa looked at her and sniffed, "I called Mom from town a little while ago. She said something about that Tony you're engaged to. Some big blow-up between you? Screw that up, did you?"

"Mind your own business."

"And what about Zoe?"

"She's at that event here. Supposed to be all about Agatha Christie and her work. But she thinks it's about her and her cruel family she doesn't even know. She thinks they invited her to kill her. Sounds reasonable to me. I'd jump at the chance to go somewhere people are plotting to kill me too."

"Sounds crazy to me. But who am I to talk? Back here in the woods."

"Guess we're all crazy in some way. But"—she reached out to hug Lisa again—"what I came for was to see my sister. Mom's trying to tell me how to live my life. Zoe's mostly mad at me. Tony acts like he got me on some marriage market. Thought this would be far enough to get away from all of it. Guess I was wrong."

Lisa took Jenny's flailing hands in hers. "Sorry. No more. I won't ask another question about anybody. We're going to have fun. My Finnish women have invited us to their Saturday dinner. They're so excited. Just remember to make a fuss over every dish they serve you. All the same—you hear? No one dish too much. No one dish too little—if you have to cram it in. They take their cooking seriously, and each one has a special recipe she won't share with anyone. Just be sweet and kind—the way you always are—and you'll be a hit."

"When are we going?"

"Seven thirty."

"I don't think I've ever known any real Finns before. Should I be nervous?"

"Don't be. Nobody bites. They'll be looking you over. There'll be some whispering behind your back. But they'll get over it. So, just smile. Keep smiling. And keep filling your mouth."

Lisa laughed. "They're Finnish descendants. When the mines closed, they stayed on. They're from the original families. Well, most of 'em. Some 'marryin' in,' as they call it. They blend with the rest."

For the hour and a half they had before they were to leave, Lisa introduced her sister to the world of making documentaries—

photos hung on a clothesline; scripts filled with ideas that were crossed out and rewritten—over and over. A mess.

"And out of all of this you get a film?"

"Not just a film, Jen. Sometimes I get a story like this one— women holding on to a rough life no one should be living, to a world they love, and people they love. More than anything else, they're loyal to their own. Fierce, these women. Now that I know them, I believe they'd kill to avenge their own."

Chapter 16

Ten minutes more of standing, waiting expectantly for someone to greet her, and Zoe slouched down into the bumpy floral cushion of one of the chairs, wondering for just a minute if the whole thing was an illusion as she rolled her eyes toward the ceiling. Maybe like her rocking chair dream—only not nearly as good.

Ego. All of it. Nothing to do with her and her mother. No cruel relatives and a score to settle. She liked being asked. She'd liked being called an 'expert.' She'd liked that she would be a *featured* expert.

Over her head, from a wooden beam, a cobweb swayed. More cobwebs in the corners and one hanging from a light. So much for Bella Webb's skills. And dust on the end table beside her. What would her room be like? Under the bed? The sheets?

A sign she should have gone with Jenny. Settled. She'd be out of there tomorrow—that was a promise to herself. One spider in her room, and she'd be out in the drive directly. Easy enough to come up with a killer disease or a blinding headache. She'd say she'd had them since childhood. Or she'd tell Emily Brent something more important had come up.

Almost a tiny satisfaction, thinking of facing down Emily.

There was a noise from out on the porch, something dropping and then a loud "Damn it to hell!" and the front door burst open.

A middle-aged man in a mesh cowboy hat stepped into the room and dropped his suitcase to the floor, a raincoat on top of the suitcase. He looked around, hands on his hips.

In a loud voice he announced: "What a place! Glad I got a ride. I'd never have found it. Christ! I thought . . ."

He looked over her way. "Who are you? Must be that Zoe Zola I've read about. Heard you were the size of a gnome."

Not waiting for her to say a word, he stuck his hand out and then forcefully—too forcefully—shook hers. He pumped her hand again until she pulled away.

He pulled off his wet hat and shook it near her, exposing wet hair pulled into a messy man bun at the back. The movement of his half-shaved chin above her head was odd. She had a view of crooked, small teeth that didn't match the rest of him.

"Who are you?" Zoe demanded.

He laughed. "You haven't done your homework, have you, my tiny dear one? I am Anthony Gliese. Other than being an executive editor at Conway books, I've written a few books myself."

He waited, staring down at her, seeming to hope his name alone would ring bells. "*The Psychosis of Agatha Christie*, for one. And surely you've heard the uproar over my book on Virginia Woolf?"

He crossed his hands over the fly of his khaki pants. His lip-closed smile was smug. "*Woolf and the Tyranny of Mental Illness.*"

He waited, then gave up when Zoe said nothing.

"Are you in charge here? Not much of a greeting, if you ask me. Poorly run." He kicked at the expensive leather bag near his feet, then looked around the room. "The old boys who founded this place obviously took good care of themselves. '*Life as it should be . . .*'"

Anthony bent to smile at Zoe, to run one finger across her cheek, and then laughed when she pulled away.

He didn't wait for Zoe to work herself into a proper snit, only turned to call out, "Hello! Anybody else here? Anthony Gliese has arrived."

He winked. "That'll get somebody."

In seconds a door off the reception room opened, and an older woman wearing a stained apron stepped through, closing the door carefully behind her as if she were sneaking in.

She looked from Zoe to Anthony. "Mrs. Webb." She nodded to each of them.

"I'm supposed to take the two of you to your rooms, I suppose," the woman mumbled as she wiped her hands on her apron.

Anthony stepped toward her, amused. "Are you in charge here, Mrs. . . ."

"I cook and clean, sir. Bella Webb." She tried to smile, but her mouth didn't seem up to it.

"Emily Brent should be back soon. Emily's really in charge. And some o' the other members of the society. Don't know where they got to. Doesn't seem to be anybody here right now."

He took in a surprised breath. "Emily Brent and Bella Webb? *And Then There Were None* and *A Pale Horse*?"

The woman frowned. "Well, dat's us. I don't know about the rest."

He looked toward Zoe, making a face. "Christie names, am I right?"

"Did you say Christian names?" Bella said. "Why, yes. O' course. Me and Emily been friends for a lot of years now. Belong to St. Paul's in Calumet. Hope ya get to visit our church while yer here."

"I don't think . . . anyway, I'm Anthony Gliese," he said over his shoulder as he passed into the hall to stop at the foot of a narrow set of stairs and look up.

Bella followed behind him, taking his suitcase, lifting it, and then dropping it to push along with her foot. "Glad ta welcome you to Netherworld Lodge, sir. I know Miss Brent's hopin' for an interesting time."

"And you, little miss," she said, smiling at Zoe, "I'm guessing you're Zoe Zola. Heard a lot about ya. Somebody all the members wanted especially."

Shocked into silence by Anthony Gliese and the odd woman, Zoe grabbed up her own suitcase and followed the two of them, stair by stair, to the second floor.

The first stop was room 201. Bella Webb pulled an old-fashioned key from her pocket and unlocked the door, pushing it open on a shadowy room.

"You need anything, I'm usually in the kitchen. Emily stays mostly in her office or in the reception hall. Either one o' us'll be happy to help you."

She stopped to take a deep breath as Anthony, behind her now, rolled his eyes at Zoe, saying, "I don't have a schedule for the webinar. Not even a subject list. Or the names of the other speakers who will be here."

"Downstairs," Bella said. "Everything's on the reception desk."

"Could you bring one up to me?" His voice was suddenly sweet. "I'm exhausted. Quite a trip. I never expected to be invited to the end of the world."

"Not exactly the end of the world, sir."

He waved the old-fashioned key he held as he went down the hall to the next room and stood looking in, as Zoe had.

"How many of us will there be?" he asked from the doorway.

"Think ten, sir."

"I would have thought eight."

He grinned at Zoe. "You've got it by now, haven't you? They've planned the event around Christie's books. Certainly *And Then*

There Were None. We're probably that terrible group of murderers gathered on Soldier Island. Every morning another one of them— gone. I hope they don't carry their theme that far."

He laughed as he entered his room, then leaned back, smiling directly at Zoe. "You ever get bored in that lovely room of yours, come knock on my door. We could have fun, Miss Zola, being bored together."

He disappeared into his room and closed the door behind him.

Bella Webb whispered toward Zoe, "Don't pay attention. I hear there's always some like him at these academic things. Most really nice. But always some like him, after the women, ya know."

Back at the top of the stairs, she hesitated. "You want me to bring you up a schedule too?"

Zoe shook her head. "I'll take care of myself."

"All I know is there's drinks in the reception at seven thirty this evening. Dinner's at eight. Plenty o' time for you to settle in before the others get here. Professor Leon Armstrong's taking the lead tomorrow, givin' his talk. You know him?"

Zoe shook her head.

A large sigh. "From some New York college, as I understand. Not here yet, but you know how those New York people are—always late, always complaining about this and that."

Zoe pulled her suitcase in behind her and shut the door.

*   *   *

She'd expected a four-poster, and maybe yellow chintz and white, foamy curtains crossed at big windows looking out over a forest of sunlit trees. What she got were walls of an indeterminate blue and a small, dark, metal bed covered with an oft-washed, white-going-to-gray chenille bedspread. The bedside table was a foot square, and that foot was taken up by a gray, metal, goose-necked lamp with a metal pull chain.

The ceiling light, when she turned a wall knob, was a bare, probably forty-watt bulb—if there were still such things. There was a scarred desk and chair in front of a slightly open window, and an overstuffed armchair in another corner. The chair looked comfortable enough: a footstool in front of it and an old-fashioned floor lamp beside it.

She hoisted her suitcase to the footstool and unpacked her underwear and tops, putting them in an antique oak chest of drawers with a crazed mirror on the wall behind it. Her pants and shirts went into the narrow closet, where an extra blanket took up the entire top shelf. Her one pair of extra shoes went to the closet floor, beside a large box pushed toward the back, a box she didn't pull out because it had nothing to do with her.

When the suitcase was empty of everything and her cosmetics were lined along the top of the dresser, she set her computer on the desk, put her pens alongside it, then arranged her notebook beside the few Christie paperbacks she'd brought with her. She closed the window, though the rain had stopped. It was still cold and damp in the room. She shivered while she walked around, looking at the faded photographs of men holding guns that were hanging on the walls.

She sat at the desk, staring out the rain-dotted window at miles of nothing but treetops. Netherworld Lodge was more remote than she could have imagined. She hadn't brought enough material with her. She'd come for a confrontation, not a real Christie event.

Of course, the others would talk about the ordinary things—Christie's childhood and her marriages, her disappearance after her husband's cruelty. Of course, they'd take on her obsession with murder—Zoe knew she was particularly good on the subject. Especially with the book she was writing.

They would cite books and articles, and she had nothing with her.

She was to do the summation on the last webinar. That could be her out. She'd simply listen to the others, put in a snarky comment or two, add a few of her own facts, and that would be that.

Or maybe there were books here at Netherworld. She'd have to take a look around.

Such a mix of emotions. Back and forth. Old guilt. New guilt. Hoping to redeem her sins—neglect of Evelyn among them. Hoping to distinguish herself as a scholar.

The sky lightened. Enough so she could see more of where she was, out to what looked like the shingles of a brown roof not too far off. That was all. Maybe a strip of blue water where the trees and water and sky mixed together in muddy layers.

Chapter 17

She heard a knock at Anthony Gliese's door and then low voices.

With an ear to her door, she listened as Bella Webb delivered the schedules to him.

There was a muttered "Thanks" and footsteps going down the stairs.

She opened her door a little. Enough to tell her there was no one in the hall and Anthony's door was closed. Almost tip-toeing, she went down to the reception room, still brightly lighted and still empty.

*   *   *

On a small oak desk, she found a stack of stapled daily schedules: first meals and other events—with films offered in the evening:

8 AM Breakfast in the Copper Room
9 AM Free time until lunch
1 PM Lunch in Copper Room
2 PM Webinar rehearsal—Michigan Room
2:30 PM Technical: Webinar prep completed
3–4:30 PM Webinars, ending with questions from
      subscribers

4:30–7 PM Bus to Calumet (except Sunday; see Emily Brent to arrange transportation on the Lodge bus. Leaves at 4:50 PM. Returns by 7:00 PM)

7:30 PM—Cocktails in the Reception Room

8:00 PM—Dinner in the Copper Room

After dinner films offered in the Michigan Room:

Saturday	*Evil Under the Sun, 1982, Peter Ustinov as Poirot*
Sunday	*Witness for the Prosecution, 1957, with Tyrone Powell, Marlene Dietrich, and Charles Laughton*
Monday	*Death on the Nile, 1978, with Peter Ustinov as Poirot, and Mia Farrow*
Tuesday	*And Then There Were None, 1945, with Barry Fitzgerald and Louis Hayward*
Wednesday	*Murder on the Orient Express, 1974, Albert Finney as Poirot; also Martin Balsam, Ingrid Bergman, Lauren Bacall, and Richard Widmark*

Webinar Schedule:

Introductions of all participants by Mary Reid of the Northern Michigan Agatha Christie Society; includes a short biography of Agatha Christie. Mary Reid will also field questions at the close of the webinar.

Sunday, June 17, 3–4:30 PM
Dr. Leon Armstrong

Chairman, Department of English, Ralston College, Upper
    Fairmont, New York
Publications: *The Murderous Among Us*, Michigan
    Press
Webinar topic: "The World of Agatha Christie"

Monday, June 18, 3–4:30 PM
Dr. Louise Joiner
Professor of English Literature, Amherst College
Publication: "The Metafiction of Agatha Christie," *New
    England Journal of Literary Studies*
Webinar topic: "Agatha's Agony"

Tuesday, June 19, 3–4:30 PM
Dr. Nigel Pileser
Professor of Literature and English Department Chair,
    Colorado Reserve University.
Publication: *Agatha Christie and Nihilism*
Webinar topic: "The Lost People of Soldier Island"

Wednesday, June 20, 3–4:30 PM
Professor Aaron Kennedy
English literature and language, University of Southern
    California.
Publication: *The Fading Fiction of Agatha Christie*
Webinar topic: "The Aging of Agatha"

Thursday, June 21, 12–1:30 PM
Zoe Zola
Literary detective and writer, using new techniques in
    biography

Publications: *The Universality of Emily Dickinson*
               Jane Austen and Marriage
               The Madness of the Hatter
               Work-in-progress: *Inside the Murderous Mind*
                 of Agatha Christie
Webinar topic:

    "The Mystery as an All-Time Bestseller." Summation of the week's coverage: what we have learned about Agatha Christie and her work; areas of dispute and agreement; new work on Christie; and a summary of questions and answers, with final questions to follow

Good to know what she was doing. Sounded easy enough—take notes and listen to questions—mostly.

The rest was about the others.

Christie Specialists at Large

Anthony Gliese
Editor, Conway Books, New York, New York
Speaker at the London Book Fest, 2014
Editor: *Christie's Countryside* by Eliot Wamsut, 2015.
Upcoming: *Christie's Life* by Ingersol Tremaine.

Betty Bertram
Graduate student, McGill University, Montreal, Quebec,
    Canada
Winning essay in Writers Place in Time
       contest: "Agatha Christie and the Battle
       for Relevance"

Gewel Sharp
Recent graduate of the master's program in English and
    language, Michigan State University
Publication: "The Detective Mystery as a Barometer of
    Popular Culture," *Signs of the Times* literary magazine,
    December 2018

Mary Reid
Owner of Ulysses Bookstore, Houghton, Michigan
Publication: *Novels with Perpetual Life*, Tollance Press, 2016
Mary Reid will act as moderator of the webinars.

Anna Tow
Editor, Tollance Press
Publication: *Creation of a Mystery*, Tollance Press, 2008.
    Novels with Perpetual Life by Mary Reid

She absorbed the names, her sense of familiarity with them, and
thought how she could check them out: Did that bookstore really
exist? Was there such a thing as the Tollance Press? Did those two
really just graduate? Were any of the publications listed for real?

So many things she could do, if she could only get out of this
place—her only hope being the lodge van. Even if Jenny and Lisa
came today the library would be closed—still there were fast-food
restaurants, or coffee shops where she could use her computer or
maybe ask Jenny to check everything and get back to her.

The front door being thrown wide open was almost a relief. *At
least another human being*, Zoe thought as she looked up to find a
short man in his early sixties or late fifties. Rather unappealing, with
messy, shoulder-length red hair and a red mustache. He stumbled
halfway into the room, then looked at her, his face as red as the rest

of him. His opened his mouth as he righted himself, then let loose a string of curses that made his small, round stomach shake.

"Damned place." He scowled around as if there should have been a crowd there to meet him. His upper body arced back and forth. He glared hard at Zoe, then seemed amused, his head settling back on his narrow shoulders, a half-smile on his lips

"What do you know? A person I can look down on."

He burped and the powerful stink of whiskey hit her full force, making her cough into her hand and turn away.

"Oops." The man leaned against one of the sofas. "Had a small cocktail with my lunch. Didn't realize it was still with me. Sorry."

He got himself upright and tried walking toward her, wiggling his fingers. "Professor Leon Armstrong. Ralston College."

His head fell to one side as he waited for her to take the offered hand. He closed his red-rimmed eyes until she took the limp hand with three of her fingers and shook it as hard as she could, forcing his eyes to open and his face back to life.

"Zoe Zola," she muttered and dropped the mushy hand.

His smile couldn't hold still. "Ah, you're the one I heard about. Literary detective extraordinaire. I was told you'd be here."

He frowned, puffing out his lips and flapping a hand. "Hope the others will be worth listening to. Sometimes these things . . ." He stumbled and grabbed at the wall. "You just never know what you're going to get tied up with. I could tell you stories of conferences I've been invited to. Not worth the time."

He leaned sideways, seeming to forget what he was saying. "You're really the reason I came to this God-forsaken place, you know. You and a couple of the other experts—as they call us. I've read all three of your books. Insightful work. Very insightful. Hear you're something of a real detective too. Like Christie, eh? Always get your man? Or woman? Christie was an equal-opportunity accuser."

He clicked the heels of his too-large tennis shoes together and bowed. "I'm all for a nap before cocktails. And when might those be?"

Zoe gathered the schedules and put a set in his hands.

He bowed. "Thank you, my tiny tender. Now, I need to find my room. Maybe someone can bring in my suitcase."

As he backed toward the hall and the staircase, Bella Webb was there, standing next to him.

"Leon Armstrong." Zoe gestured toward the obviously drunken man. "He'll need help getting to his room."

Bella frowned as she took the man's arm. Zoe watched the two of them jerk their way up the stairs, from step to step.

This was why she almost never went to these things. So far: Anthony—a seducer, now Leon—a drunk. Types instead of real people. She was almost at the point where she could believe anything about this gathering.

If she thought about the whole thing together, it might be nothing more than a bad publicity stunt. Webinars and crowdfunding sites, anonymous benefactors, black-edged envelopes. And a group of strangers brought together in the pouring rain.

And how *did* they manage all that rain?

Nothing to look forward to here. If she decided to leave tomorrow with Jenny and Lisa, it would be no great loss to anyone. Least of all to her.

* * *

Later, back in her room, she lay on her bed thinking. Not a decent greeting. Certainly, this event seemed thrown together by amateurs. But then there were the others who were coming. All with good credentials, publications—unless none of it was real.

When she thought about this so-called Christie society, it seemed she was in the middle of amateurs—Or fakers: webinars and crowdfunding sites, anonymous benefactors, black-edged envelopes. All of this and a group of strangers brought together in the pouring rain. She could almost hear the clash of cymbals inside her head.

More like a play. Characters—all of them so far. With more to come. Walk-ons and main characters. Subplots. A rising and falling main plot. She'd have to keep notes on the stories that would develop between the people around her—to see where they led.

She would have to watch. She would have to put events and relationships together until she was sure what was happening in this place. She would have to decide quickly if this was only a lame academic affair or a threat.

Chapter 18

Zoe was bored. Her room was small. There was nothing she wanted to read, and sitting, waiting, in the reception room got old. She'd already searched every corner of her room again. Nothing under the bed. No dust anywhere. Bella Webb must be a good housekeeper after all.

There was the box in the closet, but when she opened it, hoping for something left over from years ago, when the lodge was all rich men with secrets, she'd found photo after photo of a young girl—from babyhood on. Too many to go through. Somebody's child. Maybe someone connected to the lodge. As boring as everything else in her room.

Standing at her slightly open window, Zoe sighed. Nobody here. Nothing to do. The rain had stopped at last. The sky was dark, but it didn't roil over itself and seemed about to give up a dash or two of sunshine. A raincoat would take care of the dripping trees. A scarf. She didn't have to go far, only to where she could take a deep breath and not sense eyes trained on her. Just to be away from this room and this building for a little while.

* * *

Bella was sweeping the porch with a broom taller than she was, when Zoe—umbrella in hand—stepped outside. The day was almost nice. A slight breeze. A little warmth. Stray shots of sunshine behind the leftover clouds.

"Afternoon." Bella looked up at Zoe, stopping her work. "Good to have no rain. Been a deluge, I'll tell ya."

Zoe nodded. "Still not many people here."

Bella turned back to her sweeping, shoulders hunched. "Will be."

"I think I'll take a walk." Zoe started toward the steps. "Haven't seen the grounds, or the woods."

"All still wet. You got to be careful, ya know." She spoke over her shoulder. "Lots of bears this time a year. Hungry and angry—the bears. Not long out of hibernation, ya know. And Coyotes. Foxes—but they won't bother you. Cougars out there too. You can't outrun 'em, ya know. Hope you understand well enough where you are, Miss . . . er . . . Zola."

"I won't go far."

"Well, the thing is, you should have a gun with you." Bella nodded hard.

"Gun?" Zoe laughed. "I've never shot a gun in my life. And where would I get one?"

"Nobody goes in the woods without one. I think we got two or three old ones in the lodge, fer target shooting. Maybe some a those who're coming might be armed. Used to be, in the old days, men would pull up here with a whole arsenal a guns. Some for bear and some for seagulls. Think you should wait."

Bella sighed and went on. "Such a shame, the way the place is now. Ya should've seen it before. Well, I'd say, especially bad now, with the downpour and such. There's water over the roads in more places. River, over there to the west, is in torrent I hear. One of the workmen said it's getting deeper, even though the rain's stopped a bit. We have to be careful, ya know. Odd time o' year. Seems the water keeps rising even when the rain's stopped. All the rivers and streams and creeks overflowing, pushing out to Lake Superior. That's what does it, the way the earth up here sheds water. Maybe that's what they mean by 'watershed.' Add more rain and we could be in fer a lot of trouble."

She looked at Zoe harder. "And you being a little one, like you are, well . . ."

Zoe ignored her but climbed carefully down the steps, hoping she didn't trip and land on her nose in front of Bella.

"What a miserable . . ." she muttered as she walked toward an open space carved from the forest where there were benches and lawn chairs and what looked like a small flower garden beyond the seating area. Then the woods. What looked like thick, endless forest.

"*Lions, and tigers, and bears, oh my!*" She sat in one of the smaller chairs and thought about wild animals in the woods, water over the road, and people she didn't like.

She crossed her arms, squinted her eyes, and looked back at the house. Last thing she was going to be was no trouble for Miss Emily Brent and Bella Webb. Who knew? They could be her aunts or cousins. The kind of weird relatives that showed up in people's lives without warning.

*   *   *

There were a few faded tulips in the circular garden ringed by gray river rocks. There was one peony with brown blossoms hanging in the dirt. She counted twenty-seven weeds but refused to pull them.

The sky got darker again, but not dark enough to worry her. There was a paved path leading around to the back of the long and low green-log building. She started up the path, past a row of small windows either covered with drawn curtains or opening onto empty rooms. At the side of the lodge, wooden fire stairs came down from the upper floor, reminding her she was in an old wooden building.

She'd been through a terrible fire once before. She hoped there were "No Smoking" signs hung everywhere and that somebody would keep an eye on Leon Armstrong. Men who drank and smoked had a habit of starting fires in their beds. Her window was small. No fire escape on her side that she'd seen. She looked from the lodge to the woods. *Lady or the tiger?* she thought and wondered how fast she could run if she had to.

She thought seriously about where she'd brought herself.

* * *

A large white van and a dark SUV were parked at the back of the lodge, near what looked like a kitchen. There were cardboard boxes and metal tins and garbage containers stacked near a propped-open screen door. Voices and the clatter of dishes being moved came from the doorway, but she saw no one inside.

Beyond the door, she circled over a wide pebbled area to a closed shed at the back, and beyond to a place where three dark and grassy paths fanned into the woods.

Zoe took the first path, setting off slowly between the trees. Nobody was going to scare her into staying inside for the next five days. No sense thinking about cougars and bears. Still, she didn't want Bella to be right. *Fifty–fifty proposition,* she thought as she walked slowly, looking back and forth. She might meet a cougar with bloody fangs or a bear on its hind legs. Or she could have nothing more than a pleasant walk.

Chapter 19

The path was wet, and her white tennis shoes were quickly muddy, but she wouldn't turn back. Let them call out the National Guard—if they could get there. She was feeling good again. Taking in deep breaths. Running when she felt like it. Swinging her arms.

She skipped over every puddle she could and stayed to the middle of the grass. Tall pines and firs shut out the overhead light. *Maybe virgin pines and fir.* She tented her hands above her eyes, trying to see up to where the trees ended, cutting an entwined stencil against the sky.

The smell of the woods was damp and piney. Fallen limbs lay everywhere, and then deep shadows that moved with the wind as other quick shadows flitted from tree to tree. It wasn't quiet. Not what she'd expected. There were birds singing songs she didn't recognize. Trees brushing one another. Overhead branches shook as they dripped water on her head.

She walked faster. Took longer steps, and then a hop; a stop to bend, studying tiny yellow and blue violets. She felt good about herself and her bravery in the face of imminent danger. Best she'd felt in a long time.

The path opened into a wide clearing of nodding grasses and tall brown reeds. The ground was firm, so she stepped into the clearing. There were no snuffling bears. No growling cougars. What she heard was a hum—or sort of hum that kept getting louder, as if coming at her.

Voices. People, in this place where she'd seen so few.

Zoe scurried back into the trees, off the path. Getting away. Her small feet slid in places, but now she was at a full run, legs pumping, her upper body overtaking her short legs until she righted herself.

Something hit her shoulder from behind, a hard prod, something thrown at her. Or a branch fell, She was knocked forward, arms flailing, shock overtaking her system as she tried to stop a face-down plunge into the wet weeds.

When she sat up there was no one near her. Many broken branches lay over the ground but nothing or no one else. When she looked down, at her right foot, the ankle had turned in an odd direction. She was soaked, and immediately cold. Her hands were covered with wet grass and leaves. She sputtered, looking around, then sat up. She lifted her right arm, testing to see if there was pain there. Nothing much. But her right foot throbbed. The odd turn to it wasn't as bad as she'd thought but it hurt again when, trying to rise, her other foot skidded sideways. She grasped a small tree and held on, pulling her body up while she tried to catch her breath.

"Hey there! Are you okay?" The humming she'd heard became a shout.

A woman Zoe's age came running from farther up the path, to kneel and look into Zoe's face.

"What happened?" the woman—dark eyes wide, pretty face knotted into a frown—asked. "Should I get someone?"

The woman's black hair hung in streamers around her face as she put a hand behind Zoe's neck, her other hand under Zoe's shoulder, and stood her upright, bringing a groan from Zoe when her hurting ankle was dragged over a small hillock.

The woman smiled, brushed her hands together to get the dirt and grass off. "You're Zoe Zola. I was looking forward to meeting you. I'm Doctor Louise Joiner, from Amherst, Massachusetts. Not medical, you understand. I can't do a thing about that ankle. Looks like it might be swelling."

Zoe examined the hurting ankle already bubbling over the tennis shoe. Maybe sprained. Didn't feel broken. But sprain or break, either way it hurt.

She looked at Louise Joiner and smiled. "Emily Dickinson's home. I've been there."

Louise frowned, not understanding.

"Amherst, where you teach. That was Emily's home."

Louise Joiner thought a minute, then smiled—a pleasant face, short brown hair. She looked very much like a professor to Zoe. "Oh yes. And I read your book on her. Made me shiver, the way her poetry does."

"Well." She was back to business. "Let's get you to the lodge and Emily Brent."

Another woman came down the path toward them, her face displeased. "There you are. For goodness sakes. What's going on?"

Middle-aged and plain; brown hair cut short and left to stand up around her head, the ungainly woman looked unhappy Zoe was there at all.

"Louise and I heard the noise." Her thin arms, in a khaki shirt, were crossed in front of her when she stopped short to eye Zoe.

"What happened?" Her legs, in khaki shorts, were planted wide apart. "Should be more careful. You're awfully little. Coulda been trapped out here. Nobody else out."

"This is Zoe Zola, Anna." Louise introduced them. "And this is Anna Tow, Miss Zola. She owns Tollance Press."

Zoe, leaning hard against Louise Joiner's side, took the limp hand Anna Tow held out to her, shook it once, and dropped it.

Anna Tow's large, bald eyes stayed on Zoe. "So you are Zoe Zola. I figured. Heard a lot about your work, not that I agree with all of your ideas. Some too far out there"

"Could you help us, Anna?" Louise cut her short. "We should get Miss Zola back to the lodge."

"Hmmp." Anna stepped closer, trying to lean far enough forward to get an arm around Zoe's waist. "All kinds of holes to fall into and logs to fall over. Must be what you did. But why go off the path at all? Seems . . ."

"Anna and I met in the woods," Louise Joiner said, smiling down at Zoe. "Just like we've now met you."

"But she shouldn't be out here." Anna sniffed as she looked Zoe up and down. "Not if you're not used to rough hiking. What happened? Looks like you've got a problem with that ankle. Your own fault."

"Anna. Excuse me. I don't think this is the time to bully." There was a slight edge to Louise's voice as she took Zoe's arm, supporting her as they moved back toward the lodge.

"What about the wild animals? Anything could've got her," Anna grumbled from behind them.

Zoe looked over her shoulder at the woman with a large nose and an unhappy face. She opened her mouth to mention that wild animals ate nasty women too, but said nothing, instead turning to thank Louise for the use of her arm while her clothes dripped, her ankle throbbed, and her bad mood deepened.

Chapter 20

The rain stopped. The moon played tag with the clouds. It was time to go to dinner, Lisa told her.

Jenny climbed into Lisa's Jeep and they were off, fast, down sandy roads, under trees where Lisa had to warn Jenny to duck or be lost in wet, low hanging leaves.

"That's where we're going." Lisa pointed to a large circle of buildings ahead gathered haphazardly—some built kitty-corner to the others. It looked like an old Western movie set, one with a showdown in the middle of the street, except there were no people. Each of the three streets was empty. The windows of the straight and narrow white houses were lighted like dollhouses—a lamp in every front window.

Lisa pointed to a peeling building set off from the others down one of the three dirt roads. "Saturday night supper, which is a good thing since I only have one egg left in my refrigerator."

"Probably only room for one egg to begin with," Jenny sniped.

* * *

Lisa parked, got out, and ran up a set of raw-wood stairs with Jenny behind her. She pushed the heavy double doors open and walked into the church to a hail of "Well, what do ya know?" "Here she is now." "Our lady picture taker." "Who's that you brought with ya?"

coming from long tables with women—young and old—lined along either side, some with babies in their laps.

The place smelled of kerosene coming from a small stove in the middle of the big room. Over that was the smell of food, half meaty and half sweet and syrupy.

Lamps along the walls flickered.

"We was jist wonderin' if ya were comin' to supper." A happy-looking large woman with deep brown hair done up in fat sausage rolls leaned back and clapped her hands in front of her face. "I was about ta eat the last bit of food."

Lisa turned to Jenny. "Don't pay attention. They all love to tease."

"Who's dis ya brought with ya?" Another heavy-set woman, this one with a large red scar down the side of her face, smiled and rose, swinging a leg back over the bench. She looked Jenny up and down, then grabbed her hand and whirled her around. "Ya sure can tell she's related to our Lisa, no matter what anybody says. Jist look at that black hair she's got."

She laughed and hugged Jenny with strong arms.

"My hair's thin as seaweed, Inka," Lisa jumped in. "I told you she was coming. We don't look a thing alike, and you know it."

Another one at the table—a lovely young women with a cooing baby in her lap—called out. "Jist as beautiful. One or da other. Both beautiful girls. Bet your mother's proud o' the two of ya."

"Marya," Lisa told Jenny.

"Now, stop holdin' 'em up." Leena, older and plumper, and maybe in charge, gestured to them. "Come on now—get yer plates. Help yerselves to the food over there on da tables. And take plenty, yah." She scratched an itch on the back of her neck, then laughed at them.

Long tables, laden with platters of fried chicken and two platters of scavenged-looking turkey carcasses, held the place of importance, dead center, on the middle table. The other two tables held deep pots of turkey soup and bowls of salad, mashed potatoes, gravy, half-bowls of green beans, jars of what looked like jams or sauces, and baskets half full of bread. Jenny was wondering where to start, when Lisa leaned close to whisper, "Take a little bit of everything, or somebody's feelings will get hurt."

Women along one side of the table rose to make room for them to sit, making shooing motions for the others to move. Jenny couldn't shake the feeling she was trapped in a movie scene, something written by Lisa.

The women were dressed like rural women found anywhere in the United States. Some in over-large cotton pants with loose cotton blouses. The younger ones wore old jeans with T-shirts selling seed corn or advertising a tractor pull in some small town. They looked alike—some with dimpled chins and long blonde hair and big, round eyes. Every one of them, young and old, was shiny clean. Jenny could smell laundry soap and recognized the smell of a hot iron.

"How'd you ever find this place?" Jenny turned to Lisa, making the women laugh and poke one another with sharp elbows.

"Raise your hand," somebody ordered.

One of the women raised her hand tentatively, as far as her chin, and then spoke in a soft voice.

"I think that maybe it's my fault." The soft, shy woman dipped her head. "I'm Kirsten. My cousin Janne was visiting and said he knew Miss Lisa here. So, Janne's the one to mostly blame fer all a dis movie business, not me."

Laughter.

"I'm grateful for Janne," Lisa said and bowed her head to them. "We travel light, the two of us. Couldn't do anything without him. Janne's the one who told me I just had to do something on you women. He was so right."

The women demurred in low voices until Marya burst out, "I'm not so much for this whole thing," she said as she held her baby to her breast. "Everybody here is hopin' ta trade our newfound fame fer an audience to buy our jams and jellies. They're hopin' for a contract. I think we'll all be sorry one day."

She turned to the others. "Contract, joo?" The others turned unhappy faces away.

"I don't mean to be mean or anything, ya understand. Just that, well, ya don't bring in others if ya want to keep the life ya got. That's what I say."

"Ah, Marya, now," Inka, the large, laughing woman, chided. "We're doin' our best to get along here, ya know."

Marya pulled her fussing baby from her breast and held him tight. "Sometimes the 'best' ain't the 'best' anymore. Sometimes things have ta change on their own."

"Not our way," another woman said, though she smiled at Jenny and Lisa. "And talkin' about our business in front of strangers ain't our way either."

Marya put her head down, buried her face in her son's neck, and said no more.

"Sorry, Lisa," Inka said. "You've just seen one of our rare disagreements. Marya, there, ain't from this place anymore. I think she's forgotten how hard it is to sell our jams and such, what with us being out here where people don't come so much anymore."

Whatever the disagreement was about, Jenny and Lisa ignored it and kept eating until they could eat no more and groaned, rubbing their stomachs as the women around them laughed.

Jenny couldn't remember the last time she'd been so full. She felt as if she could roll off her bench and lie right down on the floor. She didn't understand what a young girl named Katja, clapping her hands in front of them, was asking, so nodded yes to "Jalkiruoka?"

More large plates arrived in the hands of women who formed two lines to make sure Jenny and Lisa got a slice of every cake and pie and some from every single dish of cobbler. Then, eyebrows raised in expectation, they watched as Jenny and Lisa tried each dessert and gave the cook a thumbs-up while smiling with gerbil cheeks.

At one point, while they watched the children play a game with wooden spindles in the middle of the floor, and the mother's looked on with pleasure, Jenny asked Lisa where the men were. "There must be men," she said. "Where there are babies, there are usually at least a few men."

"This evening was just for us, for the women. The men know when it's best to stay away."

Jenny thought about the kindness and decided she would like their men as well as she liked the women.

* * *

As dark came on, Inka, who seemed to be the leader of the group, announced it was time for the big fire. The long tables were cleared. Dishes were wrapped with cloths and packed away in bags. When the place was clean and orderly, the women wrapped shawls around their shoulders, or shrugged on large, homemade sweaters. The children were stuffed into jackets.

They left the large building together, turning off the kerosene heater in the corner, then the lamps, one at a time, to go outside and down the rickety steps and stroll the three streets of houses—one after the other, each woman proudly pointing to her own house.

It was almost ten o'clock when the men came from the houses, one by one, nodding and giving a kind of grunt when introduced to Jenny. They exchanged a few words in their language. Lisa had no trouble keeping up, then told Jenny they were just talking about the rain. "Too much of it,' they're saying. 'Bad for the crops. Could be they rot in the fields.'"

Jenny could only smile. *Could be they rot in the fields.* She wondered how many generations back she'd have to go to hear a family member warn of such a thing.

The slow, thin men built up the bonfire where all three streets came together. The gathered wood was set alight with burning torches. There was muttering and complaint until the flames licked high enough to satisfy all the critics.

Older women and very old men appeared from the houses and dragged stools fireside. Others settled on blankets or wooden boxes, watching the flames go higher.

There, at the center of town, there was little sound as the sun went down. Women with whimpering babies or small children excused themselves to go home. Only the sounds of the after-dusk breeze, a few settling birds, crackles from the logs, and the snap of burning wood broke the dark silence.

In a while a nodding woman or man was shaken awake and told, *"Whyn't you go on home ta bed?"*

The dark grew deeper and somehow more unsettling. Marya, her baby sound asleep, wrapped around with a wool blanket, leaned close to Jenny, the fire turning her skin a burnished red. She searched Jenny's face. "I hear ya have a friend at that thing. That thing over to Calumet. Netherworld Lodge. We never went there—not a one o' us. That place is fer the rich men, like most fancy places are. They go out and shoot da deer, take their dead bodies home, and instead o' eatin 'em, they stuff da head and neck and hang 'em on da walls. Only garbage left. Garbage without blessin' the animals fer the life they give. Stupid, ya ask me. We've learned." She nodded along with her own thoughts. "We know from the Indian—ya supposed ta give yer thanks. But they hang 'em on their walls. Might as well stuff their dogs."

Women beside her, back in the growing shadows, made lazy sounds of agreement.

"Yer friend over der, she enjoyin' her event? Hear she's one o' those little people. Hope nobody over to that lodge gets mean with her. Rich people—they get mean easy."

Jenny, surprised at the depth of Marya's scorn, didn't say anything. But Marya wanted something more. "Doesn't she like dat place? Me, I wouldn't go der if you paid me. Not for all da money in the world."

"She likes it." Jenny said. "She's really interested in Agatha Christie—that's who the event is about. Writing a book about her."

"Agatha Christie, eh? That's who they gonna talk about fer five days? I heard o' that one. She good? I mean, she writes good books? Like cookbooks?"

"Not cookbooks. But she's a well-known writer."

"Seems I heard something about mystery, eh? Dat it?"

"Yes, murder mysteries."

"Eh, murder. We have murder up here. One bad one. Really bad. Not too long ago either."

"There is murder everywhere." Leena stretched her arms high overhead and yawned.

"But, ya know, this one was worse than bad," Marya said, a little roughness in her voice. "A young girl from here got to go to da University a Michigan. Lots of people chipped in ta send her, they did. Everybody liked that girl. Hard worker. Good—very good—grades. Den dey found her body. He did things . . . Never caught him—the man who did dat. Dey tink he moved away from dat university. Police stopped lookin', dat's what I hear. Mother and father left behind like two lost souls. Shame. Murder ain't a subject fer a book, I don't think. Yoo, I won't read Agatha Christie. Should've written nicer books. Then she'd be more famous. I would've heard about her."

No one could answer. Marya had rambled too far. The night was colder now. The dark was dangerous.

Marya was quiet. Finally she apologized. "Sorry if I offended anyone here. It's just we had such hope in that girl. And a man snuffed her out. I hope they get him one day and put him in jail fer the rest o' his life. Nothin' else. I don't believe in this takin' the law inta yer own hands. Never know who can get hurt dat way, don't ya agree, Lisa?"

"That's enough now, Marya. Think it's time ya took the little one home, don't ya agree?"

Without another word, Marya gathered her baby to her, straightened the warm blanket over his sleeping body, and left them without a good night to anyone.

Leena, who'd been quiet all evening, leaned in close. "Don't pay her any attention. We think she's pregnant again. A little soon, some would say. Bad moods."

She turned around to ask the other women what they thought. Mostly they laughed. "Ah, yeah, poor Aimo. He'll be sorry fer all his fun a couple of months ago."

Everyone laughed and the women got up from their seats.

*   *   *

Lisa drove slowly through the woods, stopping often as a porcupine or a skunk crossed in front of the headlights.

"You really like those women." Jenny made the comment through a yawn.

"Wouldn't be spending almost a year with them if I didn't."

"There's sadness there. Kind of like a place waiting to be wiped off the face of the earth."

Lisa nodded in the dark. "Sadness, yes. But bravery too. And something else. I haven't put my finger on it yet. Something else. Almost medieval."

Lisa was quiet for the next mile. "They're rigid when they have to be. They don't think much of the police—or the laws. Like they know better than to trust anybody outside their group. I guess that's why I feel so honored they're letting me film them, the way they are. Not the usual way outsiders get treated. But that's because of Janne. He came from there. The women trust him. Now they trust me too. I sure don't want to screw that up."

"But that Marya . . . the one with the baby and pregnant with another. So sad. And what was she talking about, that 'snuffed out' stuff?"

"Everybody has their bad day, I suppose. Could be postpartum depression."

"Or maybe 'pregnant again' depression."

Lisa laughed. "That's what I mean. Everybody has a bad day, like learning you are pregnant when you've got a four-month-old at your breast. Wouldn't make my day."

Before they were back to the patch of deep woods where Lisa and Janne'd parked their trailers, a bolt of lightning shot from side to side, across the road.

"More rain," Lisa said, looking warily at the darkness overhead. The next rumble shook the Jeep. "It's got to stop. My work's held up already. We were supposed to film in the old cemetery, where their ancestors are buried. But I didn't even try. The streams are flooding. I heard today parts of Houghton are underwater. Everybody counts on summer tourists to keep them afloat all year long. Poor enough without the coming of a Biblical flood."

* * *

Janne's trailer was still dark.

Inside Lisa's tiny trailer, Jenny checked her phone—nothing. She didn't expect to hear from anybody. Zoe didn't have service. Mom was probably still too mad at her to call. And nothing from Tony.

That was the best way, after all. They would stay apart until it didn't hurt so much anymore.

None of his calls to return. Nobody to tell again she needed time to think and nobody in her head saying she better get her head straight before she lost the best thing going for her.

No Tony saying he missed her.

She was tired and didn't care if she had to share a bed and kick Lisa to move over like she used to do, or if she didn't have more than a few inches of room.

She felt sad. Maybe for that Marya, a life ahead of her of one pregnancy after another. Maybe for Lisa—so little money from her documentaries, but still filled with belief that the world would one day see all that she saw.

That was it—sad. It wasn't easy to pretend she was here just to see Lisa. Tony's angry face their last night together surfaced at the worst of times—especially when she was tired and wanted to sleep.

Maybe tonight would be different. Maybe she'd forget everything going on and sleep from too much food and too many drinks of something that tasted like a cross between hard liquor and tea.

She lay as still as she could, listening to Lisa's slight snore—a good, familiar sound. And she almost fell asleep as she pretended she was never going home and had nothing to think about but living in the woods with a group of women who sat around roaring fires, holding their babies close, and telling stories of how life would always be just as they knew it, and nothing would ever change. A father would never be killed by a driver high on drugs. And husbands would always be true and never cheat on their wives. Husbands would never leave and make it hard for that wife to ever trust again.

Chapter 21

Emily Brent did have an elastic bandage for Zoe's ankle—but none a child's size.

"I warned you. If you don't know the area, you could get yourself lost." She'd frowned over the swelling ankle Zoe stuck out in front of her. "And all I've got for you are these big-sized things we'll have to fold in two and wrap as many times as we can."

Bella came out to the kitchen, hands clasped under her apron, to shake her head over the small extended leg and put in her two cents, telling Miz Zola it wasn't a good time to be out in the woods, with all the rain and such.

"Lookin' fer trouble. That's all yer doin', ya know."

Zoe took the comments and criticisms, though she couldn't remember either one of them warning her. She made a pained face that should have quieted them, but didn't.

"Too many holes and places where the path's worn away, ya know. And there's the fallen branches—hit you in the head and there you'd be." Bella turned away.

"It wasn't a branch," Zoe said, though she was getting bored with both of them and needed to take a shower before dressing for cocktails—so she'd be taking the bandage off in a few minutes anyway. "It felt as though someone deliberately pushed me."

"Now, who would that be, do you think?" Emily's voice covered a hint of sarcasm.

"Mighta been a deer. Poor things," Bella nodded. "They get startled and go a little crazy when they hear people in the woods. That coulda been it, ya know. Coulda startled one of the creatures as it was trying to leap around you."

"Could've been." Zoe was ready to end the conversation. They didn't like hearing about a possible attack. Much better for it to be a deer, running into her in fright—though Zoe knew what she knew, and that was no deer that had pushed her face down on the ground.

Bella nodded. "Don't know this country. Not as easy as it looks. You might want to stay where you're safe."

* * *

Anthony was in the shower, singing loudly about the girl he left behind. She knocked at the door. She needed to at least wash the leaves and slime from her arms and legs, and it was getting close to seven thirty.

He sang on.

She knocked louder and then beat the door with her fists until the shower went off. There were a couple of curse words she chose to ignore before the door opened, and Anthony stuck his dark head out.

"What the hell do you want, Shorty?" he demanded, as his upset red face peered around the door edge, his wet hair dripping over his ears. "I don't have a stitch of clothes on."

"I'm not interested in that. I fell in the woods. My ankle's hurt but wrapped. I need to take a shower. And don't call me 'Shorty.'"

He looked her over and grinned. "Sure thing, Shorty. "I'll be out soon. I can hand you a towel."

He shut the door, then opened it with a towel in the hand he stuck out to her.

"What's this for?" She held up the rather used, wet towel.

"To keep you quiet until I'm finished in here." He grinned at her.

"How long?" Zoe demanded, but he didn't answer, only shut the door in her face. She had no place to go but back to her room to wait.

* * *

Later, at the cocktail hour, when she got down the stairs and had a view of the entire reception room, Anthony was already holding court from a lounge chair, bending forward to talk to a very pretty blonde girl in a red-flowered dress. Anthony's hair was pulled back into a kind of man bun; his wrinkled, opened-neck sports shirt looked as though he'd packed it in his pocket. He slouched in the chair, one of his sockless feet, in a moccasin, draped over his other knee.

She looked down at herself: pretty nice for someone just rescued from a mudhole: black top, white pants, white flower earrings, a white flower in her wildly curly hair, and a big red belt around her middle.

If nothing else, she would get attention, she knew. She usually did, no matter where she went. Especially on these academic nights when all the people dressed up and were on their best behavior. Nights after the first things could go a hundred different ways.

Everybody but Leon Armstrong looked ready for a party. Poor Leon wore the clothes he'd arrived in; his wild red hair still flew around his head, and his red mustache looked damp and unappealing, most likely wet from the large glass he held in his hands as he stood alone next to the bar and watched the others.

Louise Joiner stood talking to Anna Tow and a tall man in gray pants and a deep purple sweater. They moved around the room, backs to the others, looking at the books and then at the photos hung on every wall. Zoe watched Anna Tow, sizing her up as the kind who would find one person she could hang on to for the duration of the webinar. The woman was unpleasant, she decided. Drab. Sour. Maybe nice enough, in her own way, but *nice* wasn't one of Zoe's favorite words. She hoped no one would ever called her nice, not even behind her back. There were words to strive for, and then there were words that diminished a person until she felt small and . . . well . . . *'nice enough'*—like this awful Anna Tow.

Anna and Louise held drinks and discussed the photos of men in various types of hunting gear while talking to the tall man who stood beside them. The tall man would bend from time to time to catch what one of them was saying, then shake his head—obviously disagreeing.

Everyone except Leon Armstrong was busy talking. He was busy drinking and grabbing tiny lobster rolls from Bella's platter as she came from the kitchen, making a circuit of the room, offering appetizers from her tray.

Zoe stepped to the last stair and watched the other people she'd come to spend five days with, though she knew few of them and suspected each of them of luring her there to teach her a final lesson—one poor Evelyn had never learned. What the lesson was, Zoe wasn't sure. Maybe only that she was born different—*the sins of the father.*

She was sure someone had pushed her or hit her with something. She'd felt something against her back. From someplace in the woods.

As she looked around the room, watching the groups talk, some laughing, she knew she'd made a mistake about this place. It had been hardheaded of her to come. She'd vowed to find out why they'd tortured Evelyn and why they were after her. But how did she do that in five days? When would it start, or had it started already—with that blow against her back? Maybe trying to disable her so she couldn't leave. A warning shot?

Or, this could be exactly as advertised. An academic triumph for a group of Christie fans in Northern Michigan's backwoods. It wasn't so far off the usual. Always at least one drunk to be seen to and one lech chasing the youngest attendee. There would be one know-it-all and then a has-been writer with a terrible book, asking others to read it and comment—offering a great favor. There could be one panel where the leader stopped the discussion cold to pull a number from a bowl, run out into the audience, and award a copy of his book to a surprised person, taking the time to autograph the book before finally returning to the stage, with a little laugh.

But maybe not at a webinar where the hour would be controlled.

There should be the poet who carried his booze in a paper sack, but not here: no poets. And she remembered the woman who'd come wrapped in nothing but a dozen scarves at a New York conference. The woman had announced the removal of one scarf a day until, on the eighth day, she was ushered off the campus. There might even be two feuding writers amid a group of their friends, crying and declaring they were leaving this awful place, until properly assured of equal importance.

And one terrible panel—this from a conference in Wisconsin—where the first panelist spoke for fifty-five minutes of the allotted hour while the leader sat fidgeting, her face red, but without the firmness to stop the oblivious woman.

Zoe sighed. She'd promised herself—no more of these events, but here she was, her hatred and curiosity having gotten the best of her. And now she was meeting more people who might or might not be who they said they were; who might or might not be in on some ridiculous joke; or might or might not want to hurt her or, at least, teach her a final lesson she had no need to learn.

She hesitated on the bottom step, looking over the reception room. If she could only get on the internet, she'd look them all up, investigate much more than she had. Maybe she would figure out who they were exactly and why she'd been invited—even fooled—into attending by an invitation that looked like an announcement of a death. Or a warning to stay away, from someone who had taken the invitation to the post office. There could be someone on her side.

Maybe someone trying to help her. But with a push to her back? With a painful ankle that would more than likely keep her there?

Agatha Christie was how they'd gotten her. But how did they know she was working on Christie? And then to call Christopher Morley?

And the remote setting? Of course, that would intrigue her— *Upper Peninsula of Michigan.*

And then the rain—that couldn't have been part of the plan. But there was the water-covered bridge. The lack of phone or internet. The characters in Christie's novel were all strangers. Strangers with secrets—like her secret for coming here. Those strangers began to die. One by one. Terrible deaths.

She shivered as Louise Joiner and Any Tow, over near the shelves of books with that man she hadn't met yet, began to laugh.

Anthony Gliese must have been drinking for a while. His voice was loud. He stuck his glass high in the air when he spotted Zoe, saluting her. Beside him, a young blonde girl hung on his every word as he leaned forward and bent his head to hers, then laughed again, softly this time.

The girl had to be in her late-twenties, very pretty, if a little plump and pink and dewy. Not the type Zoe was drawn to: the little-wide-eyed-blonde sort of girl. Or more likely—the dewy-eyed hopeful writer being drawn into the good-looking male editor's hopes of a bedmate for the duration of a dull literary event. Sometimes it only took the promise of a glance at her manuscript or a word to an agent she hoped to sign with, and she was hooked. After all, what was a little virginity, or self-respect, when her name could be lifted up among those of the best writers in the world?

To Zoe, having sex with someone or not having sex with someone really didn't matter. Only the pain that was caused by using other people. Or by being used. She'd seen all of this enough to be cynical about good-looking editors and pretty women trading something for nothing.

Between Louise and Anna, the tall, craggy-looking man, maybe in his middle fifties, leaned back from time to time, turning from one woman to the other to make loud, disparaging remarks in the kind of nasal, autocratic voice that made Zoe's skin crawl with little bumps.

The pretty girl with Gliese looked over at Zoe and got up to come toward her, a soft hand extended. She was not much taller than Zoe, but not a dwarf. Still, having someone close to her size let her feel normal.

"Gewel Sharp. I'm such a fan," the young blonde gushed, taking Zoe's hand in both of hers and shaking it again and again. "I love what you're doing with writers. At first I didn't get what one of my professors at U of M was talking about—he loves your work, by the way—until I read your book on Emily Dickinson. What insight! And after all the critics have written books on her and all her friends have told their stories, it took your work to capture a mind bent toward the future. All that wisdom in her poetry. If only we knew the code."

She held Zoe's hand, shaking it again. "I have a feeling you might know that code. Am I right?"

Zoe didn't answer, too busy thinking different thoughts: *Someone close to my size. Well—almost. At least my neck won't hurt trying to talk to her.*

"Christie's a writer apart, don't you think? I mean her stories seem so simple, but they aren't. Can't wait to hear your summary of the webinars," Gewel went on. "We might come up with such new things. I want to write mysteries myself, you see."

Zoe smiled at the excited young woman. "I hope you're writing."

"Oh, I know. I am. I'm in the middle of my first novel. But then I read someone like the writer Louise Penny, and I know I'll never make it. I'll never write the way she does."

"Don't try to write the way Penny does. Write the way Gewel Sharp writes."

"I know, I know. Be myself." The girl's eyes filled with emotion. "But writers like Penny and James, Rendell and Christie stand alone, don't they?" Gewel dipped her head as she spoke. "And still with us, in a way. That's what I've found. Always a new Christie book to read or come back to. Or a short story I haven't seen before. She is constantly different."

Zoe found herself warming to this girl: Gewel. Maybe ten years younger but very different, filled with what Zoe must have been filled with once—that zeal to be successful, to prove herself to all of 'them.' And most of all, to be accepted. It made her hurt, just a little, to have lost some of that.

Zoe smiled at the excited girl. "We'll have some interesting times this week. Can't wait to hear what you have to say about Agatha."

"Me too. Oh, me too. I don't mean *me*." Gewel laughed, then blushed. "I mean listening to you and the others."

At a wave from Anthony Gliese, Gewel took Zoe's hand and pulled her to where Anthony sat beside the man Anna Tow and Louise Joiner had been with earlier.

He introduced the tall, almost ugly man as Professor Aaron Kennedy. "From USC."

Aaron Kennedy made a move to stand, then collapsed back into his seat, too overcome for good manners. He put out a limp hand to take Zoe's, shook it as if she were asking a lot of him, then curled his lips into something of a smile. "And you are?"

"Why, this is the famous Zoe Zola, Aaron. She's playing cleanup on the last day. We'll be put into good order, I imagine. Shown the rights and wrongs of Christie study. I'm sure we'll be told what we really meant to say. In other words, we'll be cleaned up, put in our places, and sent away to sin no more. Am I right, Zoe?" Anthony laughed as he pointed to a seat across from Aaron Kennedy. She shook her head and stood where she was.

"I hope no one will be changing a word I say." Kennedy's oddly colored eyebrows—shot through with white—went up into inverted V's. "My work has been years in the making. I don't think it fair to leave myself in the hands of . . ." He leaned back and looked Zoe over. "I wasn't told there would be . . ."

"Ah, but Aaron. Surely you've heard of Zoe Zola! Her books delve to the interior of the artist, discovering the seeds of the work. Very new form of biography."

Aaron Kennedy made a face that involved his nose wrinkling, his thin lips pursing, and those funny eyebrows gathering over his nose. "I see. But I still say I don't want my words changed. I have invested many years into my work on Christie. I would say I'm the preeminent scholar, even though I find Christie isn't aging as well as people think."

"Have you checked her sales?" Zoe felt her back bristling. There was always one who had to be the contrarian to get attention. She wasn't going to like this Aaron Kennedy and, despite trying to control herself, would end by taking him on—head to head. It always turned out that way.

Kennedy waved a flaccid hand at her. "So many tics in her work—repeated again and again. A shame. Many arcane references to her life. People won't stand for it for long."

He turned to Anthony. "I teach a genre fiction course at USC. I've included Agatha Christie, but sadly, I find it's time to move on to the more famous mystery writers of our time. Take Stephen King, for instance. I could create tremendous resemblances between his work and the more famous of the Russian writers. The women writers—well, I'm finding they quickly date themselves or devolve into silly love stories like Christie did under the pseudonym Mary Westmacott."

He turned to Zoe and smiled a superior smile. "But why do we even discuss these women in the same breath with male writers? The trouble with women writers is genetic, you understand. Nothing at all to do with female servitude, as some have put it. Not at all. Women will never make great writers. And please don't give me any of that 'Poor souls, held back by male critics' baloney. It is nothing but a matter of talent—or lack of it."

Zoe bit her tongue as long as she could. "Dear, sir," she said with caustic bite, "unless men write with their penises, I doubt there is anything different between the work of the two sexes except that women bring more of the senses to the page—other than shooting big guns and blowing up everything around them—which I always find suspect in the mysteries of men. Women know about childbirth and loving another more than oneself. They have a reverence for life no male writer can hope to achieve."

"Now, little lady, you don't know who you're talking to and I hope . . ."

Behind them, the front door opened, and a middle-aged woman walked in and stopped to look over the gathering before closing the door behind her. She wore a plain brown raincoat. Her hair was brown—sticking out from under a brown rain hat. She waited, suitcase at her feet, as face after face turned her way.

The room was almost silent.

She stammered, "I'm . . . I'm Mary Reid. I think I know most of you. I should have been here earlier. I'm actually a member of our Christie Society and one of your hostesses."

Zoe hurried over to the poor woman, happy for the interruption, and for the enraged look she left behind on Aaron Kennedy's face.

"Mary Reid. I own Ulysses Bookstore in Houghton." The woman bent toward Zoe, putting out a hand and vigorously shaking Zoe's. She asked her name and threw a hand to her mouth when she heard.

"Oh, Zoe Zola. Just the person I want to meet. I hope you'll come to Houghton, to my bookstore, one day. You have so many fans up here. The whole English and creative writing faculty at Northern Michigan University. I swear, Miss Zola, you would be a hit."

Zoe smiled the bright smile she gave when meeting especially perceptive people like this Mary Reid.

Chapter 22

The Copper Room was large and austere, the paneled walls decorated with copper works. One, at the head of the room, was shaped into Michigan's two sections: Upper and Lower Peninsulas. One, on another wall, was a large work of various-sized pine trees. Another was a copper rendering of a mine shaft, complete with a silhouetted man, a pick axe on his shoulder. The room was both formal and earthy, maybe Zoe's favorite room so far.

The oak table, set in the middle of the room, was large. The chairs around it were plain, yet the table was set with a long, ornate tablecloth. There were translucent white dishes at every place, glassware etched with "NL," and heavy silverware set atop brilliant white napkins.

At the center of the table, a large copper platter held a bowl of blue wildflowers—at least Zoe guessed they were wildflowers since she didn't recognize them as any cultured flower she'd seen before. Under the draping wildflowers were figures of children: playing, skipping, sitting, falling. One with a hand clutching his throat. Ten figures. Not soldiers, as in *And Then There Were None*. She felt a tightening in her chest and told herself children couldn't disappear as the soldiers had in Christie's book. Children wouldn't mark a guest disappearing and presumed dead.

Ten little soldier boys went out to dine
One choked his little self and then there were nine.

Nine little soldier boys . . . She tried but couldn't remember the rest of the poem. But whatever the last little soldier boy's way of death was, that would be hers. She was the tenth guest and the last of the presenters.

She looked around the table at the others. Anthony Gliese and Gewel Sharp were there, taking seats next to each other. Professor Leon Armstrong lurched into the room and bent to read place cards, squinting hard as he searched for his name. The professor's red hair was still uncombed, his eyes blurrier than before. When he found his place next to Aaron Kennedy, he smiled at the man, waggled his head as a greeting, and sat. Kennedy made a disagreeable face, moving as far as he could get from Armstrong.

Leon noticed nothing, only asked Aaron to please pass the wine.

She knew enough about all of them now to make judgments. There was no one who looked like her, no one who seemed to hate her—except Aaron Kennedy, and she was proud to claim that woman-hater as an enemy. And no one who seemed particularly murderous, though someone had tried to hurt her out on the path, no matter what the others said.

Zoe settled back in her chair, alone at one end of the long table, and wondered whether to point out the figurines, and make a joke of them.

Mary Reid, tilted head, flushed face, and wide-open eyes, sat beside her. She quietly touched Zoe's arm, then pointed to the figurines. Zoe nodded and smiled.

"Décor," she whispered behind her hand. "Imaginative."

Mary signaled that she got it and settled back to look over her schedules before the food came.

Nigel Pileser sat in the chair around the table corner from Zoe.

Louise Joiner, with Anna Tow right behind her, was next into the room, nodding at everyone. She was followed by Emily Brent, who took the second to last chair as a thin, ungainly woman hurried in behind her, looking left to right around the table and bursting out with apologies as she searched for her place.

"So sorry." The woman looked up and nodded in all directions. "So sorry. Got held up. From Canada, you know. Betty Bertram?" She gave her name as if asking a question, then glanced from face to face around the table, nodding at each name given to her. Her own face turned a bright red, her head soon lowered as she pulled out the chair near Anthony Gliese.

Emily Brent, seated now, leaned forward. "I was wondering what happened to you."

"I know." Betty blushed again. "The plane was delayed and then canceled. Rain. Everywhere. Nothing but rain the whole way here. Finally came by way of Flint. Took a bus to Houghton and then hitched a ride from there to Calumet. Those people lived in Calumet and they never heard of this place."

Words spilled out until she cut them off abruptly, mouth hanging open as she looked at each face turned her way. She took a breath and began talking again.

"Luckily, I found that car in town, waiting to bring me here. Never for a minute did I imagine this place would be out so far. I suppose I've missed quite a bit. Well, first of all, I'm Betty Bertram, as I said."

The woman was thin to the point of emaciation and had the undecorated, plain face of a country girl. She nodded again and again to the people around the table, repeating her name. "Betty Bertram. Graduate student. McGill. Canada, ya know."

She sat very straight and robotically introduced herself to each person at the table. "Betty Bertram. Graduate student. McGill."

Her thin brown hair was pulled back into a ponytail, with wisps sticking out along the sides of her head. The white blouse and denim skirt she wore hung on her thin body like old clothes in a second-hand shop—the shoulders of her blouse drooped halfway down her arms. Her very long-fingered hands jumped from the table top to her lap and back as she spoke.

Zoe, a master of knowing people at first sight, felt a twinge of pity for this new woman. With the academic hyenas she'd identified among them—Professor Pileser, for sure; maybe Anna Tow; Anthony Gliese, no more than a playboy; Aaron Kennedy—she could be in for a mauling.

Zoe sighed and gave her name as the woman's eyes fell on her. Poor thing. There was almost a begging quality to the woman's narrow smile.

"Oh, I know who you are," she said quickly. "Oh, not because you're a—no, I mean I've heard of you. I was so happy to hear you'd be here. I've been looking forward to this since they first asked me to come, and I said yes when they told me that Zoe Zola would be here. A whole new way of writing a literary biography. What a coup. What a—"

"Mary Reid. I own the Ulysses Bookstore in Houghton," Mary interrupted. "A long-time devotee of Agatha Christie and all the writers of her ilk."

The introductions went on.

"Emily Brent. I'm your hostess. We've spoken many times." She was a little short with the odd young woman. "I'll see you to your room after dinner."

"Oh, no, don't bother. If you'll just tell—"

Emily cut her off. "After dinner."

Gewel was next. She gave her name and mentioned her recent graduation and her hope to write mysteries. "I'm mostly an onlooker among these famous critics." She was close to gushing but closed her mouth to sit grinning a self-conscious grin.

When it was Leon Armstrong's turn, he bit his lip as if unable to remember his name—drained his wine glass, and frowned, slipping down in his chair.

Betty nodded and ticked off another finger anyway. She was keeping count.

Aaron Kennedy seemed put out by the whole thing and gave his name as if it were one word, adding nothing.

"I'm excited to meet you all," Betty said. "I would have done anything to make it here on time. One of the worst moments of my life was when they said my plane was canceled."

"And why the anxiety, Miss Bertram?" Professor Pileser leaned forward, hands folding slowly in front of his plate as his curious eyes focused hard on her.

"Oh, maybe because Agatha Christie knew people as hardly anyone has ever known them. I mean right off. Soon as she met them and then, ya know, she used their characteristics and personalities together, so her characters were never boring. Never old hat, I guess you would say."

Professor Pileser leaned far back in his chair. Zoe thought, at first, she saw what might pass for pity on the man's face. But more likely it was relish at how easy this woman was going to be swallowed whole.

"You've got to be kidding, my dear," Kennedy said. "You truly thought Christie that perceptive? But then how do you explain the Tommy and Tuppence novels? Seems to me that pair together are the silliest two not only in mystery but in any literary genre. Why, if you ask me—"

To the gratitude of all, Emily stood, rapped her knuckles on the table and welcomed her guests to Netherworld Lodge and the first Agatha Christie Webinar. She described what they would be doing together this week and touted the area around the lodge as perfect for thought and reflection.

She ended her brief talk with a reminder that Dr. Pileser would be leading their first webinar the next afternoon.

Bella Webb began the dinner quietly, carrying in a tureen of leek soup and filling each of the bowls. Except for desultory laughter between Anthony and Gewel, most of them were quiet, talking in near whispers to the people closest, except for a moment when Nigel burst out with a "Damn wrong!" to Betty Bertram. Her face turned red and she mumbled, "Sorry" to everyone around her. After that she said nothing through the meat and vegetable, then salad, and dessert course, as others praised the stuffed quail with grilled asparagus, the tomato and mozzarella salad, and then a perfect gateau of cherries, whipped cream, and chocolate icing.

The rain was the greatest topic of dinner conversation, as it had been falling for the last hour and didn't look as if it would let up any time soon.

Zoe spoke little throughout the meal. She was tired. She was worried and emotionally drained. Her ankle throbbed. Nigel Pileser and Aaron Kennedy talked the most—loudly, and only to each other. The women nodded and smiled. Anthony leaned forward to take on Pileser, mocking something he'd said.

That brought in Aaron, who took nobody's side but argued anyway. Zoe barely paid attention, only watched their faces—the passion they brought to whatever it was they argued about.

Because Emily recognized an uproar brewing between Anthony and Aaron, she stood again and asked if anyone had questions.

"What about the lodge van?" Zoe called out. "Will it be going to town tomorrow? I need to look up some Christie books I didn't know to bring with me."

Emily spread her hands and shrugged. "Not on Sunday. For the Monday trip you'll have to talk to the heavens, my dear. A little prayer wouldn't hurt. As for us, we'll soldier on, won't we? The students running the webinar assured me they've set up a failsafe internet connection and have already installed the equipment we will be needing. Not to worry about that part."

Even Nigel Pileser, his broad face red, his eyes sleepy, seemed satisfied as he thanked Emily for the very nice dinner.

The last of the wine was finished. They rose, one by one, and headed for the film room to watch—after all that wine and meat and a perfect sweet—Christie's *Evil Under the Sun*, 1982. With Peter Ustinov as Poirot.

Aaron Kennedy groused all the way that personally he would much prefer to see the banned version of *Ordeal by Innocence*, though no one paid any attention to him.

Part 3

Netherworld on Sunday

Chapter 23

Awake at midnight. The bad ankle throbbed. Then one o'clock. Not a minute's restful sleep in between. Zoe's mind wouldn't stop going back and forth over their first day. Not a stellar opening for the event. What a menagerie of human beings. She didn't envy Emily Brent herding them through the next five days.

She was grateful the first evening was over. It was always the hardest to get through, especially with people who wobbled their elbows to take up more room; almost silent people who sat watching the others as if someone were there to eat them. And then, so quickly, alliances being formed—women finding safe women to talk to; men finding other loud men to argue with; and over-sexed men finding over-sexed (and willing to make a deal) women to spend a few nights with.

She let her mind reel—back and forth. Were any of these people members of the Jokela family—Evelyn's sisters, cousins, aunts, uncles? Any of them her own blood?

The thing to do, she told herself, was to take it a day at a time, and if she smelled anything wrong, she would call Jenny and Lisa somehow and make a break for it. Or she'd strike off into the woods. Or, if she couldn't get a hold of Jenny or Lisa, she would use her suitcase as a raft and paddle back across that creek.

Almost too tired to think anymore, in too much pain to shut it out, and too confused to wonder what she'd gotten herself into, Zoe got out of bed and pushed the window as high as it would go. She lay back down and let a wet breeze bring on goose bumps. The smell of more rain was in the air—along with the cool, wet feeling that left her skin damp, her hair stuck to the side of her face.

Far in the distance, she heard thunder, and then came a stark bolt of light, cutting the sky and outlining bloated, dark clouds. Tired almost to the point of not caring what these people were planning, she let her mind turn slowly to pictures of the faces around the dinner table and then tried to connect names to the faces. Odd that all had a familiar ring to them: Betty Bertram. Louise Joiner. Mary Reid. Gewel Sharp. Somehow connected. She had already gone through the sketchy Christie files she'd brought with her and found no connections.

She drifted off to sleep, only to pop her eyes open a few minutes later. Anthony—the playboy in *And Then There Were None*, and Anthony Gliese—certainly a playboy, here to make a conquest.

The line "Well, anyway it wasn't my fault. Just an accident." The character had hit two children with his car, killed them, and showed no remorse.

She got a pad of paper and a pen from her computer bag and sat in front of the window, beginning a list of names:

Gewel Sharp. She racked her brain. Nothing. She thought through the novels she knew best—no Gewel or Jewel. Young. Blonde. A fan. Target for Anthony Gliese.

Mary Reid. A common name. Reid. Reid. Reid. Or Reed. Reed. Reed.

Aaron Kennedy. Not a clue, but a terrible, rude man. Maybe from *And Then There Were None*. Have to find a copy of the book. One of the others might have it. Or the library.

Betty Bertram. Oh, so familiar. A sad woman without the backbone to stand up for herself. She'd let Pileser knock her down with one sentence. He would have to be dealt with. The thing about being different—and Betty Bertram was different—was that you had to learn to use it. You had to learn to narrow your eyes to warn people and, if they weren't warned, to drop a devastating bomb on them. She'd learned, since Evelyn's death, that everybody in the world was ultimately alone and responsible for his or her own life.

Louise Joiner. Something here she couldn't put her finger on. Joiner: carpenter.

Anna Tow. Pull. Tug. Carry.

Leon Armstrong—Edward George Armstrong. Harley Street doctor in *And Then There Were None*. The doctor was a drunk. He murdered a patient by operating while drunk. *Bingo!* Maybe she was right and there was a puzzle or a game going on here.

So much more to discover.

Nigel Pileser—silly name. Probably real or she would have remembered coming across this one before.

She put her pad and pen away and crawled back into bed. She needed the library in Calumet. Monday. After the webinar. No sense asking the others. She didn't know who was in on whatever was going to happen. She didn't know who was completely innocent. She would take the lodge bus right after their webinar. An hour and a half—long enough to find what she was looking for: the names and their Christie connections.

If only the ankle would stop hurting.

* * *

She awoke sometime later in the night to voices whispering beneath her window.

Someone said. "Ya sure? Dat's her room?"

Someone else, a woman's voice, said only, "I'm pretty sure."

Zoe's body stiffened: *"Dat's her room?"*

She couldn't move.

She listened as hard as she could, but the voices stopped. At some time she fell asleep, lying stiff, and awoke to rain being blown into her room and thunder echoing over the forest.

When she was as damp as she could take, she scrambled to close the window and look at her watch: seven AM.

Breakfast in an hour. She didn't need another shower. All she could think about was Jenny coming with Lisa. It was all she had to cling to. In her damp bed, she leaned against her pillows and closed her eyes for only a minute.

When she awoke next, it was eight thirty.

Sunday. First full day and she was already a half-hour late for breakfast.

Chapter 24

Janne was back, knocking on Lisa's door early. Jenny frowned as she answered. A man standing there, deep in the woods, wearing a red plaid shirt and jeans, long brown hair pulled back into a ponytail. He wore a broad, happy smile.

He walked in without an invitation, held out his hand to take hers, and said, "Janne. And you're Jenny. Nice to meet you. Your sister talks about you a lot."

"And I've heard a lot about you. All good, in your case."

*   *   *

They were having coffee when Lisa crawled out from the bed at the back. She and Janne hugged, but as far as Jenny could see, it was the casual hug friends share, and she felt less happy. Lisa was her older sister. Time to be making a move in life, if she ever intended to.

Janne had come for breakfast. He'd brought a homemade coffee cake with him. His mother had sent it, along with greetings to Lisa.

"Outside?" Janne motioned toward the door. "Beautiful morning. Rain's gone again."

So they ate under the trees, sitting around a white folding table Janne set up. Toast and fruit and yogurt and coffee cake. A good solid breakfast that would keep them going until sometime that night, after dark, when the women of the town might feed them again.

After breakfast, Lisa said she had a piece of the documentary for Jenny to watch. Not edited yet, Lisa explained. But she could see what they had, and she wanted Jenny to see it.

"It's just Leena, sitting by the fire, telling her family's story. We'll go there tomorrow if it doesn't rain," Lisa said. "To the cemetery. So much of who they are is buried there."

Janne nodded. "They're my people—all of them. I come from here. I only found out how special we are when I left. And more now, through Lisa's eyes."

He smiled again. "I was happy she saw it when I brought her here to meet them. And then when she saw the possibility of this film."

Later, with breakfast finished, the table folded and put back under a tarp beside the trailer, they went inside to see the piece.

It opened in the dark, with a circle of orange flame at the center of the shot. The flame grew until it was a glowing fire, and there were voices around it, though the woman talking was never shown—only the flames as they grew and then died.

The older woman had a deep echo in her voice. The fire crackled. A bat buzzed the woman's head. She swatted hard at it, but not too hard. Somehow Jenny knew that hand wasn't raised to hurt.

"It was winter when my mother's twins died. The men, dey used shovels to clear away three feet o' snow, and den dey used dem pick-axes to cut into da frozen ground. Two small graves. And my mother so weak dey had to carry her home. Dis land ain't easy to anybody. It is, dat's all. The rest is what the people make of it. And what we make is our own place. Dat's why I stay. No place else could ever, not in a million years, be home. Where ya bury yer children is where ya live."

Jenny, moved by the woman in the stark film and the silence around the three of them, said she needed to walk for a while. She wanted to climb a hill and look around—at where she was. "Maybe I'll get a signal and can make a call."

"We'll go see Zoe later," Lisa said, her eyes on her sister. "Janne and I can work this morning. But watch yourself. You know there are animals everywhere."

Jenny nodded but didn't feel afraid of anything.

* * *

She followed a trail cutting up a small hill, a narrow sand trail between thick trees. The air was fresh, from the rain, but what started out to be sunshine was already filming over, thin clouds coming in from the west.

She climbed in sand, imagining the trek through deep snow. What she didn't want to imagine was losing two babies at once and burying them under the snow.

At the top of the hill, when she tried to call her mother, her phone signaled no service. Dead.

She sat in the sand and thought about Dora: husband taken away from her; her own kind of acceptance of life without him. She let herself think about loss. People could pass out of one another's lives, like those dead babies. So little time for memories when you buried children in the frozen earth.

But, she thought, *no one said she had to bury herself. No one said she had to become invisible. Give up everything and everyone. Tony's never asked that.* He had only asked her to share his new adventure. He'd only offered her a place with him.

She'd come up here, to Lisa, to think, and she was thinking.

She walked the path downward now, not realizing how steep the climb up had been. The sand was deep and hard to walk in.

It was a different place, going back where she'd come from.

When she fell, she began to slide and then to tumble. When she stopped falling, she sat up and felt the bump on her head and began to laugh. Something in her whole time out here mirrored her life so far—and her choices and her future, all bumps and bruises.

If she could get a phone signal, she would call Tony right then. It was her bargain with fate.

No signal.

A sign not to let the emotions she was feeling—being here with these women from a different time—take over her brain.

A sign she still had a lot of thinking to do.

Chapter 25

From the pile of papers and brochures and newspapers in front of her, Lisa pulled one out and slapped it. "Remember, you told me about seeing the opera house in Calumet? I was there. Janne got tickets the first week we were up here. *The Mouse Trap*. Isn't that odd? An Agatha Christie play. It's closed. Too bad."

"I've seen it before. In Chicago. Love that we're not supposed to tell who the murderer is when the play's over. I can't imagine there is one person left in the world who doesn't know."

Jenny looked down at the shiny brochure Lisa pushed her way. The playbill for *The Mousetrap*. She scanned the cover: the cast taking a bow. She looked closer. One woman, middle-aged, maybe sixty, smiled as she held the hands of the other cast members.

She knew her. Different in the photo. Not as old, but still definitely Emily Brent, the brusque woman of Netherworld Lodge.

Jenny opened the brochure and quickly reviewed the list of actors, but Emily Brent's name wasn't listed.

"But I know her." Jenny said to Lisa, pointing to the cover.

"From where?"

"From Netherworld Lodge."

"A critic?"

She shook her head. "She's Emily Brent, one of the planners of the event."

"Odd. But I suppose anybody interested enough to belong to the Northern Michigan Agatha Christie Society would be interested enough to play a part in *The Mouse Trap*," Lisa said.

"I recognize the role she's playing—Mrs. Boyle, a kind of nasty old lady."

"Check the cast names?"

"I did. A woman named Susan Jokela Wintor played the role. Emily Brent is lying to all of us."

Jenny made a face. Something was ringing a faraway bell inside her head.

"Why would the woman lie?"

"Look at this other one: Mollie Ralston, the role of the woman who owned Monkswell Manor with her husband, Giles. Her name is Mary Lamb. Odd name."

Jenny bent over the playbill. "Here's another. Detective Sergeant Trotter. His bio says he's a lawyer right here in Calumet. Harley Lamb."

"And the bios of the two women?"

"Nothing. All it says here is that they've both played these same roles before. In Chicago and Boston."

Jenny drew in a quick breath. "I might have seen them. I could have recognized them both if they're at Netherworld."

"You wouldn't, would you? Stage makeup and all?"

"This other one. The Mollie Ralston character. She could be there, somewhere at Netherworld."

"You said you haven't met the others yet."

Jenny shook her head. "Maybe this afternoon."

"And their names are both the same?"

Jenny nodded. "Two are Lambs: Mary and Harley."

"Mary Lamp? Doesn't even sound like a real name."

"Mary Lamb. Lamb. You know, like the ones being led to the slaughter."

"Or the other way around," Lisa said. "We've got to get to Netherworld, tell Zoe about all of this."

"She said we couldn't come until the webinar was over. After four thirty."

Chapter 26

Jenny went out to her Jeep to clean it. Nothing to do for hours.

The Jeep was loaded with dirty fast-food cups and candy wrappers from their trip. She liked to keep it clean—this first car of her own and not an old one passed on from Lisa, and not a car she was warned to keep clean by her ex-husband.

Hers alone. Not new, but only two years old. And blue. She loved blue but would never have dared to hope for such a blue, blue car if someone gave it to her.

A whisk broom and a dust pan were all she needed.

She began in the front, noticing first that Zoe had spilled something on the seat. That required a wet rag, a trip back to the house, a little elbow grease, and a few angry words at Zoe.

And then the backseat and the discovery of Zoe's box of black-rimmed letters. Like holding a terrible curse in her hands. Jenny took the box and carried it carefully into the trailer to show Lisa.

* * *

"These are what started it all?" Lisa poked the pile of letters on the table.

Jenny could've sworn she saw heat rise. Maybe letters from hell were like these. A pile of letters, sent with meanness and hatred—as if a single pregnancy hurt any of them.

"Why would they do this?" Lisa looked up.

Jenny shrugged. "Hubris. Because they could, and afterward felt proud of their high standards. Snickering among themselves at how God would surely reward them."

Lisa took one of the letters between her hands, holding it carefully.

She turned the letter over. The name was smeared, but there was an address. This one in Cheboygan, Michigan.

She picked up another and turned it over. The same. Another. This time from Alpena, Michigan.

Lisa looked up at Jenny. "If she wanted us to, we could find their names with a reverse lookup in the White Pages."

"Most go back awhile."

"I don't think Zoe ever wanted to know who they were. But maybe now. Names of people here at the event. Wouldn't that help?" Lisa looked at Jenny, who bit at her lip.

"Do you think we could do it? I mean, go someplace where I could use my computer?"

"I know a place. Sometimes I have to go there when I can't get any signal here."

"Today?"

"You mean before we go to Netherworld?"

She nodded.

"We could try." Lisa sounded hopeful. "Then we can give her the names of people in her family, and if there are any at Netherworld she can face them down and leave with us."

"Sounds so simple."

"Like I said: worth a try."

Chapter 27

Sunday breakfast: clean underwear, white pants, a crimson top, white sandals over her elastic bandage, and she was out of her room, without washing or brushing her teeth—the dull rumble of voices hurrying her across the empty reception room.

A few seats other than hers were empty. Relief. She smiled, greeting those around the table, then hurrying to her chair, climbing up, unfolding her silverware from the very large, bright white napkin, and explaining to anyone who would listen how she'd overslept.

First she turned to Mary, who didn't seem to hear her "Good Morning." Her eyes were fixed on Emily.

Next she smiled across the table at Anna, who frowned absently and looked down at her plate.

When she asked for the dish of scrambled eggs set on the other end of the table, no one heard her. She got down, walked around the chairs, reached in between the whispering Anthony and Gewel, and grabbed the dish, figuring if they were all punishing her for being late, too bad for them. She dished up her eggs, went back for a plate of toast and then a platter of fried potatoes, and sat down to eat, minding her own business. And the hell with the entire rude group. Half an hour late!

Mary Reid finally leaned toward her, bracing herself against an empty chair. "We just heard as you walked in that they had to take Professor Armstrong to the hospital in Houghton last night. A form of allergy, they said, but bad. He's being flown home today. Poor man. Now we need someone to take over his webinar. I was saying it should be one of our fine guests here. Like Anthony, but Aaron thought perhaps one of you could double up."

Zoe looked to Louise. "You're on tomorrow, aren't you? Couldn't you do yours today, leave time for one of the others to prepare?"

Louise shivered. "I don't like to change plans. It always signals trouble. I mean, I have everything ready. But . . . I suppose. Or maybe Anna could."

Louise looked around the table toward the frowning woman, who shook her head. "I'm afraid not," she said. "I put a lot of work into any presentation I give. I would need so much more time."

Louise and Zoe sighed in unison.

"Oh, for God's sake." Louise threw her hands in the air. "I'll do mine today."

"And I'll do Leon's tomorrow,' Anthony said. "Now can somebody pass the eggs before our fine Zoe Zola finishes them off entirely?"

Zoe ignored him. He was a tease, but not mean like Aaron and Nigel. Her mind was on the blue flowers and the platter beneath. She didn't want to look but couldn't stop herself .

She got off her chair and made a trip around the table. One. Two. Three. Four. Five. Six. Seven. Eight. Nine . . .

Nine little figures. The little boy with his hands at his throat was gone.

She didn't say a word to the others. If they didn't notice, they probably didn't want to.

Chapter 28

After breakfast Zoe locked herself in her room. She wished Lisa and Jenny would come soon. She wished she hadn't told them after four thirty. She was lonely, depressed, angry, and longed to talk to friends. She lay on the bed, reliving the night before. Voices. People pointing out her room. She'd closed and locked her window before leaving that morning, but what could anyone want that she had?

She got up to stare out at the vast, boring woods. Where had Leon Armstrong really gone? No way to find out where they'd taken him, who he'd really been, or why he was gone so soon. It could be another connection. Maybe a family name or some way linked to Christie.

She thought there might be a name on one of the funeral cards. Only a few were nearly legible. For most there were addresses.

She'd brought the box with her from home but couldn't remember carrying it into the lodge.

She checked each drawer of the dresser. No box.

Maybe that couple from last night . . . how? She'd locked her door too.

She looked under the bed. Nothing.

The box had to be in Jenny's car, but the bridge could be completely gone. The river might have overflowed its banks and was headed toward them right then. She might not see them for days.

The closet—yes. She pulled in a deep breath and checked the closet, knowing there would be nothing in there but the small box she'd seen when she first got here. A box—ordinary cardboard. One foot by one foot.

She took it to the desk and lifted the top.

Photographs. Loose. At least fifty, maybe more. No order to the pictures. The first she took out was of a baby sitting in a stroller. The child was lovely, soft features, large eyes. She was smiling and clapping her hands for the camera. Other photos were of the same girl—she was sure of it, the eyes were memorable—but in her teens. The rest were taken at varying times during this girl's life—maybe twenty, then about five years old, ten, eighteen. When she turned the pictures over, the same name was written on each—sometimes in black ink, sometimes in blue.

Angela Lamb.

A letdown. No name Zoe'd ever heard Evelyn say.

Lamb. Lamb. Nothing like her family name: Jokela.

She went through the girl's pictures, hoping to find something special here. Only one in the box had the girl, probably then in her teens, standing with someone else. She brought the photo close. A man with red hair. A red mustache. A younger Leon Armstrong, the professor from New York. Connected now to Netherworld Lodge.

How did his photos get into her room if they were Leon's? And why would anyone want to break in to get them?

* * *

It was time for Louise's rehearsal. No time to deal with new problems. She hurried down to the Michigan Room and took her place among the others at an oval table lined with folded name cards and headsets.

After Mary gave the floor to Louise, there was a moment of flurry as Louise hunted through her briefcase for her notes and then, flustered, spread them on the table in front of her. "I told you I would get nervous. I don't like when things get upset."

"Relax, Louise. Just tell us about your paper. We'll fill in from there." Aaron Kennedy looked bored already.

He managed to make her more nervous. She bowed her head and said nothing for at least two minutes.

When she began again, she was composed, her high cheekbones giving her a classic look, her hazel eyes calm—even a small smile as she began to talk about the agonies of Agatha Christie, beginning with the early loss of her father; then to her cheating first husband, Archie Christie; and on to the coolness of her daughter and the inconstancy of her second husband, Max Mallowan. And then to what eased her pain—writing books and plays, losing herself every day in the worlds she could control.

When she'd finished, the others made suggestions, complimented her, with Pileser and Kennedy finding a few holes, vying to be the expert's expert; but on the whole the work was accepted as very deep and knowledgeable.

For a half an hour more, the others mentioned ways they would add to Louise's talk. And then came the projected questions they might get from the paying audience across the world, with ideas for answers.

They worked surprisingly well together.

"I might add that most of the equipment was brought by boat, by our techs, if you can imagine." Emily Brent joined them. "The river is over its banks. The rain keeps falling, but we're trying to keep to our schedule. Emails to our paying participants went out yesterday, reminding them that we begin today. I've sent another, explaining Professor Armstrong had to leave and that we'll begin with Dr. Trainer.

"Oh," she added. "Remember, no cell phones in the room while a webinar is going on. They create interference, I'm told."

"Yeah, sure." Anthony made fun of the idea of a phone working at Netherworld Lodge.

* * *

At three o'clock, Mary Reid began her introductions on the purpose of the webinar, went over the plans for the four days ahead, and explained that there had been a change in the schedule. Dr. Louise Trainer was taking over for the Dr. Armstrong, who was ill and had to leave.

Louise took over swiftly, confident now, rarely referring to her notes. This was a different Louise Trainer, speaking for the first half hour, then being challenged by Aaron and Nigel, agreed with by Gewel and the others, but keeping her part of the webinar firmly in her hands.

The presentation continued smoothly, with the exception of one snit over Christie's second husband, started by Betty Bertram, which surprised Zoe, as the timid woman settled herself in, wobbled her head, and said a lot of what they were hearing today was pure bull.

Mary hurried to cover the girl's gaffe and then invited the others to ask their questions.

Aaron Armstrong took up the rest of Louise's time, and then it was the last half hour, and questions from the webinar audience.

The first question was from a Gerald in Takoma. "To go back to Dr. Trainer"—his voice cracked, then settled down—"I'd like to know who holds the rights to Christie's work now? Is it her daughter, Rosalind?"

That question was answered easily: her grandson owned the rights.

The talk was lively, only one sneering old man making fun of their research and touting a new book on Christie he'd just self-published.

Zoe quieted him by asking which university he taught at.

None, he was self-taught.

And had he visited the Christie countryside?

No. He'd picked up enough from his reading.

And how long had he studied Christie?

Over a year, as his book would show.

Other questions popped in fast until their half hour was over, and Mary had to shut them down, saying goodbye to their audience and telling them they would begin again on Monday. Same time. The topic to be "The World of Agatha Christie," as planned, by Dr. Leon Armstrong, now to be presented by Anthony Gliese, editor at Conway Books in New York.

It was over. Successful, they all agreed, though they stumbled into one another to get out of the room.

Chapter 29

It was a little after four thirty by the time the techs ran their tests for the next day.

Zoe hurried out to the reception room, but Jenny and Lisa weren't there.

Rain or not, she wanted to get into Calumet and do her research on names in Christie's books at the library.

It was these names, of people at the webinar, that bothered her most. She kept feeling she should know them but couldn't pull them from the musty corners of her mind where they'd landed.

There were books and short stories to check. How could anyone know them all by heart? And on top of that, she was certain only part of each name came from Christie.

An almost impossible task, she told herself as she stepped to the board, where the greeting had been replaced with a copy of the new schedule of talks.

A note, tacked on top of the new schedule, warned that the water was rising everywhere in the area, and the van might be delayed until Tuesday.

"Damn," Zoe whispered.

"Double damn," a voice behind her said. "I forgot my deodorant, and if today is any hint at what's ahead of us, it's going to get hot in this place."

Zoe turned to smile at Gewel Sharp.

"Interesting, don't you think?" Gewel showed her very white teeth. "We're captives. One man gone. May not be by sea, but there's sure a lot of water coming down out there. Remind you of anything?"

"Soldier Island," Zoe said, then stepped closer to Gewel, saying in a lower voice, *"And Then There Were None."*

Gewel pointed to Leon's name—crossed off the sheet. "Think he went out and choked himself? How many should we give 'em before we start running like hell?" Gewel giggled.

Zoe wrinkled her nose. "Give 'em what?"

"You know. More dead soldiers."

"Oh, I get it. You mean if somebody goes missing tonight—like 'Nine little soldier boys sat up very late. One overslept himself and then there were eight'?"

"Uh-huh. Just like that. But how do you die by oversleeping?"

Zoe could come up with a dozen different ways to oversleep herself, but none of them were pleasant. "How about poison?"

Gewel stuck a finger in the air. "One hypodermic in the arm so the person can think, but not talk or move—like a horse tranquilizer. That's the worst, don't you imagine? Or antifreeze in a Coke."

"Hmm." Zoe thought. "Poison in a gift of wine."

"Other choices," Gewel said. "Buried alive. I never really liked the idea of that one, but it doesn't fit anyway."

"Strangulation."

Gewel got serious. "Or choke on a sleeping pill. Or on a false tooth."

Zoe gave her a narrow-eyed look. "Take a big glass of weed killer before you close your eyes."

Gewel shivered. "You are truly ghoulish, Zoe Zola."

Zoe shook her head and put a finger to her cheek. "Or—if you live above your garage, just leave the car running. Carbon monoxide will get you."

Gewel turned to look behind her. "Did you notice the dancing children?" Gewel asked, her face serious. "Nobody even mentioned that one is gone."

"I saw it. The best I can come up with is Bella or Emily, setting the mood for Christie."

They gave nervous laughs and shivered as they agreed to meet for cocktails later.

* * *

Quarter after five, and no sign or sound from Jenny and Lisa. Most of the others had gone to their rooms. A quiet time. Only Anthony Gliese and Nigel Pileser stood in the hall, arguing about something that didn't interest Zoe.

She wrapped a sweater around her shoulders and went outside to check the parking area, and maybe the road coming up from the bridge.

It was raining again, but lightly. Maybe the water at the bridge had time to recede, at least a little.

She'd been inside the lodge too long, cooped up with people she didn't like or trust, for the most part. She wished the next people she talked to would be Jenny and Lisa, and they wouldn't once utter the name *Agatha Christie*.

There was no way to know if they were coming or not. No phone calls. No message by carrier pigeon.

Maybe the bridge was impassable instead of dry. Or the roads coming in were underwater. Or they'd had work to do and couldn't make it. So many reasons they weren't there yet, but they all hurt. She wanted to tell them about the voices under her window—how they were loud enough for her to hear, as if on purpose. She wanted to tell them about Leon Armstrong, that he'd disappeared. And about the one missing figure under the blue flowers. About names she'd tried to take apart because they felt so much like names she'd heard before.

The door opened behind her. Of all people she wished she could stay away from forever, Aaron Kennedy was at the top of the list.

"Ah, Zoe Zola. That was intense, wasn't it, though you have to give Dr. Joiner credit. She did an adequate job on such short notice."

She walked off the porch, down to the parking area.

He followed.

Zoe stretched her lips into a tight smile and said nothing. There were dim cars lights off through the trees.

"Still no phone service or internet." He threw his arms wide. "Those kids today somehow got on the internet. Why can't we? I don't understand, do you? Why didn't that Brent woman warn us this place was so isolated and that we were in danger of being stranded? I really think I will be telling others to skip any programs planned at this place."

"Emily and Mary couldn't have predicted floods." She didn't want to listen to much more of him. The headlights, through the trees again, were brighter.

She tootled down the drive, away from Aaron.

He followed easily at her speed.

"That's my friends. I'm sure of it. I've been waiting to see them." She pointed to the lights.

"Really? Certainly not for drinks or dinner, I hope. Are they coming to tonight's film? Did you ask first?" He kept pace with her, forcing her to slow to get her breath.

"I would think the first thing you'd do is ask permission. Even asking your friends to try to get across the sunken bridge . . . who knows what danger you've put them in? Rather a reckless thing to do, Zoe."

Zoe stopped abruptly. That was enough. She'd reached a brittle edge here with this man. Never intimidated by a tall, skinny man with bad breath, she got up close and lifted a finger to poke his stomach. She poked again, making him bend, then pushed until he took a step back, complaining.

"I beg your—"

"May I warn you, sir." Her words were bitten into small chunks. "I may be small, but I am probably as intelligent—no, I'd say more intelligent—than you will ever be. And can run my life without help from . . .'"

Her words trailed away as the lights she'd been watching made the last turn toward the front of the lodge, then stopped beside Zoe. Two women threw open the doors and rushed to hug her.

Aaron Kennedy faded away, off toward the path around the lodge, as the three of them hugged.

On the porch they stopped to huddle again. Jenny and Lisa had a story to tell, a story Zoe was happy to hear.

"So, I left the funeral notices in your car after all?" Zoe was relieved. "I was looking for them. Early this morning, outside my window, someone was talking about getting into my room. I thought it was for those notices. Something they didn't want me to find in them. But I found something else—"

"We took them into Copper Harbor with us," Lisa interrupted.

"We hoped we could look up some of those addresses on the backs of the envelopes. Get you the names of who sent them," Lisa said. "You know, a reverse address lookup."

"And did you?"

"Couldn't find a place where we could get on Wi-Fi, but the owner of a restaurant let us use his phone. Pretty strong signal."

"And?"

"We called Tony."

Zoe looked hard at Jenny, seeing nothing unusual in her face.

"And?" Zoe pushed.

"We gave him some of those addresses to see if he could find names to go with them."

"And?" Zoe demanded.

"Not so fast," Lisa said. "He's looking them up. He says he'll get them to us here, at Netherworld, as quick as he can."

"We can't get anything here. He won't be able —."

"Don't discount Tony, Zoe. He's got lots of ways to get things done. Remember, he used to be a cop."

Zoe watched Jenny's face. Not a hint of irony.

Inside, Emily Brent was the first to greet them. "Thought I heard noise out there. Who the devil are you two?" She frowned at Jenny and Lisa. "Oh, you're the one brought Zoe Zola, aren't you?"

"How'd you get here?" Mary Reid asked. "Boat?"

"Jeep," Lisa said. "Not easy. Hope we can get back out. That bridge isn't too stable."

"Can we get out soon, do you think?" Aaron Kennedy, back now, called.

Zoe led them toward the stairs. She wanted to hear the news they brought with them. She wanted to tell them things she'd discovered, but the other guests stopped them with questions.

Did they know if the rain was over?

How were the roads to Netherworld? Were they passable?

Everyone asked questions, looking for good news but getting none.

It was only a few minutes before the outside door opened again, and a state trooper stepped in, looking around.

"Yes?" Emily Brent hurried to greet him.

"Oh, it's you," the officer said. "I wasn't sure who to ask for. I've got this."

They talked awhile by the open door. Zoe was sure she saw the officer hand something to Emily. Something she stuck in her pocket.

He touched the brim of his hat and was gone.

Nigel leaned in close to assure everyone. "A welfare check," he said and nodded as he spoke.

"Good to know they're aware we're here." Pileser gave a small, superior laugh. "You never know if the people in places like this are even competent."

"I was almost tempted to ask him to take me back to civilization with him," Aaron said. "This whole thing is turning into a disaster, if you ask me."

Pileser frowned. "I would hope we're all professional enough to wade through minor adversity. The show must go on, you know. We have a webinar to do. Have to fulfill our literary duties to the masses."

"You're not thinking about the five thousand you've been promised, eh?" Aaron laughed at him.

Nigel sputtered.

"Would you really leave, Professor Kennedy?" Gewel Sharp reached a hand behind her to take Anthony's.

"I suppose not," Kennedy said. "At least, now that I know we're not stranded. Only four more days of this misery to get through."

The others looked pleased and were soon back upstairs to their rooms or comfortably seated on chairs in the reception room, some napping, others reading. Gewel and Anthony, still held hands, and talked, heads together.

Zoe excused herself. She wanted to talk to Emily Brent, whom she found in the kitchen, alone.

"I was expecting a letter. Did that police officer have anything for me?"

Emily gave her a strange look. "Unless it's coming by drone, I don't know how you expect to get it."

"But, he gave you something—"

"A list of emergency numbers to call," Mary interrupted.

"Maybe my message is inside."

Mary almost rolled her eyes. "No message, Zoe. Sorry."

She leaned down as close as she could get to Zoe. "You realize that Emily's upset you've allowed your friends to simply drop by. Food might get short soon. I hear deliveries to some of the stores in town aren't getting through. Emily's set everything up for the number we have here and says that's all she can take on. If your friends don't make it back over that bridge, I don't know what we'll do with them. Not even a room left."

"What about Leon Armstrong's?"

"Who do you think has time now to clean it?"

Disgusted, Zoe turned away. "They won't be staying," she promised.

Chapter 30

Up in her room, where she was beginning to feel a little bit at home, Zoe offered Jenny and Lisa the bed, the single chair at the desk, or the reading chair she hadn't used yet.

They squatted on the bed together and talked about the box of funeral cards.

"So, you called Tony?" Zoe asked Jenny, who nodded, chin out, daring Zoe to say another word.

"Was he surprised to hear from you?" She didn't take well to dares.

Jenny sniffed and looked away. "I only asked him to help because we couldn't get enough band width to do the search ourselves. Lost the call to him twice, as it was. He said he'd send a copy of what he found."

"I have to tell you something." Jenny leaned close. "That Emily Brent—I don't think that's her real name."

"I figured that out the first day. Must've thought it was cute . . ."

"No. She's an actress. She was in *The Mousetrap*. Right here in Calumet. At that theater we saw. Anyway, her name isn't Emily Brent. Not at all. It's Susan Winton."

Zoe felt the blood drain from her face. That name. Her stomach turned. She had to reach out behind her, to the headboard, for support.

"That's who she is?" was all she could get out.

"Wasn't Jokela your mom's name?" Jenny asked. "And two others in the cast were named Lamb. I don't know if that means anything . . ."

Zoe could only nod and think harder, then harder, until she almost couldn't think at all.

"She's Susan Jokela, my mother's sister. I guess Winton's her married name. She was someone Mom thought still liked her. She thought Susan was a friend. *And she's here.*"

"You were right, Zoe. You're here because of your family. Terrible." Jenny climbed off the bed. "You're going to leave with us today. Something's going on, just the way you thought. We'll help you pack."

Zoe looked away. She slid to the floor. The other name: *Lamb.*

"I've got something to show you. I didn't think that much of it . . ." She got up and went to the closet for the box of photos.

It wasn't where she'd left it, pushed in next to her suitcase. She moved the suitcase. Nothing.

"It's gone," she said.

"What's gone?" the women asked together

"A box of photos. They were here when I arrived. I took these." She reached into her pocket and pulled out the photos she'd hidden there. She held one up and pointed to Leon Armstrong. "That man was here yesterday. Supposedly a professor. He left during the night. They said he was sick, but he arrived here drunk and stayed that way."

"But since he was sick . . ." Lisa said, taking a deep breath, "maybe he wanted his photographs and those people didn't want to bother you."

"So, they had to sneak in today to get them?"

Lisa shrugged. She took the photo of the man and child from Zoe.

"His name is Leon Armstrong," Zoe said. "A professor at a college in New York. I don't remember which one, but it's on our schedule."

Zoe rummaged in her briefcase and brought out the sheets she was looking for. "Ralston College. Upper Fairmont."

"Maybe we could call there . . . check on him."

"But it doesn't say Leon Armstrong on the photo. It says Angela and Harley Lamb."

There was silence in the room.

"Lamb?" Jenny and Lisa asked at the same time.

Zoe nodded.

Lisa pulled the playbill from her purse. "Look at this. That's what I wanted to show you."

She first pointed to the cover photo.

"That's her, right? She's Emily Brent," Lisa said.

Zoe took the brochure and stared hard at it. All she could do was nod.

Jenny stuck her finger on Emily Brent's face. "Listed as Susan Jokela Winton. Look at the cast list inside."

Zoe wasn't listening; the words in her head were *But Susan's a good person, Zoe. Someday she might look you up.*

She finally paid attention when Jenny pointed to an inside page. She saw the name, Harley Lamb, but he was Leon Armstrong.

Zoe nodded. She couldn't clear her head enough to think. Little pieces, like shards of glass, spun inside of her. There were names and letters behind her eyes, but she couldn't get them to hold still.

"Your photo's of Angela Lamb and Harley Lamb," Jenny said.

"Look at them yourself." Zoe pushed the photo at her. "That's the man who disappeared last night. He was drunk the whole time he was here. No surprise he's gone."

"The people in this photo are named Lamb. Two people in the play are named Lamb. One played Mollie Ralston. She's . . . uh . . . listed as Mary Lamb."

Zoe stared at Mary Reid's face. Made up to look older, but definitely Mary Reid.

"And this one . . ." She pointed to the man with red hair and a bushy red mustache. "He's our Leon Armstrong."

Leon Armstrong. Detective Sergeant Trotter in Christie's play. And Evelyn's beloved sister "Susan." *Emily Brent. Her aunt.*

What else connected them to her?

Only Anas Jokela—her grandmother. The cruel woman who hated her own daughter.

"Three of them." Zoe stared at the picture. "Three connected to me. Three of the people who killed my mother. They're here."

"Maybe a—" Lisa started to say.

"You think this isn't about me?" Zoe interrupted.

Lisa closed her eyes.

"But," Zoe said after a minute of quiet between them, "who is Angela Lamb? And Harley Lamb? You think he's Mary's husband? Probably. Then Angela must be his daughter."

"Let's get out of here now," Lisa whispered close to Zoe's ear.

Zoe didn't take time to think about escaping. She thought about Evelyn and how she'd suffered at the hands of these people lined up in a play brochure.

Zoe shook her head and whispered, "I'll stay. They started this. Not me."

*   *   *

The movie that evening was *Witness for the Prosecution*. Zoe'd seen it ten times and, when Lisa and Jenny were gone, she went to bed instead.

Part 4

Monday

Chapter 31

The Finnish women set off at eleven, driving down dirt roads from their hidden town as the clouds turned from gray to bright silver.

They drove in a line of battered cars, Jenny and Lisa following behind them, out to Highway 41 and then to the sign pointing to Cliff Cemetery, where they parked beside the road and piled out, babies in their arms or children running around their legs. They trooped down the muddy side of the hill, walking to where the old cemetery lay hidden back among the trees.

Lisa and Jenny walked among them. Janne, camera slung over his shoulder, walked behind. They were going to film the women among the gravestones of their dead as they told the stories of these people who first came from Finland. The women were excited, having an important goal and whispering among themselves, asking one another what to say and how much truth to tell. How could they make their ancestors look better than they were?

"Sometimes, ya know, Uncle Asmo was known ta start a fight. How would that look on this documentary thing?"

The older women had walking sticks they'd brought with them to help on the uneven ground; they sometimes lost them in the mud and would laugh as they stumbled on down the hill.

The group formed a line as they came over a rise, Inka yelling to Lisa that it was just ahead. "We'll all be quiet, ya know. We'll whisper our stories fer yer camera."

Lisa motioned that she understood, then turned to Janne with a finger at her lips. He stopped where he was, letting the women pass him by, but then grabbed his camera and ran on ahead. They heard loud cries, and a wave of shock passed through the group.

"Aw, no, fer God's sake!" Leena, in front of the others, was bent in half, wide hands at her knees. "Jist look at what's happened here, would you?"

She crossed her arms over her body, hugging herself as if in terrible pain. The others crowded around her. There were cries and gasps at the sight of a forest of trees knocked to the ground, jagged trunks sticking dead white shards up into the air. And not a tombstone in sight. Nothing but blinding light and dying trees.

Behind her, Inka moaned, the red scar blooming up her cheek. "That's what I heard da storm did over here. I hated ta say it."

"I heard, but I thought they was exaggerating the thing," Leena said. "Ah, not this bad. I thought, *A few trees, dat's okay.* But not . . . dis."

The women cried and mourned together, holding one another, then letting go and standing straight, a slight cry coming from first one and then another until the cries became sighs.

Around them, the silence of the place was terrible—or not silence so much as noises that shouldn't be: the creaking of fallen trees and fluttering of leaves down among the hogweed.

Cliff Cemetery was destroyed. It wasn't there. Not the place they'd fondly described to Jenny and Lisa. Not a huddle of old tombstones, some fenced off from the others—as people everywhere did—by ornate iron fences.

Each to their own plot, as always—the family all together.

"Ah, never mind." Leena's disgust filled her voice. "We'll fix it, as we do everything. It'll be fine. You just listen. There . . ." She pointed here and there. "Ay, you, Kirsten. That a tombstone? There! No, over there. Go see, will ya'? Find one and we'll find 'em all."

"Everyone o' them." Marya stood beside Jenny, hugging her baby against her body, rocking him as tears wet his bald head. "Ah, how am I goin' ta find my mother? Dear Lord, didn't she have enough to put up with while she lived? And what about our Angela? Can we find her, ya think? I don't want to be the one to tell Mary. Dear Lord above. We've got to find her grave."

Within fifteen minutes, the women were drawn away by a shout from the farthest end of the cemetery.

"Found her!" One of the women was shouting. The others went running.

* * *

The mourning, like the shock, didn't last long. Nor the blame. The women worked together, pulling limbs from places where the family stones might be, helping one another, calling out to one another, directing, suggesting, lifting trees four times their size, and soon too busy to weep. Soon only their own noise surrounded them.

"I found my mother." Marya held her baby off to one side, making him grunt as she pulled the last broken branches from a crooked stone. "Ah, at last."

She fell to her knees, bent forward around her baby, and kissed the stone.

Her face, when she looked up at the women, beamed.

Lisa and Jenny and Janne, when he stopped filming the disaster, worked with the rest of them, pulling branches away, joining in to push trees too big for just a few women to move. Some shouted as they found another stone or tripped over one of the old iron fences.

They didn't stop until every woman found her people and her husband's people and cleared graves well enough to identify who was buried there—most with no names left on the worn stones; some, maybe newer graves, with names clearly incised, and with a woman beaming and pointing to where Aunt Enya lay in peace, Uncle Eero next to her. Then she'd turn away to help someone else.

Finally, with Leena's approval, Lisa and Janne stood with each woman, talking, asking questions, filming. Not to capture long stories, but to get what they'd come for—the strength of women self-exiled in an inhospitable land, and what they'd become, cut off from their own, creating their culture from trees and stones and lakes and rivers and the deep, deep snows of the long, hard winters.

For the last hour of filming, when her stomach was already groaning at her, Jenny went to sit on a fallen log, up a small rise, and watch. As she sat there, she wound her long black hair up into a pod on top of her head. She fixed it there with pins that were already in her hair and sat, chin resting on her knees, as she watched the constant movement of the women.

She was out of place, anchorless here in her sister's life. *How did Lisa do it?* she asked herself. Live in a trailer, for craps sake. And only thinking of the next story she could tell. Nothing of her "self" at all. That's what bothered Jenny most. A woman had to have a cause, a platform to stand on, in order to live.

Something to believe in.

That wasn't her. There wasn't anything specific she believed in. Her job. Maybe a different way of living. Not home with Dora. But what was there of a future? She didn't know.

She'd lost her sense of what was ahead. Somehow, because her marriage had failed so miserably, she'd forgotten who was at fault; or she didn't care or didn't have the nerve to look at what part of all that might have been hers.

She squeezed her eyes shut. All this anger . . . it wasn't about Mom; it wasn't about Tony. It was about . . .

The sky clouded over. She was tired of rain. And mud. And gloom. She wanted to go home, back to Bear Falls. She was tired of having to think things she was supposed to think about—an order coming from somewhere outside her. She'd put Tony in a box and closed it. But Tony being Tony, he wouldn't stay there. In his own way, he kept popping up, asking questions he had every right to ask. And soon she'd be standing someplace or other—it didn't matter where—with her mouth hanging open, trying to tell him about her need to try a new life without him, try this new job at the law firm in Traverse City, this new freedom, and he'd get that look—as if what he was hearing was a gunshot to his chest.

"Wish I'd known that at the beginning . . ." he'd say, maybe.

And she'd answer.

What she was doing to him now felt like revenge, but on the wrong person. If he would listen, let her tell her truth.

Marya, with her baby looking around and smiling, came up the hill to settle beside her. She sat down heavily and pulled her baby, his mouth still dampened by milk on his lips, into her lap; and bounced him a few times until he burped.

"I never imagined what it was like to be a mother." She looked at her child, dark hair standing up like a brown flower around his tiny head, blue-veined eyelids half-closed as he tried to go to sleep.

"I don't have any children," Jenny said.

She shrugged. "You're not too old ta have some o' yer own."

Jenny smiled. "I don't think I want—"

Marya almost moaned. "Don't say dat. You have plenty o' chance yet. I didn't want babies. I never thought it would be this way. Really somethin'. I always saw women holdin' their babies and thought, 'Oh no. I don't want some little thing suckin' off my tit.' But here I am, and I would die fer this child. My little man. I would kill fer 'im, without givin' it a thought, ya know. If anybody tried to hurt him, I would kill and turn away and never think about it again."

Her eyes sparkled. She pushed her chin out.

"I'd hate fer ya ta miss a thing like this, Jenny. I'd hate fer any woman ta miss it."

They watched as the others worked, lifting and moving trees they shouldn't be lifting and moving.

"You take those people who lost their girl. The one I was talking about before . . . Oh, maybe you don't know 'em. Anyway, I'm telling you I'd do anything. Don't you agree?"

Jenny said, "I don't know what you mean."

"I mean I'd lay down an' die if somethin' happened to Johnny here. I wouldn't stop until I found the person."

"Johnny!" Jenny couldn't help herself. "Where'd that name come from? Why not an Elias or a . . . Hennik or . . ." She tried to think of other male Finnish names she'd heard.

Marya leaned back and laughed. "He's an oddball but my husband, Aimo, wanted it like this. In case Johnny wants to go out into the world, away from here, Aimo doesn't want him to be different."

"And where is Aimo? I haven't met him, have I?"

"No, ya haven't. He's down with his aunt in Grand Rapids. He should be home soon. You'll meet 'im one day. Maybe."

"What were you saying about somebody who lost their girl? How? You mean up here with all of you? Was she sick?"

Marya shook her head. "She didn't live with us. Down to Houghton is where. She was gettin' on in the world too. Goin' ta college. Ann Arbor, if ya know where that is."

"University of Michigan? Pretty good."

"Pretty smart, our girl. Everybody chipped in to pay her tuition. We all wanted bragging rights, ya know. Ah, but den somethin' happened to 'er. Disappeared. The police kept sayin' you jist wait, she'll be back—they all come back. But she didn't. Hell on da mother and father, and on 'er friends and then all the relatives. We mourned. Den a hunter found 'er dead body in da deep woods, down below the bridge is where it was. I guess you could say nothin' but bones. Murdered. Front of her throat broken. Then other things nobody wants to talk about. Poor mother and poor father. To this day, they suffer like no human beings should have to suffer. Joo!" She nodded to herself. "If I coulda done somethin' . . . That's how we all felt. If there was only somethin' ta be done."

"Did they ever find who killed her?"

Her face changed. Something in the eyes—hidden there—stared back at Jenny. Something cold.

Then a slow time for her to catch herself.

"Police figured the man moved away from dere."

She watched Jenny with a different kind of look.

Jenny was thrown off by the challenge.

"Well named, dat girl. I loved her. I did. Like a sister. Strange, I think ta myself, fer her to be named in the way of the Lord. Fittin', don't ya think?"

"What do you mean?" Jenny felt a change in the space between them.

"Angela Lamb. The Lamb of the Good Lord, don't ya see?"

Jenny stared at Marya's stiff face. The prettiness was gone. Softness gone. Motherliness gone. She didn't know what she was supposed to say. It was all so—planned.

"I get it, Marya." She got up from the ground. "A drip of secret information only some of you seem to know. Is any of this really about Agatha Christie—this thing at the lodge? Or this, Lisa's documentary? Or has it been some sort of game all along? Are people going to die?"

Marya tipped her head, looking puzzled. "I wouldn't think so. No game! I would certainly hope not. This is all much too serious to be a game, Jenny. And too far into it. We are almost at the end." She smiled and kissed her baby's head. "It'll be okay. Just your friend, that Zoe Zola. I hear she's a fine person. Don't let her get hurt. You just never know. For me, I'd rather see some other way."

"You don't seem so Finnish all of a sudden."

"Really? Well, we are when we need to be. All of us. Aimo is. And now my baby. His name ain't really Johnny, ya know. "It's Jounni. Still, Johnny works just as well."

Jenny's throat tightened. "Is Zoe in real danger?"

"That depends on the choices she makes, doesn't it?"

"What's Zoe got to do with any of you?"

Marya widened her eyes, then clicked her tongue as Johnny began to complain. "Witness," she mumbled just loud enough for Jenny to hear. "Let her know that."

"To what? Witness to what?"

Marya didn't answer.

"And these others?" Jenny gestured to the women tending the graves. "Are they fakes too?"

Marya shook her head. "Nobody but me. I live down in Detroit. But mostly they're all the real thing. Finnish women who stayed behind. Fierce Finnish women. Yah, sure. And don't worry, yer sister will have herself a fine film to take to market."

She got up from the ground, brushed off the back of her skirt, cooed to her baby boy, and turned to leave, but not quite.

"By the way, Jenny. My name is Lamb too. Just like Angela. Marya Lamb. A whole gaggle of little sheep. She was my cousin. Now isn't that a funny thing fer ya ta think about?" She walked off to where a few of the others stood, brushing leaves from their family graves.

Chapter 32

Monday morning offered a dull gray sky. Gray like the other days so far. It was almost impossible to imagine this countryside in sunshine.

Zoe had missed Jenny and Lisa as soon as they'd left the night before.

She was alone—and felt it, especially when she walked into the breakfast room and nodded to everyone, and no one greeted her back.

"I don't suppose you've heard, if you just got up," Mary Reid said from across the table.

Zoe shook her head. "Nothing. Is the van going this afternoon? I really want to get to the library."

Mary shook her head. "We have another deserter."

"Deserter?"

"Louise Joiner. Her child's in the hospital. Somehow her husband got across the bridge to get her. I can't imagine what those poor people who paid to hear all of you are thinking."

"Not as if they're waiting for Lady Gaga," Anthony said, putting his spoon down in his oatmeal bowl and grinning to everyone around the table.

Zoe watched Mary's face. Nothing there except a little boredom. She didn't bother turning Anthony's way.

"She's given her talk. That's a good thing," Mary said.

"But the audience wants everybody's input," Anna complained.

"Ah, but this afternoon I get to give Leon's talk," Anthony smiled to himself. "I will have them wrapped around my little finger. No one will miss Louise."

* * *

The two women Zoe'd feared seeing most this morning were across from her, drinking their coffee but barely speaking to each other. It wasn't as hard to look at them as she'd feared—or not to look at them, keeping her eyes turned down.

She started a conversation with Aaron Kennedy, despite their last encounter, asking how his webinar, scheduled for Wednesday, was coming along. He leaned back in his chair, half-closed his eyes and began to expound on "The Aging of Agatha."

He went off on how Agatha's sales were sagging, while Zoe watched the faces around the table, no one else talking, all staring into their bowl of oatmeal or setting their spoon down, hands into their lap, and waiting for something to happen.

Aaron gave a long sigh and bemoaned again the fact that Agatha's fiction was falling out of favor.

She knew better but said nothing, planning to keep her statistics secret until Wednesday, when they were live, on the internet, and she could contradict him in public, or in her summation on Thursday. He wouldn't get a say after that.

She stopped listening to Aaron as he droned on; she nodded from time to time but was thinking about the woman across the table. She was related to her by blood. Susan's genes ran through her body but she meant nothing to Zoe.

This was the Susan that Evelyn had thought, of all her family, loved her. Maybe, at the end, the cruelest of them all.

Different from what she'd expected: eyes, body type, hair—but the hair could be dyed. Especially if she was an actor.

As Zoe watched, Gewel's eye strayed to the platter of flowers and figurines. Zoe knew before she looked what would be there.

Another playful child was gone.

Chapter 33

The upstairs hall was empty.

The air smelled of wet sweaters and dirty socks. Zoe couldn't remember ever feeling as alone as she did right then. Most of all, she missed Fida and hoped Dora was taking good care of her. Something to be said for mute animal love.

She heard voices coming from Anthony Gliese's room and fervently hoped Gewel Sharp wasn't in there with him. The thought made her a little sick. He'd promise her publication and fame—of course, none of that would ever come true. She'd seen it before.

She wanted so badly to knock and see for herself who was in there. But then what? None of her business anyway. Since when had she turned into a snoop?

She stood in the middle of the hall, head down, listening as hard as she could, but unable to identify the woman's voice—and it *was* a woman. After a few minutes, when the room went quiet, she gave up, and rather than heading downstairs, she tiptoed along the corridor, down to Leon Armstrong's room. It was worth a look. Tony's letter still hadn't come. Two people were gone. What else could she do as she waited for the afternoon and, with luck, to get away in the lodge van, and finally into Calumet.

From there, maybe she'd find a bus up to Copper Harbor. Then a car to where Lisa stayed. Or not.

At Leon's door, she knocked to be certain no one was in there. She turned the old-fashioned knob and went in.

An exact duplicate of her room, with the same bedspread, furniture, and even the same pictures on the walls. The view out of his window was the same as hers—trees and that brown roof.

She opened the closet. Empty except for a few hangers. Every drawer of the chest was empty, not a scrap of paper to say that the man had been here, if only for that brief time—less than twenty-four hours.

Alive she presumed.

Standing at the center of the familiar room, she put her hands on her hips and looked around. Nightstand. Bed. Small chair. Desk.

Nothing in the desk.

Nothing in the nightstand.

She sank to her knees, lifted the edge of the bedspread, and tipped over to see beneath the bed. A few dust balls where someone hadn't bothered to clean, a crinkled piece of paper at the very center of the uncleaned space. Zoe fell to her stomach and pushed under the bed, getting stopped as her bottom—higher than the space allowed—couldn't go any farther. She suddenly realized she might get stuck—with what excuse for being there?

She reached out as far as she could, her short fingers barely touching the paper. With one finger planted on it, she pulled until the paper was under her chin and then drew the folded paper and herself from under the bed.

Nothing but a worn business card.

Something from a past guest, maybe even another time, except the card belonged to Harley Lamb, Attorney at Law, with a half-obliterated address in Calumet and a phone number she couldn't make out.

Harley Lamb. He haunted her like a crazy ghost. Why weren't any of these names familiar?

Maybe the Lambs had nothing to do with her directly. She looked at the worn card in her hands. Maybe it went deeper than a name. Something cataclysmic—like doing away with every Agatha Christie expert in the world. And what about the Jokelas? When would those people crawl out from their swamp?

Beyond the closed door she heard another door open, whispered voices in the hall, and then a door close.

Anthony and Gewel.

If ever she wanted to scream at somebody, this was that moment.

Zoe put her ear to the door, opened it a bit, then listened. The hall was empty.

She walked down toward the end, trying doors as she went.

The first door opened onto nothing. No furniture. The window was dirty, cobwebs dimmed the glass. Not used in years.

The next—the same. Unused. Empty.

The next . . .

The next . . .

And then a room with furniture, the bed stripped and left as it was. Probably Louise's room.

Again a search, but not even a crumpled card here. Nothing to say Louise Trainer had ever been.

Nothing to say Louise Trainer was real.

She hurried back toward her own room, counting on her fingers the rooms she knew to be inhabited. Eight. The number of guests left.

Two little soldiers gone.

Chapter 34

She should have had her head up, been more on guard, instead of counting her fingers and wondering what it could mean—that they had been ten, as in *And Then There Were None*, and now they were eight.

The whole thing could be for real or not for real at all.

Turning too quickly into the doorway of her room, she ran directly into Emily, blocking the way and frowning hard down at Zoe.

"I wondered where you'd gotten to," she said, the frown staying firmly in place. "I hope you're not barging into the rooms of others."

Zoe said nothing.

"Well, anyway, I took a phone call for you." She held out a slip of paper with numbers sketched on it. "Your friend," she said. "The one from yesterday."

"How did you get a call?"

She flushed. "Phone worked for a minute."

Zoe thanked her and took the paper. Jenny's number.

The woman, still blocking her way, clasped her hands over her stomach. "I hope you don't try to make arrangements for your friends to come here because two people have left. We don't have room. Poor Bella Webb's overworked as it is. And with all the flooding problems, well . . ."

Zoe tipped her best smile, one that almost always shamed people into shutting up, to Emily.

No such luck with Emily. "Really, it would be much safer if they didn't come."

"Safer for whom? Why the devil aren't we being evacuated if it's so dangerous? I am beginning to think this whole thing, this whole webinar thing, is for a reason having nothing much to do with Agatha Christie."

The woman's face changed to outrage. "Well, really. No need to snap at me. And I didn't mean to frighten you. It's just that I— we . . . have enough to handle with the people already here."

Zoe shrugged and pushed against the woman, getting into her room, then grabbing the door and trying to close it.

"If my friend and her sister can get here, I welcome seeing them. I was paid to deliver the final webinar and take part in all other planned events. That doesn't mean every second of every day is yours. I will be down in a minute to return my friend's call. If she wants to come see me, she's coming, and her sister Lisa too. They won't take any meals. They won't get in the way of events. They won't stay overnight. They just want to make sure I'm in good hands since everything has been so odd about this whole event."

"Odd?" Creases deepened between Emily's eyes, making her look tired, but not really old. "This is my first large event for our society. Mary and I are in charge. The others are waiting to see how we do here. I hate to hear that you're unhappy with us. I really do. We've tried to be so careful."

She sniffed and bent her head toward Zoe. "Odd?" she said again. "What do you mean by odd?"

Zoe looked at her in disbelief. "What about the invitation?"

"You didn't like something about my invitation? I thought it was done quite well."

"With black edges—like a death notice?" Zoe was incredulous and tired of having these jousts between them every time they met.

"I beg your pardon." She reared back on her oxfords. "I would never do such a thing. *Like a death notice?* Really! I may be a novice at events, but not an idiot. Who would want to come to anything announced in a death notice?"

Zoe was about to say that she had come, hadn't she?

"That's what I got," she muttered and tried again to close the door.

"You should have mentioned it to me when you first called. I did send an invitation—of course—because I wanted you here, but it wasn't dressed up as death."

"Who helped with the invitations?"

Emily's face was flushed. "We needed people to do the calligraphy. Just a couple. Mostly Mary Reid and I did them. But then there were a few of the Finnish women. One, Marya, had her baby with her. There were one or two others."

"Who mailed them?"

"I don't remember. I know I didn't." She thought awhile. "Seems one of us was going by the post office."

Her faded blue eyes were wide. If she wasn't feeling outrage, she was doing a good job of acting. But she was an actor. As far as Zoe knew, they were all actors.

Zoe leaned full against the door until the woman stepped back into the hall, calling, "Lunch in an hour. Please don't be late."

* * *

Downstairs, Zoe walked straight to the telephone on the reception desk and punched in Jenny's number as hard as she could. Nothing. No dial tone.

Chapter 35

There were only six of them at lunch. No one asked about the others: Anthony Gliese, probably studying Leon's notes, and Mary Reid.

Betty Bertram announced loudly that she wished people would stop leaving. It was so unprofessional, and she didn't want to be roped into giving a webinar. She wasn't being paid enough for that, she said, and set to eating her stew and dumplings, ignoring the others.

As soon as lunch ended, Aaron and Nigel got up and left.

Anna Tow, on the other side of Betty, knocked back her wine and set her glass on the table with a heavy clunk. She leaned across the table toward Zoe, whispering, "I think the men here have decided to be snotty to all the women."

"Seems like equal-opportunity snottiness. They don't treat each other much better." Zoe said.

Anna laughed her high laugh and asked, "Are you going to town later?"

Zoe nodded. "I have some things to look up."

"Really, I'd think *your* webinar would be the easiest to do. Playing mop up on the last day. What on earth do you have to research?"

When Zoe couldn't answer, Anna got up and left.

Zoe waited for Betty to go next.

Once Zoe and Gewel were alone, Gewel quickly whispered to her, "Think someone's playing a joke on us? Are you as suspicious as I am?"

"I'm suspicious of some of the people here, if that's what you mean. I'm even suspicious of their names. I'd like to check them out."

"Who is it you're suspicious of?" Gewel batted her eyelashes at her. "Anyone in particular?"

Zoe shrugged. "A little widespread deception."

"Deception? About what? Who on earth here would want to fool us? I was talking about how the webinar schedule has been messed up."

"Oh." Zoe wanted to smile. "But I was talking about the names. Nigel Pileser—what kind of name is that? Or Anna Tow. I keep thinking: Tow, Carry, Pull."

"Or heave, yank, tug." Gewel didn't laugh.

"How about Gewel Sharp."

"Me?"

Gewel thought awhile. "Hmm. But what on earth is a Zoe Zola?"

Zoe laughed. "Not easy, is it?"

Gewel started to get up. "I think I'll—"

"He's using you, Gewel. Just a creep with a little power."

"I think you're talking about Anthony. There's nothing—"

"I heard you in his room. I hope you don't get hurt."

Gewel gave her a look, but no answer.

She left the room.

Zoe, alone at the table with the dirty dishes and a big bowl of stew, wondered how she'd made enemies so fast. And still three days to go.

She could be setting a record for herself. One enemy a day, but since everyone here seemed to be somebody's enemy, maybe she was right on target.

Chapter 36

Anthony's rehash of Leon's talk was adequate. The questions from their faraway audience were tepid. They finished right on time—with a few minutes to spare.

Gewel and Anthony, Zoe, Nigel Pileser, And Betty Bertram were on the lodge porch by 4:40. Then they were in the van and off to Calumet, talking in low whispers.

The road was pocked and washed out in places. At the swollen creek, the driver had to slow down to barely moving to get them over the still submerged bridge.

Anthony, in the seat with Gewel, turned to the others. "Wouldn't Christie be proud of us? All on a ruined road together, in this old bus—not exactly the Orient Express."

He laughed when Zoe called back, "I can't begin to imagine which one of us might be murdered."

The group quieted, turning to look out their windows and whispering when they had something to say to the person in the seat with them.

Once in town, they were reminded by their driver to be waiting back here, at the nearby bench, by six forty-five. Zoe asked for the library, pulled her computer case down the steps, and was directed to Mine Street. "The red-brick school," the driver said and then added proudly, "Fine library. One of the best on the Keweenaw."

She felt the weight of her computer bag before she'd gotten more than two blocks across the park.

Every block she walked, there was another massive structure: big, red, important-looking buildings, but almost no one on the streets. A few cars. She couldn't quite put a finger on what she felt in this strange town. It wasn't pity. More something like hope, she was picking up on. More like the red buildings were waiting, along with the people who lived there.

She found Mine Street and the red-brick school. Then found the end of the school, dedicated to the library, and went into a large room with tall, rounded windows, filled with antiques, tall plants, and wooden tables for quiet reading.

When she asked for Agatha Christie books, the elderly librarian, thin bangs etched over her forehead, smiled and leaned over the high desk.

"You must be Zoe Zola. We heard you were coming to Calumet. How are things going out at Netherworld? Everybody's heard about the webinar series. And right here, in Calumet—well, almost. Really happy to have you all with us."

She smiled wider and took a deeper breath.

She brought out all she had left of their Agatha Christie collection. "Town people've been taking them out at a great rate," she explained and set three books down. One very old copy of *And Then There Were None*. One hardcover copy of *The Mysterious Affair at Styles* with a cracked cover. And a paperback of *The ABC Murders*.

She knew these books almost by heart. Knew the characters. None were named Gliese, nor Joiner, nor Betty Bertram. No Aaron Kennedy that she knew of, nor Gewel Sharp. Nothing in these.

Where do I start? she asked herself, settling back in her squeaky chair.

There was a code for the internet. The librarian smiled when she asked, and offered to punch the code into her computer for her. Being treated as a child by the elderly woman was uncomfortable, but Zoe forgave her, knowing elderly men and women saw her as small and maybe in need of their help.

Zoe declined the help and got her small laptop up and running, beginning the search for names in Agatha Christie's work. She knew what was ahead of her: seventy-five novels, one hundred and sixty-five short stories, three poems (she could ignore those), sixteen plays, radio broadcasts, two autobiographies. Had the woman ever stopped to take a breath? And why that kind of production? What was she running from?

She took out a list she'd made back at the lodge. Every name from the symposium written down except for Emily Brent and Bella Webb. She probably had to accept the explanations of the women's names—connecting themselves to Christie's work. There were nine others—from Anthony Gliese to Betty Bertram, including the two who were mysteriously missing. She didn't know what she hoped to find, but something that could help explain the feeling of growing nerves around her, and the odd black-trimmed invitation that Emily denied sending.

Something was off, so far off her brain had been jangling from the very beginning. She couldn't get it to shut up, to let her accept that this group of ten, including her, weren't somehow caught up in a strange reenactment of *And Then There Were None*, and doomed—every one of them—to be murdered. To be about anything less than murder just couldn't be possible. She couldn't accept it, not with the elaborate preparations, the lodge, the strange feelings she got from the other guests, the names that rang so many bells.

Then another part of her brain—the more practical part—said they were trapped in a psychological study, and it wasn't about literature at all, but about being locked away together with egos and baggage on full display. Guinea pigs.

She did a search for Christie's books, then went to Wikipedia for character lists for each. Next she looked up the names and found:

Mary Reid—nothing, except there was a Gwenda Halliday Reed in *Sleeping Murder*.

And there was a Dr. James Kennedy (not Aaron) who first tried to poison Mary and then to strangle her. Dr. Aaron Kennedy. Maybe a tie to Mary Reid as the killer in *Sleeping Murder*.

But she found a Dr. Aaron Kennedy. English Literature and Language, University of Southern California. Prior jobs at the University of Utah, University of Michigan. A list of publications. Nothing on Agatha Christie, which she found odd. But at least he was an academic with a reason to be chosen for this event. He was real but 'leaving the University of Southern California as of June 1.'

Hmm. She couldn't make any connection to the event at the lodge.

She felt the beginnings of a headache but kept going.

Gewel Sharp. Nobody by that name anywhere that she could find. Maybe in some forgotten story—if there was such a thing.

She put three question marks next to Gewel's name.

She looked up the *ABC Murders,* where she found an Elizabeth "Betty" Bernard. It was Betty Bernard who was murdered by a Franklin Clarke. Nothing. No connection to Betty Bertram, but something was nagging at her. She couldn't pin it down, and there were too many others to search for.

Louise Joiner—listed as a professor at Amherst and lived on the street where the Dickinson family had lived. A list of credits. A list of classes she'd taught in the past. A list of classes planned for the fall. There was a contact number for the English Department. Did she dare call? She put it off.

Anna Tow. *Oh, phooey. Totally the wrong track.*

Leon Armstrong. Ah, *And Then There Were None*. She had that one. Dr. Edward Armstrong (close enough). A drunk. That fit their Leon. Killed a patient while operating on her under the influence. He was the one who went missing—pushed by Justice Wargrave into the sea—*"A red herring swallowed one . . ."* The seventh to die on Soldier Island. But of a Dr. Leon Armstrong, touted as an expert on Agatha Christie? Nothing.

The right track after all. How to tie them together?

Anthony Gliese. Nothing. An Anthony Marsden in *And Then There Were None*, but that was really stretching.

Dr. Nigel Pileser—no one anywhere. She searched as many Christie books as she could find online. Then, as many short stories. Nothing. Until she came to *A Murder Is Announced* and found the vicarage cat—Tiglath Pileser—and knew immediately someone or something was laughing at her.

When she sat back and closed her eyes, she visualized her fellow speakers, then checked out each again. Surely, if they were all well-established Christie critics, they would have a web presence. After all, she had a fairly extended one. For an ego boost, she began searching her own name first, separating herself from any other Zoe Zolas in the world, to read about her books, her articles, her growing national attention—then pulled herself away from posts where people said they didn't understand her work and didn't get the premise. She sniffed at the rampant stupidity let loose in the world.

Back to Gewel Sharp. Okay. Nothing on her. The girl was young, just out of college. Maybe she didn't know about self-puffery yet and hadn't gotten herself a website.

Anna Tow. She searched for her press: Tollance. And found it—two postings. *Creation of a Mystery* by Mary Lamb and another by Anna Tow. *Where were those books? She had to find them. Her head was hurting.* Anna Tow. What to believe?

Back to Harley Lamb as Leon Armstrong, an attorney in Calumet and half owner of Ulysses Bookstore. A connection between Leon Armstrong and Mary Reid. There was a phone number for both places.

Zoe wrote the numbers down and went to find the bathroom. Down a set of metal steps, and luckily there was no one in there.

She dialed the first number—an attorney's office. There would be someone there on a Monday, or at least a recording. The answering machine said only that Mr. Lamb would be back in his office the following Monday and gave the number of an attorney in Houghton in case of emergency. She was tempted to call but called the bookstore in Houghton first.

A woman answered. Zoe asked for Mary and was told that Mary and Harley wouldn't be back in the store until next Monday. When asked, the older woman on the phone said only that Mary was attending a book convention in Chicago.

Monday. Whoever was going to die had to be dead by next Monday so everyone could get back to normal.

She kept looking and found Miss Emily Brent in *Murder on the Orient Express* but couldn't figure out how the Lindbergh kidnapping, loosely used for the book, could figure into what this Emily Brent was doing.

There were a couple Betty Bertrams in Canada. One in Manitoba. A Betty Bertram in Montreal. Could be the right one. Student at McGill. Yes, that was Betty Bertram. But not a graduate with a master's degree. How had she come to be chosen as an expert?

Nothing made sense.

Dr. Nigel Pileser. *Ah. Agatha Christie's vicarage cat.* She considered whether Dr. Pileser was catlike and decided he was, with his odd moods and vicious attacks when he had the opportunity, and then an almost licking of his fur when he knew he was right.

That left only the lecherous editor: Anthony Gliese. She hoped to find something like *Elbowing the Seducer*, about another preying editor, but didn't. Gliese was listed in a search either as an actor or the Gliese 581 Planetary System. No editor anywhere. It seemed she was looking for people who didn't exist. All the fault of that black-edged invitation.

Anthony. Another character in *And Then There Were None*: Anthony Marston. A playboy. He killed two small children with his car, while drinking, but never seemed bothered by his crime.

And the rain. Nobody turns rain on and off at will except on a stage. Nobody floods roads because they want to. Without the rain, her whole theory—whatever it turned out to be—didn't hold. Without the rain, no one would have been kept at the lodge. They wouldn't have gotten so short-tempered with one another. And without the constant downpour, any mysterious purpose for the gathering was improbable.

Zoe pushed back her squeaky library chair. She'd proved that most of the people had no business at this gathering. Maybe a couple of them were real—maybe her, and Louise and Aaron Kennedy.

Actor slipped back inside her brain. Actor. Anthony Gliese was an actor. She looked him up online and found nothing. Not an editor. Nothing.

Her head was pounding now. Anything—for a couple of aspirin.

She had a question to ask the librarian.

The elderly woman came back to the counter and leaned far over to smile down at Zoe.

"There's a woman in town," Zoe said. "She's leading the event at Netherworld I'm involved with. Her name's Emily Brent. Do you know her? Is she someone from Calumet?"

The woman's kind face froze. The corners of her mouth arced downward. She wrinkled her forehead until the wispy bangs caught in her eyebrows. With tight lips and wrinkled lipstick—she said only, "I'm afraid we're closing early. You'll have to leave."

Chapter 37

Because she still had an hour before the bus was to pick them up, Zoe stopped at a Burger King on Sixth Street for a Coke. And maybe because the place was empty, the girl behind the counter leaned in while handing Zoe her cup and asked if she was with the group out at Netherworld. She smiled oddly when Zoe said, yes, she was with that group. The girl leaned closer, looked straight into Zoe's eyes, and asked in a whisper, "Did it happen yet?"

"Did what happen?"

"I heard . . . oh, well . . . guess not. Never mind."

Her face flushed, the girl turned her back and called out to a man in the kitchen, ignoring Zoe.

* * *

Because there was internet, Zoe searched again for 'Ulysses Bookstore, Houghton, Michigan.' They were pushing Agatha Christie books, but no mention of the webinar series nor that the owner would take part. A line near the bottom of the listing named Mary and Harley Lamb as owners. No Mary Reid mentioned.

She looked up events at Netherworld Lodge. The history was there, and the photo she'd already seen. Nothing about an Agatha Christie event. When she looked up conferences and webinars on Christie, she found there was one in Exeter, one in Cambridge, and one planned for September at the Newberry Library in Chicago. Nothing in Calumet, Michigan.

She wasn't surprised at what she'd learned but was still disappointed. All along, somewhere inside, she'd been hoping that it was real, all planned somehow by people who wanted to meet her, some maybe related to her. Or at least planned by people who wanted to make amends for the way they'd treated Evelyn. Or they wanted her dead once and for all.

She took out her copy of the schedule, the introductions to everyone, along with their credits. She pulled up what she knew of Dr. Louise Joiner and dialed the number listed for the English Department.

A woman answered.

Zoe asked if Professor Joiner was available. She was told that Dr. Joiner was in class and couldn't be disturbed.

"I'll be happy to take a message and see that Dr. Joiner gets it," the woman said.

"Tell her that Zoe Zola called, from Netherworld. Z-O-L-A. I'm just calling to see how her daughter is."

There was silence.

"And let her know I hope we'll see each other at another literary event."

"I'm sorry, miss." The voice was chilly. "Dr. Joiner doesn't have a daughter. Is this a crank call? What is Netherworld?"

"Eh, she was just here, at Netherworld Lodge in Upper Michigan. We were doing a webinar on Agatha Christie."

"Dr. Joiner's been teaching a summer class. She hasn't been gone as much as a day. If this is a joke—"

Zoe hung up. *Doesn't have a daughter. But back at school on Monday.*

*   *   *

When she returned to the corner where they'd been dropped off, she was the only one there. No benches to sit on, so she sat on the ground and went over what she'd learned. She picked a leaf of grass, straightened it between her fingers, and blew into it, hoping to make a mighty noise the way she had when she was a kid. She blew again, getting a weak little sound, as she thought about reality and perception.

The headache she thought she'd beaten was back, moved down now into her eyes. Cluster. Cluster. Cluster. She'd had them before.

When the phone in her shoulder bag rang, she jumped at the chime, then thought how smart she'd been to keep the useless thing charged. Lisa's name came up in the caller window.

"I didn't know if I would get you or not." Lisa broke into talking. "I've got Jenny here, right beside me."

Lisa asked how she was and if she'd learned anything more.

"Shuttle bus got out today, though the roads are still pretty bad. I'm in Calumet."

Jenny came on the phone. "Listen, I found out who Angela Lamb is. A woman named Marya, with Lisa's group, told me."

Zoe caught her breath. "With Lisa's group? The Finnish women? But how would she know to . . . It's like everybody who lives here knows something's going to happen. Okay, tell me. Who is she? Another relative?"

"No. Well, maybe yes. A young girl from up here was murdered in Ann Arbor maybe three years ago. Terrible crime. Went to the University of Michigan."

"Murdered? But what has she got to do with—"

"Her name was Angela Lamb. They never found the murderer."

"Angela Lamb? So, related to Mary and Leon? But what does that have to do with me? Am I related to her too?"

"Probably. Looks like you've got a big family all of a sudden. Remember next time: be careful what you wish for."

"I never wished for any of them."

"Anyway, do you want to get out of there? We're both worried. Especially now. We could reach you in a couple of hours. We could skip dinner with Lisa's women. And I talked to Tony. He gave me what he had."

She looked up to see Nigel crossing the street toward her.

"There are more Lambs in Houghton. Jokelas are all over up there. Mostly near Copper Harbor. You find anything else?" Jenny asked.

"I went to the library. I'm waiting for the van back to the lodge now. So far, I've found out that the people around me aren't who they say they are. Some of them are Christie characters or just a play on the names of Christie characters. I learned that nobody named Mary Reid owns the Ulysses Bookstore. People named Lamb do."

"Lamb again."

"Mary and Harley Lamb."

"And Angela?"

"Who knows if they belong together? Who knows anything about them? These people are devious. I wish I knew why."

Jenny was quiet for a very brief minute.

"Dora said to tell you that Fida is depressed. Won't eat much. Sits by the door and whines."

"That cheers me up. She misses me. I should never, ever, have left her. All because of that damned envelope."

It was agreed that they would find a way to talk Tuesday morning, even if Jenny had to come to the lodge.

"Lisa's got interviews. But I'll be there. How's the bridge?"

"Van got out. I'm waiting for it now, to go back. But I'm early."

"Rain predicted tonight."

"Wouldn't you know it? Whatever these people are doing or planning or scheming, I still can't figure out how they make it rain."

* * *

The rest returned, packages in their arms. The van pulled up, early, and they were on their way back to the lodge.

No one seemed happy. Only tired.

The words *"Did it happen yet?"* rang in Zoe's head. And then the name again: Angela Lamb, a murdered girl, a ghost.

Chapter 38

The lodge was quiet when they got back. There was no Emily, her keen eye watching over the reception room. No Bella slowly pushing a dust mop across the splintered floors.

All the people had to be sleeping or working or out on a destination of their own, except she had no idea where that could be in this isolated place.

There was the smell of dinner—that was encouraging. Someone would be around soon. Zoe decided to confront Emily or Mary about what she'd found out. She couldn't hold her questions and fears in any longer.

"Did it happen yet?"

Angela Lamb.

Strange things were beginning to fall into place.

The lodge was as it had been when she first got there on Saturday. Her third day. She didn't belong here. She was in the middle of a nest of enemies. Except she had no idea why.

Why Aaron Kennedy. Maybe he was there just as she was, unaware of what was really going on.

Louise? She was gone. And didn't really exist.

And Leon Armstrong—for the same reason. He had another name; owned a bookstore with his wife, Mary Lamb; and was an attorney.

But who among the others? More relatives who wished nothing good for Zoe?

After a while, she gave up waiting for Emily Brent to show herself. Anyway, what was she going to say to her? Emily Brent was a Jokela. *The* Susan. Evelyn's friend. Her cousin.

"Did it happen yet?"

What was *it*?

And did the whole town know something she didn't know? The librarian—strange how she had become so unfriendly.

She yawned. More walking than she usually did in a whole week. And she still had her headache.

If Emily came back, she didn't know which to do first: ask for two aspirins or accuse her of lying about this whole event.

After waiting another a few minutes, she couldn't sit still any longer. She went to the kitchen and pushed the door open. The room was dark despite a pot bubbling on the stove, the lid bouncing.

She went to her room, telling herself that later, when Emily returned, maybe even while they sat at dinner, she would call her Aunt Susan, as if by mistake, and see what happened.

Susan Jokela Winton. The name felt greasy in her mouth.

She went to her room and kicked off her tennis shoes. She yawned, standing at the window, looking out on the familiar scene.

At least a half an hour before cocktails. Time to take a nap and clear her head before facing the next part of someone's grand plan. Maybe they had their own Mr. Owen here, the killer of *And Then There Were None*, among them.

The sound of a raised voice from the floor below shocked her. Without bothering to change for cocktails, as they'd all been doing, she got her shoes back on and hurried downstairs.

They weren't angry voices. Anthony was laughing as Gewel twittered behind him. Even Nigel's voice was amused instead of

complaining. He was asking someone if they'd seen the shrimp platter. And then it was Aaron, accusing Anna of hiding it from them.
Anna's voice was aggrieved as usual, but not hysterical. The others
laughed.

At the bottom of the stairs Zoe hesitated, watching them as they
partied easily together. She raised a hand only to have Anthony wave
her down, calling out, "Hey, here's our little one. Let's see what she
thinks of our plan for the rest of the evening."

A rather drunk Gewel, who giggled again and again behind her
hand, forced a gin and tonic in a smudged glass on Zoe. Gewel
leaned forward, holding on to Anthony's arm, then smiling up at
him.

"Anthony just found out that I'm a singer. And a dancer. That's
how I put myself through college."

"She's going to sing and dance for us as soon as Bella finds a
couple of CDs. Oh, and a CD player. Can't stream anything in this
place."

Which he found very funny.

"Maybe jazz—right, Gewel?" He bent close to her. His mouth
brushed her cheek.

Zoe thought she'd accepted what this thirty-something jerk was
doing. She thought she'd agreed with herself to butt out, keep her
nose in her own business, but now thought, *Poor kid. Looks like a
kitten with a damned vulture hanging over her.*

"And, while we wait, let me tell you what Gewel and I have
come up with for tonight. No movie. We've seen all of them anyway.
We agreed that—except for people turning up missing around us—
things have gotten a little boring."

He nodded to the men.

"And since we can't drink twenty-four hours every day."—
Anthony looked very pleased with himself—"why not?"

Gewel took the floor. "There are now eight of us, and we are trapped here—not on Soldier Island, as in *And Then There Were None*, but here, in our lovely Netherworld Lodge." She glanced over at Emily, who ignored her.

"We can accuse each other of crimes. Offer evidence. Maybe put on short mini-trials. Announce verdicts—especially death sentences." Anthony was thinking hard.

"Well, not real things. I mean, nothing too terrible."

Gewel's sunny smile was gone. "Let's keep it to crimes we've heard of though murder seems to be the most interesting."

"Doesn't that sound like fun?" Anthony smiled around at everyone. "Maybe we can do an article together afterward, announcing our results."

Bella was back, unloading a CD player into Anthony's hands.

She gave Gewel a small stack of CDs, making her squeal, "Ooh! Ella Fitzgerald."

The CD went in, Gewel turned on the player, and the voice of Ella spilled into the room. Everyone moved back to the walls, giving Gewel room as she shed her shoes and closed her eyes, lifted her head, threw her blonde hair back from her face, and began to move to the voice filling the room with blue notes.

She didn't sing. As they all watched, she danced—one sinuous movement after another. One low bend and a slow rise. And another. Little Gewel Sharp was transformed into woman with a capital *W*. Not what Zoe'd expected from the young woman who gave off the feeling of being vulnerable.

Her dance was different. She was different.

Another one masquerading as someone she wasn't.

There was loud clapping when the music ended, and Gewel sank to the floor in one flowing movement.

Mary Reid, who so far had kept her distance from Gewel, was one of the first to hug her and thank her for the really outstanding dance. "You have so many talents," she complimented her, making the girl blush.

*   *   *

Later at dinner, the talk was of Gewel's success and how she should think of turning professional. "You're that good, you know," Mary Reid gushed again and again as Anthony proudly nodded. "I told you so."

With only the eight of them and Emily, the talk was more intimate and relaxed than it had been before. A leaf had been removed from the table. All sat closer to one another.

Even Nigel was heard to laugh a time or two and proposed a toast to both Emily for her gracious hospitality and Bella for her fine cooking as he shoved a fourth dumpling into his mouth in proof of his admiration. He then combed his dark mustache with his fingers and eyed the dumpling bowl again.

They were a riotous group later, trooping into the Michigan Room.

Betty Bertram had her hand on Nigel's stiff arm. She happily sang to her own tune:

> *Ten little soldier boys went out to dine;*
> *One choked his little self and then there were nine.*

Gewel took up the lyric:

> *Nine little soldier boys sat up very late;*
> *One overslept himself and then there were eight.*

Anthony sang:

> *Eight little soldier boys travelling in Devon;*
> *One said he'd stay there and then there were seven.*

The others hummed their way to the last line as they took chairs, ranging them into a circle.

Gewel belted out the last line: *"He went out and hanged himself, and then there were none."*

Anthony put a hand around his neck and pretended to choke himself, falling out of his chair to the floor, his tongue hanging out.

"Our Professor Armstrong choked himself on booze," he said as he got up. "Does that count?"

Betty put a finger into the air, announcing her turn to talk. "Where do you all think Dr. Joiner really went? Just wanted to get out of here? Or was she murdered, the way some of us are thinking?"

No one answered. A few looked guilty. A few snickered and sank back in their chairs. Zoe, being the soberest in the group, rested for what she sensed was ahead.

Anthony put his hands in the air. "Our challenge tonight is called 'J'accuse!' For our esteemed Bruxellois, Hercule Poirot."

He dimmed the lights.

He kept his guttural voice.

"Now the soldier boys have stopped their wandering ways." Anthony scanned the room. "Though next we might expect the trip to Devon, where one of us will stay."

His dark eyes searched the faces around him. "I wonder who will be next?"

"What silly business is this, Gliese?" Nigel, testy, called out.

"Simple, dear doctor. We will accuse each other of crimes and hope to make it stick. Anyone may use the crimes Agatha thought up for the novels or come up with our own dastardly deed. Surely we're aware, by now, of the ugly depths in every soul in this room."

Anthony raised his hand to stop the edgy laughter, then leaned close so Zoe could smell his breath. "I thought to accuse one of us of doing in our departed cohorts. But now I've spoiled my show. So tell us, Zoe Zola, what would you accuse me of, my pretty?"

Zoe thought, but not too long. "Bad acting," she said.

The group laughed harder than her little joke deserved.

Anthony turned to Gewel. "Then, Gewel, my dear, to reward you for your magnificent dance, why don't you go first?"

The room was almost dark. Anna sat hunched in her chair. Aaron stood by a window, looking at his reflection in the half-lighted glass. Betty moved to sit next to Zoe, leaning close. "Could I charge Kennedy with self-inflation?" she whispered.

At another time Zoe might have laughed but couldn't now. There was something deadly serious in the room with them. Maybe only the red faces and worked-up excitement, or something else.

Gewel, quite the actor, swung slowly back and forth, looking from face to face as her own face straightened and took on a look of decision.

"You, my pretty." She pointed to Zoe. "Let me see. A mother. You had a mother, didn't you?"

Zoe didn't let on she felt anything. She held herself tight, expecting cruelty to begin.

"Ah, yes, a mother who . . ."

Zoe got ready to move fast at Gewel.

"Lived a blameless life. Loved you madly, I imagine." Gewel stepped away, bowing and smirking at the room.

Allowed to breathe, Zoe said nothing.

"That was cheating," Nigel complained. "I thought we were going to keep this at least mildly entertaining. Weren't we supposed to talk about murders we've taken a look at? Maybe come up with something new?"

"Then I'll take you, Betty Bertram," Aaron Kennedy said in a voice meant to be ghostly as he turned back from the window.

Startled, Betty blinked and blinked.

"Oh, Canada . . ." he sang, then let the anthem fade away as he drew close to Betty. "You're from McGill. Montreal, Canada. And what is Canada known for? Hmm." He put a finger on his chin and thought hard. "Maybe cold. Snow. And icy streets . . . And maybe murder, aye? Oh no . . . someone you knew was murdered."

He came in closer to her face.

Betty blinked again and clutched the arms of her chair.

"*J'accuse.*" He pointed a finger at her. "Wouldn't go to the funeral, would you? Such a shame. Your only friend."

"*You shut up!*" Betty popped out of her chair, knocking into him, then running out the door.

Nobody moved until they heard an upstairs door slam. Even then they looked away from Aaron, their faces either sorry or confused or disgusted.

Aaron made a show of innocence. "I seem to have hit a nerve. Only making it up, of course. Too bad the poor thing's such a miserable sport. No clue any of it was true."

He went to his chair, waving a hand behind him. "I'll sit the rest of your game out."

It was Anthony who smirked now, moving them on. "No one willing to take a shot at me? I'm surprised. I thought, of course, I'd be first. I've seen the looks on your faces." He turned from person to person "Prudes and prisses."

"Oh, I'll take you on, Anthony Gliese," Mary Reid said. "Let me think a minute—I'm sure I'll come up with something."

Anthony's laugh this time wasn't as self-assured.

Mary rose from her chair and walked toward Anthony. His face reddened as she got closer. "I see a long line of young women. So easy to take advantage, isn't it? And then so pleased with yourself, except maybe the one you talked into leaving her husband and three-year-old daughter. Did you think she believed you would publish her book? That you'd make her a literary sensation? So easy to take advantage of a woman's dreams. Nothing asked but a few rolls in the hay. But you had no intention of publishing a third-rate writer, did you? Wasn't that what you told someone in your vaunted publishing house? Who told someone else? And then the item hit a gossip column in New York. And the woman became a sensation, not literary, and then she went out the twenty-third window of a building."

"Ridiculous," Anthony, humor gone, snapped back. "I've never done such a thing. I never would."

"This is a game, Anthony. You thought it up." Mary turned abruptly and went back to her seat, leaving Anthony red-faced and, for the first time, angry. He reached a hand out toward Gewel, who wouldn't take it.

"Now, Zoe. It's your turn. Right up your alley, I imagine," Emily said. "You write about the psychology of characters in novels, don't you? Give us a good one."

Zoe rose and turned to Anna Tow.

"Oh no, not me. I don't think I want to." She put up a hand to Zoe.

"I think . . ." Zoe began in a deep voice, "I see water."

Anna's hand went higher. "I don't want to do this anymore."

"Water. And someone floating in the water."

Anna pushed her chair back, directly into Anthony. "I don't know what's going on here but it's just . . . cruel."

She was gone.

Those left in the room were quiet. Finally, Anthony made a face at Zoe. "Looks like you were on to something."

Zoe turned to face those still in the room. She smiled at each of them. "I've got a feeling she would have run no matter what I said."

"Well . . ." Pileser swiped his hands together and stood. "A terrible waste of time and effort if you ask me. This isn't the sort of thing one usually does at academic affairs. Why, I remember once, when I was at the Iceland Writers Retreat, someone brought up a bit of silliness like this, thinking it would be an icebreaker, and was summarily asked to leave."

"Interesting. But don't they expect 'icebreakers' in Iceland?" Aaron asked, then chuckled, folding his arms over his chest and waiting for the laughter.

Pileser left the room. The others soon followed.

* * *

Later, when Zoe couldn't sleep, she lay in her bed, listening to the leaves in the wind. She heard creaking in the hall. Because she was curious and because the noise—probably footsteps—kept up, she opened her door and stuck her head out. Across the hall, Anthony, in a red silk robe, was going into Gewel's room. She heard their low voices.

And then the door closed.

None of my business, she told herself again and again as she crawled back into bed. The girl was old enough to know better.

Zoe squeezed her eyes as tightly closed as she could. She didn't want to hear anything more that night. She didn't want to think of a gullible girl-woman—alive or dead.

Instead, she slept.

Part 5

Netherworld on Tuesday

Chapter 39

At three AM she sat straight up, pulled the chain to her lamp, and looked around as if something was about to jump on her.

"Where did I put it?" she said aloud, swinging her legs to the side of the bed, and sliding to the floor.

At first she tried to visualize where the thing could be. Since this wasn't her house and not her own bedroom, there were no normal places to hide something or to put it away for a future time.

First her purse. It wasn't there, though she emptied the purse on the bed and shook it until the last paperclip fell out.

The top of the chest: nothing in her growing pile of welcome notes and schedules and menus. Nothing under the dirty underwear she'd thrown there that morning.

Standing at the center of the room, rotating slowly, was the best she could do: a chair with a pair of jeans thrown across the back; her suitcase, open at the bottom of the bed. There was the window chair—empty. There was the small stack of shirts and pants she'd slung down on a towel laid on the floor of the closet because she couldn't reach the shelf, which never mattered to her since she didn't wear fussy things anyway. Everything was wash-and-wear and no-wrinkle, and if they wrinkled, she just wouldn't look down her body.

Anyway, there was nothing tucked among them.

She turned around again in the middle of the room, whirling as if to catch something behind her. Open closet. Window chair. Suitcase. The other chair with a pair of —

The jeans. Yesterday's.

The business card was in a back pocket. She dug it out to smooth between her fingers: Harley Lamb, Attorney at Law.

And Mary Lamb, the actress.

Angela Lamb, the . . .

An illegible address. A worn away phone number.

Harley Lamb. An attorney in Calumet. She could call him again, leave a message, let him know she was on to what he and his wife were doing.

Or she might say to Mary Reid: *I'm on to you. You're not at all what you claim to be.*

She looked at the card again. The whole thing could be harmless—a trick to play at an Agatha Christie symposium: *Won't that be fun? Won't these people remember us after that?*

She smoothed the faded card again between her fingers. She would hand it to Mary, tell her she found it in her room, and watch her face.

* * *

She tried to sleep, to give her overactive mind a rest, but facts bounced behind her eyes like a dust storm. The storm growing, about to hit her directly.

Emily Zokela Winton and Mary Lamb leading a symposium on Agatha Christie. Why? Because they'd played Christie characters in a play? Because they knew Zoe was writing a book based on Christie?

Maybe this whole thing was an offshoot of *The Mouse Trap.*

A new drama, or farce, and everyone with a role.

Maybe there were hidden cameras. Cinéma vérité.

She looked at the ceiling, following the molding from one wall to another. And then around the door. The windows. Under the lampshade. Headboard. Everywhere a camera might hide, she searched and found nothing.

The thought of being watched was chilling, like the constant, unchanging landscape out her window. A camera wouldn't blink or tell a lie. And the group that would be at breakfast, unchanging, would be in their assigned places, looking up, on cue, when she walked in.

People whose real names she didn't know and whom she didn't trust.

She sat at the edge of the bed to think. First, she needed to know if Dr. Leon Armstrong was still in a hospital. Where? Which hospital? There'd been no updates. How could she even ask? But of course, she could. Wouldn't any normal person ask?

Then Louise Joiner. A real professor. They'd kind of gotten to know each other, but Louise had never mentioned a daughter. Not even a husband. And no daughter existed.

She tried to put herself into the head of Louise: mid-thirties, established at a university. Unlikely she'd be involved in something shady, or silly, or . . . deadly.

Chapter 40

At breakfast, when she tried to hand the business card to Mary, she frowned down at Zoe and brushed her hand away.

She called "Susan" across the table to Emily, trying for her attention before the woman found a way to escape. Too late, and she was gone.

She asked the others if they'd heard whether Leon was all right. A few looked up from their plates and shook their heads.

Zoe fell back in her chair and swung her feet from side to side in frustration.

Aaron Kennedy leaned toward her, saying, "By the way, Zoe, her name is Emily. In case you don't remember. Must be the stress of this place. Good thing we'll all be gone soon."

Across the table, Anthony lifted his glass of orange juice to the others, one by one. "Miracle of miracles—we're all here this morning. Nobody with the plague, nobody fell out a window, nobody kidnapped during the night. I'd say that's worth a toast."

The others said "Hip hip hooray," but without enthusiasm.

"Well, I, for one, might have welcomed a good case of plague." Nigel's face was long and miserable. "I have to do a webinar this afternoon and, if truth be told, feel completely ill equipped for the job."

Betty Bertram made fun of him, while Anna tried to sympathize as she passed a bowl of grits.

"Professor," Zoe said, "you must have done a million such things in your career."

"You'd think so, wouldn't you? But I've always dodged these new technologies, or whatever you might call webinars. I'm not the greatest speaker in the world, as you might have noticed. Nor the prettiest."

"Baloney," Gewel said.

"A lie," Anna said. "You seem content with who you are."

"Balderdash," somebody else said, then snickered.

"We'll be there to help." Zoe felt she should add something. "Surely you don't mind giving your talk on . . . crap sakes, I've forgotten the name of your talk."

"We settled on 'The Lost People of Soldier Island,' remember?" He said this to Emily, who'd just come back into the room, coffeepot in her hands. "I'm to compare a few of the scenes in *And Then There Were None* with those in *Murder on the Orient Express*."

"Ah, yes," Zoe said. "A fascinating topic. Both novels with a large cast of men and women. Both settings isolated. But completely different stories. One to kill off a lot of people who deserve it. The other to kill one man. If I didn't know what our situation was here at Netherworld Lodge, I'd swear there was a pact to do what the characters did in both those books."

She looked slowly around the table, watching the reactions.

"What a silly idea," Anna Tow scoffed but kept her eyes down. "A pact. Between people who've never met before?"

"Two people suddenly missing?" Zoe said.

Nigel interrupted with his worries as the others ate their scrambled eggs and grits, and toast with thimbleberry jam from the monks in Eagle Harbor.

"The larder's gettin' a little slim," Emily warned.

"Not as slim as ya might think." Bella nodded as she handed the bowls and platters around. "Only some of the staples. If we had a house full o' hens, we'd be just fine."

Emily, coffeepot in hand, hurried behind Zoe, who was quick to ask for a refill.

"You forgot me, Aunt Susan." Zoe smiled a warm smile as she held out her cup.

No one at the table seemed to notice.

Emily said nothing. She filled Zoe's cup, then moved on quickly.

Chapter 41

With nothing to do until lunch, and still waiting for a call from Jenny, Zoe went to her room and gathered her research from the library and Harley's business card.

"Did it happen yet?"

This was her proof that something was going on—too many lies, too many coincidences, too many odd things happening. Two speakers gone.

But none this morning.

* * *

In the kitchen, she found not only Mary but also Nigel, his arms crossed, a distant look in his washed-out eyes. The look of rabid condescension he always wore was gone. Instead, he watched steadily out the back door, where rain splashed on a little pad of cement, as he spoke in a low voice to Mary.

Both of them turned as she walked in. A few beats were missed during the look of surprise they exchanged. Nigel said her name.

"Well, Miss Zola!" Nigel called out. "You've caught me here, probably obstructing preparations for our lunch. All because my raincoat has mold on it."

"May I do anything for you, Miss Zola?" Mary turned from the stove.

Zoe nodded. "When you have a minute."

"No, don't leave," Nigel said. "I've been reassured I can simply wipe the mold off. That's really all I came for."

He gave a small laugh, bowed his head to Zoe, and was gone.

There was a long moment while Mary looked down at her hands and then over at Zoe.

"Would you like to sit down?" She motioned to the table, a nervous tic making her right eye quiver again and again.

Zoe climbed up on one of the wooden, spool-backed chairs, set the business card in front of her, and waited for the right words to come.

Mary didn't ask what she wanted. She didn't look at her. She was fascinated with her right thumb, which must have had leftover nail polish because she picked at it obsessively.

"I don't know what's going on here, and it's beginning to scare the hell out of me," Zoe said.

"What are you talking about? I thought everything was going very well."

"Your name isn't Mary Reid, is it?"

Mary's face relaxed. She half-smiled. "Oh, you've heard I was in *The Mouse Trap*, here in Calumet. I hope that proves to you what a Christie fan I am."

They exchanged cool smiles. "So, what is your real name?"

Mary lifted her chin and smiled. "Mary."

"Lamb?"

She hesitated.

"And Emily is Susan Jokela Winton, your mother, I imagine. You do own Ulysses Bookstore, with your husband, Harley. Or Leon Armstrong."

Emily's smile slipped. She said nothing, waiting to hear what was coming next.

Zoe put the card on the table.

"What's this?" Mary asked.

"A business card I found upstairs under the bed where Leon Armstrong slept. Harley Lamb."

Mary gave a low laugh. "So, you caught us."

"Doing what?"

She shrugged. "A game. Hyping the event. *The Daily Mining Gazette* promised they'd run any stories coming out of the webinars if they were of real interest.

"So, that's what I decided we needed: hype and mystery. After all, this place is so far away, and we've tried hard to promote what we're doing up here. I thought, if we make it really mystifying, and people get a little spooked . . . well, the stories might go nationwide, which is good for our Christie group. It's a fundraiser for the arts council."

"But why Emily Brent? Everyone must have recognized it. And Bella Webb too. What's Bella's part in this whole thing?"

"And . . ." Zoe thought hard about what bothered her most. "Why was I the only one to get a black-trimmed invitation? What do you know about me?"

"Only that you're almost famous. Known for solving some pretty difficult murders. That you are working on a book about Agatha Christie. Emily thought maybe you'd enjoy our event. I thought so too."

"And the invitation?"

She shook her head. "I didn't do that. I swear. I sent you a regular invitation. I can't say what happened."

She thought awhile. "Maybe it was a bad joke. One of the other invitees?

"What did we do, Mary? You knew us when we lived in Cheboygan. Our mothers were sisters. We're cousins, the two of us."

Mary's head was down. She waved a hand in the air. "We were babies. I don't remember . . ."

"Why was I asked here? Do you hate me? What's going on? Or do you want to be friends—want to make up for how you all treated Evelyn?"

"I can't tell you."

Zoe waited a minute before asking, "To embarrass me? Was it to exact some kind of punishment? For what? Please tell me what I did? How did you find me?"

Mary looked around at Zoe, her tired face softer now. "It happens I know someone in Bear Falls."

"Bear Falls?"

"A very nice older woman. We met at a political rally a while ago and stayed in touch. One day she mentioned this almost famous author who moved to town. She told me your name. Who else is named Zoe Zola?"

"Who is she?"

"Myra Cavendish."

"My postman's wife?" Zoe was incredulous.

"She said you'd solved some pretty difficult murders, and that she heard you were working on a book about Agatha Christie. Here we are, with this Agatha Christie webinar. It was my mother's idea to invite you. She thought maybe you'd be intrigued."

"By the black edging on the invitation?"

She shook her head, "I didn't do that. I swear. Maybe Aunt Bella. She didn't like the idea of going against their mother, Anas. But just before you got here, Aunt Bella said it might be a nice surprise for you, at the end."

"After all these years? After all the cruelty?"

"There was no cruelty, Zoe. They lost touch is all." Her smile was a happy one.

Zoe saw she believed what she was saying. "And where are Dr. Armstrong and Louise Joiner? Who are they? Is anyone here real?"

Mary sighed. "They had to leave. I might play games with my name, but I didn't cause them to disappear."

Zoe watched her face. A worn face, with more lines than she'd had before. The eyes trying to avoid hers were ringed with dark shadows. Zoe wanted to believe her, really wanted to like her, but there was too much in the way.

"What am I missing here?" Zoe asked.

The woman gave her an odd look. "What do you mean? There's nothing. I want this to be a successful event—for our arts council. If I went too far, I'm sorry, but I think it's going very well now."

"A lot of anger."

Mary shrugged and looked out the back window.

"A lot of attacking each other's scholarship," Zoe said.

Nothing from Mary.

"And their names—they're not real."

Mary relaxed. She almost smiled. "There's nothing going on, Miss Zola. But if it makes you happy to think there's something beyond the seen, well, go ahead. We only have a few days left. Please let me know if you come up with anything. I might use it for publicity for the series. Now, I have to cook. Emily's out looking for mushrooms."

At the kitchen door, Zoe turned back to look hard at the woman she didn't remember. "I don't believe a word you're telling me, you know. Are we playing out a version of *And Then There Were None*? Is that what you're doing? You have cameras on us . . . I don't know . . . A new version of the book? Oh, and the black-rimmed invitation—if you didn't send it, who did? And your name—why do you need to be anonymous, Mrs. Lamb?"

Mary made a gesture toward Zoe, then pulled her hand back.

Zoe waited. Nothing. "What's going to happen tonight?

"A surprise. A wonderful surprise."

"Goodbye, Mary," Zoe said. "I'm going to find the reason we're here, you know. If that means you have to kill me, then I suggest you get on with it."

"I would never hurt you, Zoe." Her face was sad. "I will only do what I have to do. Nothing more."

"And what is that—'what you have to do'?"

She didn't answer.

"Right now, I have the feeling that no one's leaving Netherworld until whatever has to happen has happened."

Mary's back stiffened, but she said nothing.

At the door, Zoe had to ask, "Please tell me how you made it rain?"

The woman didn't turn.

Zoe left her, shaking her head.

Chapter 42

Zoe fumbled for the handle of the screen door. She pushed and stepped over the threshold all at once, then turned, stomped across the porch and down the steps. She kept going, into a light rain, across the driveway, and out to the road she'd come in on.

She ran her ungainly run until she couldn't run anymore. The trees were still and dark. The leaves dripped a constant patter.

The road was empty in both directions, but anyone could have been hiding, watching her.

She heard the creek before she got there. Water still flowed unimpeded over what should have been the low bridge. The plank road lay beneath the fast-flowing water. She'd never make it through that way in her sandals. And if she did get across, where could she go? There'd been a house where they'd first turned in here. Maybe there were people . . . but what kind of people? It felt like enemy territory. No matter how far she got, it wouldn't be far enough, not on her own.

When Zoe turned back, she walked much slower. Maybe there were other roads or paths. That one she'd taken her first day, toward the river. There was still that one to try.

Back in sight of the lodge, she hid among the trees to see if anyone was on the porch or standing at the front of the house—looking for her.

No one was there. She could get back in . . . but . . .

Keeping the lodge in sight, she moved from tree to tree, never taking her eyes off the building. No noise came from inside, and when she was around back, near the kitchen, no noise came from there either.

She stepped out of the shadow of the lodge and ran as fast as she'd ever run for the woods beyond, along the path she'd taken when Louise—or whoever she was—had rescued her.

When she was safe, she forced herself to calm down, to keep her mind on what she had to do and where she had to go. The river. Had to be the river. Maybe a boat.

She couldn't handle a boat. But she could follow the river out of there.

The path curved, looked dangerous in places where the water had risen and lapped at both edges of the sand. Ahead of her, the path curved again and started downward.

There was no choice but to keep going unless she hit the river and it was impassable, so far over its banks she would stumble into it—something she'd been afraid of for years, childhood nightmares of being in water, then sinking down to where she couldn't see.

At one curve, the path went straight again. She caught a glimpse of something large and dark ahead. *Maybe a fallen tree* is what she thought at first. And then she stopped because the dark thing was a house, a log house built low to the ground. The roof she'd seen from her room.

Maybe there was a working phone inside.

Maybe people. Renters. Caretakers.

Maybe . . .

*   *   *

The old house was made of hand-hewn logs, with a moss-covered porch, a low front door so that most people, other than her, would have to stoop to get in. No rockers here. No sign of anyone.

She ran to the porch and grabbed on to the railing. Maybe she could hide here until she was sure people from outside had come to rescue her.

A single step. She could hide and rest and think before going all the way to the river.

So many thoughts, she didn't look up when she put her hand out for the door handle and shook it.

When she did look up, Louise Joiner stood beyond the window, her hand holding the inside doorknob. Zoe heard the click of a lock.

Her first instinct was relief. She began to smile until she realized Louise had locked the door on her.

She stepped back until she reached the edge of the porch, then climbed down to the ground and stood a minute, waiting; maybe she'd been wrong, and Louise would fling the door open, and ask her to come in where it was safe.

She didn't.

There was movement at one of the front windows; a curtain was pulled back. Leon stood there, bending forward to look out at Zoe, then hold still, staring at her with no expression on his face.

She backed off the porch, then walked to the path, looking from side to side. Only once did she glance back to see Louise at the door, watching her.

In a few yards, the path came to an end, and another one started off in another direction. She took that path because she had no choice. She didn't run.

* * *

First she smelled the water—a cold, musky stink.

Then the sound hit her, like rocks rolling down a mountainside. The sound grew until she saw the river ahead, water boiling over itself. Another turn in the path, and quieter water here at a bend, protected by a thicket of trees, some leaning, ready to topple.

The path curved slightly. A blackened wooden pier was in front of her. A rising floor of old boards. It stretched out over the river, but on one side boards hung down into the water; a few of the supports on that side were gone. It didn't look safe to walk on as the river smashed into it, and water leaped higher than the floor of old planks.

She looked one way up the river. Rows of slanting trees hung out over the water rushing around a wide curve, turning abruptly toward the north.

Behind her was the forest, with pools of standing water everywhere.

There was no place to go. Her feet sank into the sand and water covered her shoes where she stood. She stepped up on to the pier; the boards held, but the whole thing groaned when the river hit it.

She jumped back into the weeds and water and sloshed to where she'd come out of the forest. Maybe there was another path. One she'd missed that would take her out to a road where there were cars. And real human beings.

She squished slowly back the way she'd come. One tired foot in front of the other.

This path ended at the low cabin. No sound came from the house. No figures stood in the doorway or at the window.

With her head down, she kept walking to the lodge, inside, then back across the reception room, with a trail of mud and sand and water behind her.

She heard the door to the kitchen open.

She didn't look. Didn't have to. Emily's voice followed her up the stairs.

"Lunch in half an hour, Miss Zola. Don't be late."

Chapter 43

Gewel stood at the top of the stairs, looking at her.

Zoe would have stopped, but the shock of what she'd just seen made her pass Gewel by. She kept her head down and watched her feet move. There was no one she could trust. And no way to get out of there. Everything was illusion: what she thought, what she'd talked herself into, everyone she thought was normal. It was only as real as they let her believe.

"How are you holding up?" Gewel, her hair uncombed, no makeup, said to Zoe's back as she brushed past her.

"A very long week." Zoe said over her shoulder.

"Only five days."

Zoe muttered to herself.

"And this is Tuesday," Gewel said.

"Two days to go. We'll never make it."

"Zoe!" Gewel's voice followed her. "We have a surprise for tonight. A big one."

Zoe was at her door, feeling in her pockets for the old-fashioned key.

"Zoe? Bella's a medium, did you know that? Can you imagine? She does séances. That's what we're doing tonight. And who do you think she's going to try and contact?"

Zoe didn't turn from her door. "Noah?"

"No. Seriously. She's going to try and reach Agatha Christie. Won't that be exciting?"

"Wow. Can't wait." She leaned her forehead against the door.

"And for tomorrow, our last night, we'll have Anthony's Murder Games." Gewel said, then asked, "What's wrong, Zoe? Something happen?"

Zoe hesitated with her key in the lock. "Nothing wrong, Gewel. I wish all of you a wonderful night—an amazing time. I'll be asleep. I'm too tired."

"Zoe? What's happened to you?"

She closed the door behind her.

She lay on the bed, closed her eyes, and fell asleep. Then someone shook her.

* * *

"Zoe." Betty Bertram's worried voice said as the hand gripped her. "It's time for lunch."

Even the thought of being awake hurt. She opened her eyes to a long face, surrounded with streaked blond hair, hanging above her. To avoid being seen, Zoe covered her eyes with her arm.

"Come on, Zoe. Bella sent me to get you."

"I'm not hungry."

"Then don't eat. But you have to come to the table. You signed a contract."

Zoe moved her arm enough to see Betty, leaning above her. "Contract? I signed a contract that I have to eat? Crazy."

"No. No. You have to take part in all the planning. Things are being changed, and you have to be there."

Zoe thought back to anything she'd heard about change and remembered Gewel yelling something at her.

She moved her arm and looked up. "Gewel said something about a séance tonight? Okay. I'll be there."

"That's not the way it works here, Zoe. You know that."

Zoe forced herself to roll to the side of her bed and sit up.

"Never signed such a contract."

"But you have to get up."

She felt an arm around her waist and tiny Betty pulling at her. When she stood on her small, bare, cold feet, she shivered.

"Ten minutes, Zoe. Emily said no more than ten minutes. They're holding lunch until you get down there."

The woman was gone. Zoe found her suitcase on the closet floor and opened it. She dumped the clothes to the floor and pawed through her things until she had a clean white shirt with a big red heart embroidered on the back. Jeans—not too clean, but she'd only brought two pairs with her. Underwear. No socks. She would wear her sandals.

After dressing, she took her brush from her makeup case and ran it over her hair. When she was ready, she took a deep breath. With no car she couldn't get away. With no Jenny, no Lisa, no Tony coming for her, all the forest beyond the window was as wide and impenetrable as the strongest fence.

She had to go to lunch and then to the webinar. She would take part in everything they ordered her to take part in. Two days to go, and she knew things the others didn't. Or didn't want to know.

All of them? she asked herself as she very quietly stepped into the hall. The sound of voices—indistinct—came from below.

* * *

One step at a time until she got to the Copper Room.

Someone laughed. "You sure can sleep, Zoe."

It was Anna Tow, laughing at her.

"I went for a walk this morning." She smiled and talked until she got to her end of the table, hoisted herself into place, and looked from face to face close by. Her eyes were still bleary, seeing only eyes and then noses and moving mouths.

She was soon in conversation with first Anna, at one side of the table; then Nigel, who wanted to know what she thought of the séance idea; and then Mary, who was saying nobody had approved it yet. And then, in the middle of all of that, an argument grew until Aaron stood angrily and said he wouldn't have agreed to come here if he'd known it was to be about such nonsense.

"I don't . . ." Zoe started but was then unsure of what she was against.

"Look." Anthony was on his feet too. "We all have some concerns with things going on here. We've had people come up missing. Been without the internet. Anna and Betty swear Agatha Christie is haunting them. Bella says she's done séances before and offered to contact Agatha's spirit."

"What if we don't like her?" Gewel asked.

Gewel and Anthony were giggling when Bella entered with the first of the lunch dishes, a platter of mashed and buttered squash.

"I don't have to do it, ya know," she said while setting the platter down with a thump. "Don't have to do anything. It's just that, since I was born, I've had this gift, and I'm willin' to use it if ya need me."

"Imagine if *she* is here." Betty's face was pale. "What a story it would make. Newspapers. TV. This place would be famous. People would flock to the programs. We'd be known worldwide."

"And we could ask her directly if we were right about that second husband. Max. And if she ever loved him or just wanted to travel through the Middle East, writing her stories."

"And what about when she got amnesia, or whatever it was, after her first husband left her for another woman? We'd have firsthand research." Anna's eyes were big.

"Do you women care about nothing but gossip?" Aaron sniffed. He crossed his arms.

"What does it matter?" Zoe smiled from one to the other. "Two days and we'll all be gone."

The others took her remark as agreement. They laughed and talked as they dug into Bella's stuffed meatloaf with the buttered squash, which did nothing for Zoe's rolling stomach, so she sat, listened, ate nothing beyond the first forkful, and kept nodding.

* * *

First they had to help Nigel through a rehearsal. He was nervous about this webinar thing, getting his talk down; then they discussed what they could bring in to back him up and then their questions.

"Better questions than before, I hope. Solid questions that will lead our online guests to be more interesting. I can't do everything, you know." He looked away.

It would be an interesting event, they assured him.

"Don't forget your notebook, Zoe," Nigel reminded her as the webinar was about to begin. "You'll have plenty of my quotes for Thursday."

* * *

Nigel wasn't boring, as she'd expected. His talk on "The Lost People of Soldier Island" plodded through a series of interesting facts on Soldier Island and then about a train trapped by snow in the wilderness.

Zoe made a few notes, then doodled in her notebook. She hoped for good questions from their audience. One young man named Arizona John always gave her decent quotes and would again

She doodled circles with faces in her notebook when she thought there was enough to say about Nigel. Her first circle was Gewel, wearing a veil, her distinctive, almond-shaped eyes flirting. Anna, with an unhappy look, staring at Nigel. She drew a blue bow in Nigel's mustache. A red bow taped to the bald spot on Aaron's head. Emily Brent in a helmet. Mary Reid was sad.

When Emily Brent frowned her way she quickly filled in each circle, feeling spied upon.

A séance ahead, gathering for a happy hour with Agatha's ghost. Cocktails. One of them would drink too much.

Later, at dinner, someone would start an argument, probably over the séance.

And tomorrow? Aaron Kennedy would tear into poor Agatha Christie then—ah yes, murder games. Thursday morning she would tie the webinar all together, make sense of it, and they would all say goodbye and be on their way—as if it never happened.

A shame. An end to all the good times they'd been having.

Chapter 44

Zoe was tired and in no mood for a silly séance, but they'd given her no option except to attend. Anyway, she felt more and more that she had to keep watch.

If they had anything planned for her, it had to happen soon.

She didn't change her clothes. Didn't wash her face. She brushed her hair, put on her shoes, and went down to find join the others on their way to the séance.

In the hall, Betty came from behind, took Zoe's arm, and squeezed it. "I'm so excited. Can you imagine? What if Bella contacts her?"

"Agatha will probably disapprove," Anna Tow groused, from ahead of them.

"Why? There's been nothing but homage here." Betty pulled a long face.

"You've heard Aaron. He makes fun of her. Can you imagine what she'll say to that?" Anna said. "Talk about a woman's wrath!"

Gewel knocked into Zoe's small body on the way to a seat, almost tipping her over. "Sorry. I'm so excited."

* * *

The floor-to-ceiling curtains were pulled across the windows, making the room dark except for one floor lamp lighted in a corner. The table was pushed to one wall, the chairs placed in a circle.

The room didn't smell of food this time. The air was stuffy, filled with the stink of mold. Copper pieces on the walls glittered in the low light. They looked, to Zoe, tarnished and old. Nothing was new here, nor seemed of much value. She was getting the feeling of the rooms as settings, something from a much larger stage.

Everyone was quiet as Bella walked in from behind them and went to the front. She wore a white robe that hung straight to the floor, hobbling her. The white turban on her head slipped as she walked, to be caught and pushed back into place.

At a break in the circle, she pulled an old chair around to face her audience. She sat down with a rustle of satin and a grunt.

She arranged her robe, tucking her feet in her everyday loafers under it, and looked out, toward the ceiling.

Anthony stood, half-falling over. He giggled and threw his hands into the air. "Could we get started? Our Gewel has the rules Bella demands we follow."

He bowed to Gewel.

She stood, smiling at her audience.

"Bella asks that we hold hands until the séance is over. She will be contacting a dead spirit and no one must talk or move. When the spirit is here, you may ask a question in a low voice, then wait for the complete answer. Otherwise keep silent until the trance is over."

She nodded when she stopped talking, emphasizing the rules.

Zoe didn't dare look at anyone. She would be rolling on the floor, laughing. She was holding Betty's hand on one side. Anna's on the other.

"I hope ya listen to Gewel, here." Bella frowned from face to face. "Ya must be silent. If Agatha Christie's going to come tonight, it will be through me and me alone. When yer sure she's here, ya can ask all the questions unless I pass out from da strain. Then da séance is over."

"Can I record what Agatha says?" Betty asked.

"Heavens no! She's a spirit. Who knows if her voice will even record? Sometimes, ya know, it's just for the ears of the listeners."

She looked around the room. "Okay? That's it? You all hold hands. Now I'm taking myself into a trance. I'll be calling out to Agatha Christie, the way ya asked me to. I'll keep asking her a question. Mary gave me some suggestions—what to ask. When you hear her answer, you'll know she's taken over my body."

Nobody moved.

Bella talked to herself, in a very low voice, which, after ten minutes or so, began to change, got higher, and slowed.

"So are ya here with us, Agatha?"

For a long time nothing happened. There were squeaks and grunts and other uncomfortable noises until a high, nasal voice said, "Well? What do you people want from me? I'm very busy, as you might imagine."

The voice wasn't Bella's. The accent was upper-class British, with the faintest touch of disdain to it. And maybe a bit of frustration and anger underneath.

"Dame Agatha?"

Somebody spoke but Zoe didn't recognize the voice.

Zoe opened one eye. All she could see was Bella, nothing or no one else.

Nobody's to look at me, do you hear? There, you. If you can't follow the rules, I suggest you leave the rest of us alone.

Zoe swallowed hard and shut both eyes as tight as she could get them.

"Now, just so you all know I'm not without contact," Dame Agatha said. *"I've followed the terrible things you're doing at this uncivilized place."*

There was an imperial sniff and a moment of quiet.

Along the circle of seats there was nervous movement.

"Especially you. What's your name? Nigel somebody. I've been insulted and maligned and have been thinking about contacting my solicitor, but I don't know where he's gotten to.

"I would have expected a much better greeting here, in America, where my work is very popular. So, what I'd like to ask—no, demand— is that you stop this insult, talking about me with so little knowledge, and go back to your homes. Or . . ."

"Or what, Ms. Christie?" Zoe spoke up. She opened her eyes and was determined to keep them that way.

Bella's outraged face was gray, and haughty. *"Mallowan. My married name is Mallowan now. Or I will see to it that every one of you is made into a public fool. And stop your attempts to learn my secrets. You can't."*

Agatha was quiet. And then came a deep sigh.

"My disappearance was manufactured by me. I believe you all believe that fact. I needed to rest after what my husband did to me. I knew I would be found before long, and what better way to shame him than by having his craven cruelty exposed to the world. I am not now, nor have I ever have been, a weak woman. Sometimes not even a very nice one."

There was an even deeper sigh. *"There, that should be enough for the pack of you. I don't have the strength to stay here very long. But, if I don't hear you've stopped this silly business you've engaged in and disperse, I will be back. Especially tomorrow afternoon, for Professor Kennedy's webinar talk."*

"Sir?" Bella's blinded eyes sought out Aaron Kennedy. *"I will take it as a personal attack if you make things up about me. Don't think I haven't heard you. "The Aging of Agatha!" Indeed! And other things you've said. You don't think me perceptive? Because of my* Tommy *and* Tuppence *novels? And might I ask, sir, which novels of yours I might read that I can laugh at? Oh, I'll bet they're in a drawer. Bundles of them. All unpublished. What is it in you that makes you think your non-talent superior to my enormous outlay of stories? Come, sir. Tell me what you've added to the world?"*

Aaron didn't laugh or answer. He slid down in his seat, unclenched Anthony's and Nigel's hands from his, folded his arms across his chest, and glared at Bella Webb.

Bella breathed very fast and dipped her head low, almost to her lap.

Betty cried, "Not yet! I have questions."

No one moved. No one leaped to help Bella. No one said a word until Bella righted herself, white turban hanging to one side, and blinked many times, looking from one person to another in the room.

"Well?" she asked. "Did anythin' happen?"

There was nervous laughter.

"Yes, Bella." Gewel was on her feet, her hands on Bella's shoulders. "Quite a bit. She doesn't like what we've been doing here. Maybe it's time to stop and let everyone go home."

"Ridiculous!" Emily stood. "Two more talks to go. Professor Kennedy tomorrow and then Zoe Zola. We've looked forward to what both would say about Agatha and about what's been learned here this week. We can't stop now."

"We can, Emily. And we should." Zoe called out.

"Nonsense." Emily turned to the seated people. "We want to hear Professor Kennedy, don't we? Our webinarians want to hear him. After all, they paid."

235

Zoe watched as Anthony put his arm around Gewel's shoulders and pulled her close. She watched as Aaron Kennedy examined his nails and looked at no one. She saw Nigel searching for a face turned his way so he could complain about Agatha's solicitor coming after him.

They all sat still as Emily helped Bella from her chair and out of the room.

Chapter 45

Dinner, afterward, wasn't quiet.

Anthony was in rare form—or still half-drunk from the cocktail hour. He greeted everyone with a kiss on the cheek, even Aaron and Nigel, who pushed him away and wiped their faces.

No one mentioned the séance at first. It was after they'd eaten and pushed back their plates that Aaron Kennedy looked from face to face around him and began to laugh.

"Well, isn't our Bella something? What a show! Even I began to believe her for a bit. And I half-expected it—Bella's attack. The perfect target because I don't particularly like her backwoods cuisine, and I've let her know. What you all witnessed was a powerless woman's revenge." He threw his head back and laughed.

"Oh, I don't think so," Gewel said.

"Me either," Anthony agreed. "Sounded exactly as I expected her to sound."

"Any upper-class English woman. Really. I picked out a few words Agatha wouldn't have used like *webinar,* but otherwise I think she was a perfectly fine Agatha."

The argument picked up speed until Aaron was laughing hard, and the others were angry. Bella cleared the table without a word to anyone. She shuffled in and out, not looking left or right, nor standing up for herself.

Gewel stood, hands balanced on the table. "Please. Please. We are here until Thursday. "Today was to be fun. Tonight you may all watch the movie, if that's what you want to do. Tomorrow Aaron will deliver his talk. Which, I'm sure, we're all looking forward to . . ."

"Except our dear Agatha," Nigel called out.

"And tomorrow night," Gewel said, ignoring him, "we'll play Anthony's game of murder. Does everyone agree to go along with the rest of our plan?"

Nigel grumbled. Aaron frowned. Betty sat up to hear better. Anna looked perturbed, and then fierce.

"I don't care what the rest of you think," Anna said. "Agatha was here today. I felt her. She's been with me over and over since I got here. Her books have been moved around in my room. Even this morning, I noticed she'd opened *Five Little Pigs* and left it like that. I'm sure she wanted to talk to us."

"And I've felt her during our webinar," Betty said. "Not in a good way, either."

"I wanted to ask her about those two missing figures. One of the figures had his hand to his throat. And what else?" Gewel turned to Anthony for help. "And this weather. Was she responsible?"

No one was really missing, Zoe knew. She wanted to tell them but didn't. When she thought about seeing the two of them at that cabin, she wondered if she'd been hysterical. Maybe there'd been no one there at all. She was beginning to doubt everything she saw and heard.

Mary Reid was smiling. "It had to be one of Agatha's little jokes."

"But whatever it was, I'm ready to move on." Anthony was back at Gewel's side. "An interesting addendum to our event. Maybe tomorrow we will solve a few old cases together. That should make the Christie Society happy."

"Ah, no. We're still doing that?" Aaron groused.

Anna shook her head. "How about you, Zoe?"

Zoe had no real opinion—an old movie or a game. Both seemed like good ways to pass the time they had left.

Gewel raised her hand, wiggling her fingers for attention. "As Anthony told us, tomorrow night is ours. It's what we know best. You have to admit, we're all pretty adept at murder."

"Personally," Pileser said on his way from the room, "I think the only murders not solvable in this day of DNA and cutting-edge forensics are those where good luck intervened for the murderer."

Kennedy said, "Ah, but, Nigel, you're discounting the superior mind."

He threw his head back to stare at the ceiling. "Never discount genius. There'll always be people—men and maybe a few women—able to outfox the police and any investigator he comes up against. Like so much in life, nothing is ever completely equal."

Anthony put his hands in the air. "Ladies and gentlemen, Anna Tow has asked to say one thing before we go up to rest."

They stopped to listen.

"I've got something on my chest," she said, following this with a sniff. "I just wanted to say that I don't like the way Professors Kennedy and Pileser attack everybody, especially the women. Like we don't know what we're talking about."

Anthony put a hand on Anna's back. She elbowed him away and had a few more words for the two professors who were snickering, trying to cover their smiles and then outbursts of laughter.

Anna put her hand up again. "Okay. You two can laugh, but I've said what I wanted to say."

The end of her long nose was red. Her thin lips were drawn into a childish line that might signal tears.

"Okay." She went down the hall, stopping to turn to the two men and flip them a finger, making them bend over with laughter.

*　*　*

Zoe was still laughing later as she straightened her pile of research and made notes for her talk on Thursday. What was she going to say? Nothing new here—well, some things. A few observations on similarities in Agatha's books, places she used, and how the sadness of her life set up some of her characters. She'd noted those facts. Aaron would probably go for the jugular in his talk—poor Agatha. She almost wished Agatha had been real. Then she could protect herself. Maybe, in a magnificent display of supernatural fireworks, she could smite the man and send them all home in a flash.

Two webinars to go: Aaron Kennedy's and hers. And then a plane, boat, or automobile out of here.

She wondered who Gewel Sharp could really be, other than a very smart woman. Her name was stuck in her brain. Nagged at her.

She sat back in the chair, drew a writing pad close, and let her mind range over the people she'd been thrown with for the last few days. Starting with Gewel.

Gewel Sharp. Gewel Sharp. For Gewel . . . a sapphire, opal, topaz, emerald, ruby.

Ruby. Ruby The name stuck. And sharp—Keene? *Ruby Keene.* The Body in the Library. *The dancer murdered and left in a quarry while another young girl was murdered and her body left in the library at Gosington Hall.*

She slouched down in her chair and smiled at her own genius.

No such human being as Gewel Sharp. That little dance of hers was a clue to her name. Why? Only a joke? Everyone here a joke, but her?

She rubbed at her eyes. She rubbed at her forehead. She thought about Fida, the one who helped her make sense of her thoughts. Zoe missed her.

In a few minutes she was in bed and fast asleep.

Part 6

Wednesday

Chapter 46

At breakfast, nobody mentioned that Mary wasn't at her place. Her plate sat in front of her usual chair, untouched. Bella didn't pick it up, nor clear it at the end of the meal. It sat there like a memory marker: the place where Mary used to sit.

Zoe said nothing about Mary, pretending along with the rest of them. She had no appetite for the thick bacon and fried eggs. No appetite for talk about the weather. Not even for how they were going to get out of there the next day.

Even with the sun finally coming out, everyone seemed tired. There were wide yawns, a lot of whispering to the person close by, and a lot of food removed, uneaten, from the table.

One by one, people excused themselves and went out to the reception room to find a partner for a card game or more coffee.

She stayed where she was, sipping her coffee and watching the others leave. She waited until Bella was back to gather the dirty dishes and hover over Mary's place setting, not moving the plate, glass, utensils, or napkin.

"Where's Mary?" Zoe asked, then asked again when Bella pretended not to hear her.

"Sick," Bella said. "Can't come out of her room."

Zoe didn't say a word. She was beyond treating anything here as normal. If they wanted Mary to disappear, then let them do it. She was probably at that cabin with the others. Nothing to worry about. As long as she could get away after her talk in the morning.

"I wanted to talk to her about the plans for tomorrow. Is the bridge fixed? How does she want to get us out of here?"

"I wouldn't worry. I'm sure she's got ya taken care of. We're all leavin', ya know."

"But I'd like to be sure."

Bella shrugged and left the room with the dirty tablecloth gathered in both her hands.

Bella was back with a new tablecloth. "What do you want from a sick woman?" The woman's eyebrows shot up when Zoe asked again.

"She's not here, is she?"

"Don't know." Bella set the wilting flowers back at the center of the table. "But I know you though—ya won't leave it alone. All I can say is Mary asked to be given time to herself. Just leave her in peace."

*   *   *

Mary's room was on the same side of the hall as Zoe's, down farther, beyond the shared bathroom. It wouldn't hurt, she told herself standing in the hall, to knock and make sure she was all right.

She stood listening to low voices coming from Anthony's room and figured Gewel was in there with him. The woman wasn't exactly a kid—somewhere in her early thirties, if she had to guess. Old enough to know better.

She listened at what she thought was Mary's door; she'd seen her come out of this one from time to time.

Not a sound. Maybe she was sleeping and wouldn't be too happy to see Zoe's smiling face.

Zoe knocked anyway. She had the excuse that she was worried Mary was unhappy about what happened downstairs.

No answer. Room 208. It had to be Mary's. After this, the empty rooms began.

She knocked again, the knock hollow and loud in the long hallway.

Nothing.

Zoe turned the knob and opened the door, being very quiet.

The bed was made. Everything here was as it had been on the first day in Zoe's room. Same indeterminate blue walls; small, dark metal bed covered with an oft-washed white-going-to-gray chenille bedspread; same bedside table and goose-necked lamp with a pull-chain. But all of it as if it had never been touched.

She stood in the middle of the room and looked around. No personal things on the chest or bedside table. Nothing on the desk. Nothing draped over the bed. Maybe, when she got sick, she'd packed to leave.

But nothing in the closet, not even a suitcase, not one piece of clothing hanging on one hanger. No one was staying here. When she ran her finger over the back of one of the chairs, it was dusty. There were cobwebs stretched across the upper glass of the window.

She'd seen Mary going into this room. How could she not have stayed here?

She backed out and closed the door behind her. There was no one to ask. She wouldn't get the truth from any of them.

Two people had disappeared but were staying in that cabin. Maybe they were prisoners. She shouldn't have run.

What was she going to do about what she knew?

Another one gone—or never there.

And then there were none.

* * *

"She left last night, I think."

Emily Brent stood at the head of the lunch table, hands together in front of her. "I have no idea why—or how she did it. Her note said she felt she had to go. Someone was waiting for her. She'd almost forgotten her promise to meet him. That's what she said, but I don't believe a word of it."

"Bella said she was sick. That she was in her room?"

Zoe was ignored.

"Awful." Anthony heaped hash on his plate. "You said there was no way out of here until , , , what? . . . The Army Corps of Engineers or somebody fixes that bridge?"

"Or National Guard, I would imagine. They'll be here when they can." Emily's cool eyes turned to him.

Zoe watched them. She'd never known this before—being in a place where everyone lied. Nothing normal here. She felt she was living in a novel—everyone with their role. A cruel novel. Maybe a Christie novel. She couldn't be sure who was real and who wasn't. Maybe no one. And no truth anywhere.

"I imagine we'll hear, Zoe. Maybe when Mary gets home," Emily said.

"Will she call us?" Zoe couldn't help the sarcasm.

"Now, Miss Zola, you know our phones are out or I'd be calling her."

"And so, we don't give a flying—" She stopped herself. "So, we don't try to get to the police or ask for help. A woman leaves. Maybe floating far away by now . . . What's really going on? And don't worry, I don't expect a truthful answer."

"What are you talking about?" Emily demanded. "Really, Miz Zola, I wish you'd—"

Zoe turned to the others. "I've been in Mary's room. I don't believe she ever stayed here. The room hasn't been used."

"Nonsense," Gewel said. "I've seen her myself. Many times, going in and out."

"Dust and cobwebs. She didn't stay there."

Zoe stared at Gewel Sharp, who looked back with her nose in the air, challenging Zoe to something.

"And you"—Zoe went for her—"are you Gewel Sharp or Ruby Keene? I didn't realize the little joke until very recently. Probably neither one of them. I've been with you for four days, and I still don't know your real name."

Gewel looked surprised. "I never thought about it! You're right. My goodness."

Zoe felt sick to her stomach as she turned to the others. "What games will we play tonight, in our Murder Games? There has to be something special, doesn't there? Something driving this whole thing? Who are we supposed to be when we play our games?"

"Oh, Zoe." Gewel waved a hand at her. "You're so distrustful."

Distrustful. That's what the woman had said: *"You're so distrustful."* The words ran on fat little feet, circling in Zoe's brain. Distrustful. Dis-rust-ful. *Dust. Rust. Lust.* A many-faceted word.

Emily's hand was on Zoe's shoulder after the others left the room. "You'll still do your job, won't you?" Her voice cracked. "Are your remarks ready?"

"Not until after Aaron Kennedy speaks today."

Emily shook her head a few times. "But you'll stay until tomorrow, won't you?"

"Describe my choices."

Emily gave her a direct but blank look. She clucked her tongue. "What I meant was, we'll all be so disappointed if you get angry and leave. You can even tell us about your own work. The Agatha Christie book, if you'd like to. That would be fascinating."

"Hmm." Zoe tipped her head sidewise, thinking. *I can't swim. I don't have a boat. Can't fly. Looks as if I'll be here until we all leave. If we do leave. Guess I can talk about my book.*

Zoe knew she should have brought up the people at the cabin. But that fact was hers.

* * *

Upstairs, she looked at the roof in the woods. Two people there. Maybe three by now. Zoe stared at the wild, wet forest, in all directions. They were between a river and a creek. *Was this damned place an island?*

She'd seen the overflowing creek, gotten through it—maybe she could again. The river—no way out.

North—was she facing north? Or was it west? Which way? Which way was Oz? Where were the flying monkeys? The Wicked Witch of the West. Which way?

She covered her eyes so she didn't have to look at endless miles of nothing. If she couldn't get away, she had to outsmart them.

With her computer open on the bed in front of her, Zoe made a list of the people here:

Bella Webb. She didn't have a big part to play but was named for Bella Webb in *The Pale Horse*. Maybe only there to play the medium.

Emily Brent—already established—a character from *And Then There Were None*. Related to the dead girl.

Gewel Sharp—Ruby Keene. A silly play on words.

That's as far as she knew.

Dr. Aaron Kennedy—A Kennedy from an Agatha Christie novel? She remembered at least one Kennedy, but what was the use? None of it meant anything.

> *Ten little soldier boys went out to dine;*
> *One choked his little self and then there were nine.*

And a figure gone from the table, exactly as in *And Then There Were None*.

> *Nine little soldier boys sat up very late;*
> *One overslept himself and then there were eight.*

A figure missing from the table. Louise Trainer gone.

> *Eight little soldier boys travelling in Devon;*
> *One said he'd stay there and then there were seven.*

Mary Reid gone. But could be Gwenda Halliday Reed in *Sleeping Murder*.

Anna Tow—another trick name? Tow. Tow. Tow. Tow . . . maybe Carry? There was a Frances Cary in *The Third Girl*. She killed...somebody...pushed her out a window. Louise Charpentier—the woman she murdered. Louise Charpentier—the word in French meant "joiner."

Louise Joiner and Anna Tow, connected.

Leon Armstrong. The first to disappear. Dr. James Armstrong in *And Then There Were None*. In the novel, Armstrong killed a girl. He operated on her while he was drunk. Leon Armstrong had been a drunk.

Anthony Gliese. There were Anthonys in Christie, surely, but she couldn't remember any that fit except Anthony Marsden from *And Then There Were None*.

Professor Nigel Pileser. Too distinctive a name to ever forget. Christie's cat: Tiglath Pileser. The vicarage cat. What a joke on her.

She looked at the names. No hidden message. She couldn't get the lineup of letters to make a sentence that made sense. She added her own name but nothing with two Z's meant anything.

She wrote down their twenty-two initials, with Bella and Emily, and tried to make them spell words: *gasbag, lamp, lag, plat, rags* . . . It went on and on.

Staring at the letters in front of her, she sounded out any word she thought could be among them: *lap, lamp, beg, jar.*

She divided the letters—first initials from last: *LLAMBAGANBE.*

Ball. lam, bang, nag, gall . . .

A useless effort.

Still, she tried with the second row: A J G R B K S T P W B—*bag, gap, stag.* Only one vowel to work with: *Tag. Jag. Rat.* . . .

Names. Names. Names. What else could they mean? And who were they, if not who they claimed to be?

A knock at her door brought her flying off her bed and yelling out to whoever was there to come on in.

Aaron Kennedy stuck his head in. He stood in the doorway, eyes wide. "I'm sorry to disturb you, Zoe. I'm going to start my webinar in a few minutes. I . . . er . . . wanted to ask you if you've noticed anything strange about this place."

The professor was dressed as she imagined he dressed most of the time: the sweater with patches, the baggy pants, the pipe in his hand, though she knew he didn't smoke—or hadn't the whole time he'd been here.

He stood straight, head back. He prepared to look directly down his nose at her.

"Strange?"

"All of the names straight out of Christie. I'd say that's a little strange. Three people have disappeared. I thought maybe, when I've given my talk tomorrow afternoon, I might leave immediately. Have you been told if the bridge is all right to use? And I'll need a means of transportation. Are those two girls coming back for you? If so, I'd like to tag along. I want to see the end of this place as quickly as possible."

"I know how you feel. Nothing's normal or right. But I don't know yet about leaving because there's still no internet. No phone to call my friends. I don't have my own car."

"Really. Must be intermittent, the internet. I was online this morning, seeing if I could get a car here, but the site said there was flooding in the area."

"Oh, dear. But I'm sure my friends wouldn't leave me."

"Let me know, if you don't mind? I really want to leave as soon as possible."

He flapped a sheath of papers at her. "'The Aging of Christie's Fiction.' Want to hear it? You can pull quotes."

"'From Graham Green to P. D. James,' he began, "the mystery is as much a part of the literary canon as what passes for literature today. But only the best last. Agatha Christie, having been a bestseller for all of these years, we would imagine she would be at the top of the pantheon of mystery litterateurs, at least the top female litterateurs. Unfortunately, we see the reign of our premiere writer now falling into competition with the likes of P. D. James, with Patricia Cornwell, Sue Grafton, and Louise Penny, and therefore a diminishing interest in Christie studies."

"Dr. Kennedy." Gewel's voice called from the stairs. "Please come down. It's time."

He smiled at Zoe, bowed. "Maybe I waited a little too long to ask for help."

Everything he'd been before—brash, know-it-all, superior—seemed to be gone except for that little touch of condescension in his voice.

In the doorway, he leaned down to Zoe. "I should just run like hell, I suppose. Swim across the creek, get into town, and as far away from here as possible."

Zoe smiled up at him. "Me too. Something very different from Christie's work is going on. People are missing and—" She stopped herself from telling him about the cabin.

Someone called again from downstairs and he left.

Zoe soon followed. She had to get more notes for her talk tomorrow. She especially hoped that Arizona John would call. Out of the hundreds of questions they'd had so far, John's were best, though that wasn't saying much.

Chapter 47

Everyone was in the Michigan Room—as usual.

Kennedy stood at the front, a little stooped for such an arrogant man.

He settled his papers and played with his headphones, coughed a few times, then settled his papers again.

"Everybody is just thrilled to hear you," Anna called out, her smile unconvincing. "Though I'm not sure either Betty or I will agree. Still, it will be interesting to have another point of view on Agatha." She almost simpered at him. "Not even you, dear Doctor, can disagree with success, can you? Agatha is still one of the bestselling mystery writers of all time. And I'm sure she will be here, somewhere, to straighten you out."

He laughed, an unexpected sound from a man who rarely laughed. "Because commercial success, in my estimation, doesn't equal quality, Anna, I reserve the right to talk about my view of the work. Perhaps you don't believe that is important in a critic, having one's own point of view?"

Betty and Anna nodded over and over, as if convincing themselves with a kind of Girl Scout pledge that they would be faithful and honest and true, no matter how this man insulted them nor how hard he tried to prove his great intellect.

"And you two?" Aaron turned to Anthony and Gewel, meeting with surprised faces knowing they had no reason to be singled out.

"Oh course, man," Anthony said. "Happy to hear your ideas. Hope it's scurrilous and libelous enough to keep me awake. Rough night."

Aaron chuckled and looked down his nose at Anthony. "I don't write scurrilous and libelous material, Anthony. And I'm afraid I will stay away from knocking the poor woman, though a knock or two is in order. I'm ready to prove my point."

"Aren't you afraid of what she'll do to you?" Zoe asked.

"What a joke. Have to get Bella Webb to do that one again. Entertaining."

Nigel clucked at him. "Not going to praise her, Kennedy? But she wrote a lot of books."

"I will give her that. I will extol her ability to keep her hand moving, to the heavens, if I have to. But, I repeat, a plethora of writing does not the best quality make. I won't tell lies just because her books make millions every year, as Anna indicated. Ah, but now I'll save everything for my talk."

"Hmm." Betty made a noise under her breath.

Aaron turned to give her one of the withering looks people always gave Betty.

His eyebrows went up. "Why, Betty, I'm surprised that you're here at all after some of your comments in the last few days."

Betty sent daggers his way.

"Professor!" Zoe was livid. "I'm beginning to think it's you who can't discriminate. Betty is on her way to becoming an Agatha Christie expert. I'm in agreement with most everything she's said. Now we'll hear your thoughts and decide."

"Well, with your objections about to be drawn and quartered, and the lines of your ignorance clear, I will address you all in a few minutes." He walked out of the room and down the hall to find a lozenge for his raw throat.

Gewel muttered she would try to stay awake.

"Well, well, Miss Zola." Nigel turned to her. "The professor's talk fits right into this place, don't you think?"

She didn't understand.

"What I mean is, don't you think there's been a big buildup to something? Do you imagine this group has something to hide? There has to be more than we've seen so far, don't you agree? Think it's as big as the bombs Aaron plans to drop?"

"No idea, Nigel. But since that can't explain the disappearance of all ten of us, I doubt this whole business is little more than a press stunt."

"Ah, but then maybe you're not quite as perceptive as I am, Miss Zola. Men often are, you know, more perceptive. More so than women is what I mean. For all the talk of women's intuition, women give themselves too much credit."

She stuck her tongue out at him.

Chapter 48

"Ah, here we are." Aaron sat at the table, headphones on, one of the tech kids motioning to him.

He was slightly bowed over his notes.

When he looked up, he was smiling. "I am here to blow up all your dreams about the famous lady."

He stopped to chuckle to himself. "I'll begin where I began with Miss Zola, who was kind enough to listen to my intro."

There were no smiles on the faces around him, no forgiveness for past insults.

"'The Aging of Christie's Fiction.' I thought that the most appropriate title," he began, then stopped to cough into his hand, a kind of affectation, and began again.

"Can everyone out there hear me?" he was asking their audience, though he didn't listen for answers.

He began again. "From Graham Green to P. D. James, the mystery—now, and in some of its former forms—is as much a part of the literary canon as what passes for literature today. But only the best lasts." His heavy-lidded eyes scanned the faces at the table in front of him. "Agatha Christie having lasted as a bestseller for all of these years, we would imagine she would be at the top of the pantheon of mystery writers. At least, the top female writer.

"That's where she deserves to be, but unfortunately we see the reign of our premiere now falling into competition with the likes of P. D. James, Patricia Cornwell, Sue Grafton, and Louise Penny, and therefore a diminishing interest in Christie studies."

"Pooh!" Anna interrupted out loud. "The new doesn't wash away all of the old. She'll always have her place, Agatha will. I say you're arguing up an empty storm."

He eyed her but kept going.

"Let's take a look at falling sales."

Anna's microphone was off, but her words came through clearly in the room. "Thought you said figures weren't important, that it's the quality. 'Cause if you're going to argue that way, I'd say Agatha's got most of them beat."

"Modern women are growing in influence, but —" he went on.

"Ha, who is the most influential and who will always be?" Zoe lifted her voice behind Anna's. "You're going after straw women here."

"They are still far behind male writers such as—"

"You've got a defect, dear Professor Kennedy. Shows right off." Bella was standing near the back wall, calling out.

"Yeah, you academics don't know your ass from a machine gun. People are tired of those shoot-'em-ups. They want real people with real trouble. What's going on now is like a romp in the sandbox," Betty yelled at him. "We need more writers like Christie. Not fewer."

"Right, Betty," Anna yelled. "There's a gap in English literature, ya know. Nobody's buying what's supposed to be the best writers. Why? Maybe 'cause of people like you. Tellin' them what they should like."

Aaron pulled off his headphones as one of the techs came running over. "Don't, Professor. Can't do that."

"Really?" he sneered at the kid. "I'm not speaking in front of a pack of idiots."

Soon the others joined in, voices rising.

"You're all nobodies. I should have been more careful. I only wanted a chance to get out the word, how Agatha Christie is falling in literary regard."

He laughed at first Zoe and then Nigel, then around the room until he'd insulted everyone to his satisfaction.

"Better hurry up and explain what's happening here, to your rather ignorant audience. Or they'll all be demanding their money back. Which is what I'd hoped for all along." He laughed as he gathered his papers, then, head high, headed for the door.

"I'm leaving," he shouted at all of them. "As soon as I can find a way out of this terrible place."

"Murder Games after dinner," Gewel called after him.

Zoe turned to look at the others. They were calm. A few were smiling. It was as if Aaron Kennedy's tirade had never happened.

Chapter 49

Cocktails were to be announced soon. Gewel and Anthony sat very close on the sofa in front of the dark fireplace. The others had gone for walks or up to their rooms.

Zoe took a trial step toward the reception desk, turning to see if either of the two on the sofa stirred.

She lifted the phone. When she hit the dial button, she squashed the phone against her ear and bent over it. Nobody was going to grab her hand until she knew if she'd been lied to all along.

No dial tone. She punched in other buttons. Nothing. There was a cord attached to the base it was sitting on. She pulled it, just to find the plug it was attached to. The cord came at her. The more she pulled, the more it came, until the plug bounced over the desk.

Unplugged.

Zoe tiptoed around the back of the desk. She stuck the plug in the wall, then punched a button. The phone lit up, as it should. In a few seconds a dial tone came on. Without another thought she dialed Jenny's number, listening to it ring twice.

"You're not allowed to touch our phone." Someone behind her yanked the phone roughly from her hand, and the cord pulled across her throat.

Zoe grabbed the cord and held on, turning, pulling at it to keep from choking. She turned to look into Gewel's fierce blue eyes. She wasn't smiling, wasn't coy, wasn't anything but determined. Anthony was behind her and reached around to pull the phone from Zoe's hands.

Gewel clucked her tongue. "You know we were told not to use this phone, Zoe. You've got to wait until we're rescued, along with everybody else."

She was scolding her.

Anthony shook his head. "That's not what we're supposed to do, Zoe. Can't break the rules."

When the cord was pulled from her neck and wrapped around the phone, Anthony held it out of Zoe's reach. She stepped quietly, almost daintily, away from them, not turning her back until she was across the reception room, to the open front door, where she stood, head tipped to one side.

"Now, Zoe. There's no place to go until they come for us. Stay here. We can listen to music."

"No, we can't, Gewel. I have to get home."

"But we want you . . ."

Back to Oz. "Of course, you would.'

This was nuts. Perfectly crazy. Nothing meant anything, and yet some of it had to mean something. She put her hands to her head and pushed hard at her temples, trying to distract herself with pain.

* * *

Later, close to dinnertime, when she was up in her room, away from those two crazy people who'd attack her, she heard her name being called from downstairs. Emily's voice wasn't subdued or strained as she yelled out "Zoe! Zoe Zola!"

At the top of the stairs, Zoe looked down at her, waiting.

"Zoe? Miss Zola? You've missed cocktails. Now we're almost to dinnertime. Bella's fixed a special surprise for everyone. Please come down."

Zoe lay back on her bed and closed her eyes. Of course, she would go downstairs. She had no choice. Something had been decided on—with Anthony and Gewel, with the others, with the lodge, with the dead animals in every room. She knew, the way she'd known things all her life, that something was about to happen and she was a part of it. Maybe a larger part than she could imagine.

Another call from downstairs. Gewel's sweet voice. "Zoe. Dinnertime."

No reason to change her clothes. She didn't have anything different left to wear, and what anybody wore, or said—or pretended to be—didn't matter.

Lamb. And there was a Jokela—Emily's name. She whispered the word as she picked up a satchel holding pages to edit, in case she had to leave or in case she needed to throw it at someone.

She shut her bedroom door behind her—no use locking it—and hesitated at the top of the angled staircase.

* * *

Emily was watching for her when she got to the bottom of the steps. She hurried over to put her hand on Zoe's shoulder, leaned down, and declared for all to hear, "Bella's made *Leipäjuusto*. It's a celebration, ya know."

"Really?" Zoe pretended great surprise. "What is it? And what are we celebrating?"

"Bread cheese."

"We're celebrating bread and cheese? Astounding."

"A very special Finnish dish. You should know more of your heritage. Served with cloudberry jelly. Since this is our last night, Bella wanted to do something special. Besides the *Leipäjuusto* for an appetizer, she's made *mustamakkara* for dinner."

Gewel held her hands out as she walked in from the hall. She smiled sweetly. "You look rested, Zoe. I'm happy for that."

"What's *mustamakkara*?" Anthony, behind her, asked Emily.

"I won't tell until you taste it." Emily looked over her shoulder at him, teasing. "It will be familiar. Any good Finnish boy would recognize it immediately."

"Ah, but I'm not really Finnish. Only married to a Finn. I'd give my life for a single meatball."

Emily waved a hand at him. "Ech, meatball. Wait until you taste what Bella's prepared— then you can talk to me about meatballs."

As the others laughed, Zoe stood near the open front door. Something about an open door signaled escape.

She didn't dare try.

Chapter 50

They followed their noses, sniffing the air.

Betty and Anna went in to dinner ahead of Zoe, talking only to each other.

Anthony and Gewel were behind them, his arm around her shoulders as he leaned down to talk into her ear.

That left her and Nigel to go in with Aaron. Though they didn't talk to each other, having no pleasant conversation left in them. They went straight to their accustomed seats at the table, leaving three empty places scattered among them.

Zoe had the head of the table to herself.

The appetizer was presented and passed with fanfare. Bella took a few bows, waited until her bread cheese was properly raved over, then went back to her kitchen.

Zoe asked Nigel to pass the water pitcher, which he did with a smile, then leaned close to say that the table was either getting larger or they were getting fewer.

Zoe pretended to look around and notice the empty places for the first time. "Oh yes, the three who had to leave. Too bad. I was hoping we'd have a round-table discussion after I speak tomorrow. You know, Nigel, to sum up everything we've learned."

He leaned back to stare at her, his multi-colored eyebrows in the air, mustache hairs sticking out at many angles, his pinprick pupils fixed on her. "Have you really learned anything, Miss Zola? Was there a single word said that you haven't heard before?"

His voice was louder than it should have been, but no one took notice.

"And why bother to think of the commotion Aaron caused with his talk?" Zoe said.

Nigel nodded very slowly. "I must confess, I wasn't paying attention. I thought he would try to make a hero of himself, only to be different from the rest of us."

Aaron beside him said nothing. He sat as far back as he could get in the chair and once in a while made a face at what they were discussing. He didn't take part. He sat with his the edge of his napkin going back and forth between his fingers. Finally, he turned to her.

"It's too bad we landed at this poor excuse for an academic affair. I know why I came, but whatever made you want to take part?"

Down the table, Anthony heard. "I imagine our Zoe recognized true scholarship."

Aaron threw back his head and laughed. "And you, Anthony, I'm sure you don't get many requests to take part in programs. What was that last book you edited? *A Guide to Fields and Streams?*"

"Or maybe my *Christie's Life* would be a better example, Kennedy. Diminishing me does little to add to your luster. Tell us what you have added to the Christie scholarship, other than to diminish her talent."

With a well-placed *"Ta-da,"* Bella came from the kitchen with a large platter in her hands. "Mustamakkara," Bella said as she laid a platter of sausage, black and not exactly appetizing, at the center of the table.

Gewel wrinkled her nose. "What is that, Bella? Something special you've made?"

"Not with my own hands. I don't kill pigs."

"Pork sausage. I'm afraid I don't eat pork." Anna tried to smile, but Bella's face, when she turned to her, was dark enough and tight enough to scare Anna into muttering something like " I'll . . . try. I just hope . . ."

"Blood sausage." Bella looked around at them, one by one. "Killed today—if you heard something squealing—so the blood is fresh as you can get it."

She turned and left the room, coming back with a bowl she dropped heavily to the table. Zoe heard it clank against the bare wood. She waited to hear the crack of the bowl that had to follow, but the bowl survived.

"Kaalikääryleet." Bella said the word and stopped where she was, looking straight at Anna. "You allergic to cabbage rolls too?"

Anna shook her head. She kept her mouth shut as Bella went back to the kitchen and returned with a bowl of something red to go with the blackened green cabbage and the very black blood sausage.

"Rosolli," she said. "Beet root salad."

She set her hands backwards at her waist, leaned forward, and announced, "I made a *Puolukkapiirakka* for dessert. Don't eat so much, now, ya hear."

Anthony shook his head at her. *"Puolukkapiirakka!* Hmm . . . who would miss that?"

Bella narrowed her eyes hard and stood close beside him. "It's lingonberry pie, fool. For the people who don't know what's good in this world."

Anthony made no more jokes but put his hands together in front of his plate and pretended to pray.

"Who wants a blood sausage?" Gewel stood, pushing the chair back behind her and picking up the dish to circle the table, offering the sausage at each seat.

Betty tried to stave off the sausage on Gewel's platter, but she wouldn't let her. "New rule. Everybody takes something of everything."

Betty let the black sausage hit her plate, where it jiggled there by itself. She picked up the beet root salad and carefully piled it atop her sausage until nothing of the black sausage could be seen.

Next the cabbage rolls were passed and remarked over as they were cut up and eaten.

The problem with the blood sausage was still a problem when the cabbage rolls were all gone. Gewel picked at the beet salad and said it was very good—vinegary. She nodded and the others began eating their beet salad until it was gone from their plates and the blood sausage lay exposed, each plate with a plop of plump, black cigars.

"I'll try," Anna whispered toward Betty.

Anna carefully cut her first sausage into three pieces, then put one piece in her mouth. She held it there until she bit down, tasted the sausage, and her shocked and then unhappy face gave away what she thought. Without a worry about the others, she spat her mouthful back onto her plate.

"Tastes like singed dog hair," Betty said.

"That good?" Anthony tipped his head and smiled.

"I can't eat it." Betty wiped her tongue with her napkin and shuddered.

"Any other guinea pigs?" Anthony asked, then looked to Gewel, who shook her head.

"Here." Zoe took her papers from her briefcase, set them on the floor, and held the case open toward Gewel, who pushed the sausage in, thanking Zoe.

Zoe put the sausage from her own plate into the case and hurried around to Aaron, who did the same. Then Nigel. And the others, until her case was heavy, but their plates were clean.

Just in time. Bella was back to clear the table for dessert, smiling and nodding, as if bestowing her approval on the guests.

Dessert was a very good berry pie, served as Emily came back in with news of a man who got over the creek in a small motorboat. She shook her head at them as they all asked if they could get out of there yet.

"He says not yet. Tomorrow some time. It was dangerous for him to even try, but he did and is staying here until the men come to fix the bridge."

Disappointment forced the air out of the room. Someone's stomach rumbled. Like sheep, they got up, first one, then the next, to follow one another down the hall to hear Gewel Sharp, who had asked, as a special attraction, to give her take on *Murder on the Orient Express*.

Only Aaron stayed behind at the table, looking out the windows, at the unusually bright sunset, until he finally braced his hands on the table and got up.

Chapter 51

Zoe tried to get outside to dispose of the sausages in her case, but was stopped by Anna Tow, asking in a low voice, looking over her shoulder, "Do you think they'll ever let us leave?"

The voice was panicked. She sounded the way Zoe wouldn't let herself feel.

"Of course," Zoe said, reaching up to pat her arm. "Just bad luck—all the rain. No one is going to die."

The skin around Anna's eyes tightened, making her eyes stand out even more.

"Well, I certainly hope not. That's not at all what I came here to do."

Anna went off in a huff.

Zoe turned away, about to scurry outside to the edge of the woods, when Gewel began herding everyone to the Michigan Room. "No sense wasting time. I'm eager to see how you all feel about this little talk I prepared. Not what I'm normally known for, but—well, I'll explain . . ."

She couldn't leave the overstuffed satchel behind or leave it out in the hall until she could find a place to dump it. There was still the smell to deal with.

Zoe hoped Gewel wouldn't talk too long. If her bag began to smell, she would have to get up, pretend to be sick, and leave the room, dragging her satchel behind her.

Inside, nobody sat close to anyone else, and no one spoke.

Zoe climbed onto a hard chair at the very back of the room to listen to Emily, giving Gewel an introduction, stressing that *Murder on the Orient Express*, as they all knew, was one of Christie's most famous novels.

"Our own Gewel Sharp will address the group mentality that allowed all of the people on the Orient Express to plan and execute a murder no one could be blamed for. We hope she will intrigue you with what she's found about the characters and whatever she has brought to convince you that group murders don't work in fiction. But can sometimes be an only means of justice."

Gewel looked over the faces looking back at her. She began: "Though *Murder on the Orient Express* is meant to be a group murder, done by everyone and therefore by no one person, Christie, by closely examining the minds that could conceive and execute such a thing, did not at all solve the problem of the multiple killer." She cleared her throat. "There always has to be a real murderer. The person whose knife does the killing, whose bullet is the one of many found in the victim, or the first to add poison to the drink that will kill."

Zoe smelled sausage, the odor curling up from under her chair. She bent down to tighten the top of the satchel, moving it with her feet. The case left a wet lane of grease on the floor. How could she ever get it out of the room?

Zoe sat lower in her chair. How would she explain the bag of sausage if Emily or Bella caught her? What do you say when it looks as though you're stealing someone else's blood sausage?

She put her toes to the floor. Gewel had to take a breath soon. She would be fast, getting out during the questions—maybe. Nobody would notice her leaving if they all got mad and into proving their own points.

"I just want you to know about those people—and the man they had to kill."

Zoe slipped from her chair. She knew the book very well and didn't need to be reminded who the dead man was.

She tried to slip out as Aaron Kennedy walked in, but Zoe heard Gewel saying, "The whole world hated him."

She stayed.

Aaron was barely into a seat before he called out.

"And Ratchett is a man named John Cassetti, who murdered a little girl and shocked her pregnant mother, who also died. Disaster piled on disaster, poor souls. Another example of Christie's overwriting."

Gewel looked slowly from face to face. "One after another, the family left behind committed suicide or died in some fashion. More victims of this man."

She dropped her head to her chest and stood there, silent, until everyone in the room was holding their breath. "Clues to the murderer of John Cassetti began to appear: a cup, a button, a uniform, a red kimono. People are shot, even Poirot, but not seriously. Nothing seems to be done seriously on *The Orient Express*, except murder."

"Oh, for heaven's sakes. Why must we wallow in this melodrama? Mr. Poirot thinks that Cassetti died when the train was stopped by the avalanche. But then comes the genius theory—that they all killed the man, that they took turns stabbing him, and here, in Poirot's shining hour, he absolves himself of blame for not anticipating the death. Then he absolves the group of their kindred guilt and walks away from *The Orient Express,* satisfied he has proven his case and made the correct decision.

"But listen," he said, "Did the man deserve the death he got? Or was he deprived of the trial he was due? Does any group have the right to redress their own wrongs, or are we a civil society? Bigger questions."

Gewel's round eyes fell on Anthony. "What else could those people do if the police can't or won't find enough evidence against him?"

Anthony looked toward Aaron. "You're saying Cassetti should have been tried the usual way. If he had, those people wouldn't have murdered him."

Aaron laughed. "I always thought this book one of Christie's worst, to tell you the truth. She treated the legal system callously, only to provide herself with a novel to sell. Terrible of her, if you ask me."

"That man, Ratchett—he murdered a young girl, didn't he?" Betty asked. "Sounds like he got what he asked for."

"He did," Anna butted in. "I wonder if he killed more girls. That would make it even worse, wouldn't it?"

"Ah, but think about it," Nigel said. "Wouldn't you imagine the group of murderers would have told him the girl's name before they killed him? What good is revenge if the murderer doesn't know who you are? Or why he is being murdered?"

Aaron shrugged again, looking impatient. "Christie left that out, didn't she? Guess the man never knew for sure why he was being stabbed. Seems like a terrible surprise for the poor fellow. He's got my sympathy."

He laughed.

"Sympathy? Really?" Anna's disgust thickened her voice.

"Maybe it was just that one girl. And he had to do it because she hounded him or tried to hurt his reputation."

"Professor." Gewel tried to get a hold on her group.

"Let me finish my points, young woman. I find this to be an important point in the Christie study."

Nigel interrupted. "Wouldn't you say that only the first to stab or poison or whatever else they did to Ratchett could be the murderer? So there is no such thing as a group murder. It would be an impossibility."

"That's one of my points." Gewel clapped her hands. "So, no one ever knows who the real murderer is."

"But think a minute," Anthony said, getting to his feet. "What if the first to plunge the knife in didn't kill the man? What if it took until the fifth person before the victim died? Then who can call the first to stick the knife in the killer, when it wasn't until the fifth that the man died? And if the victim took his last breath then, is the fifth the only killer? Who knows when life really leaves the body? First the brain, then the body—bit by bit."

Aaron thought awhile. "I see what you mean. I do see what you mean. But I would say, in the eyes of the law, they are all equally guilty, had equal intent."

"But that would only be if the law ever found out there was a plan in place," Gewel said.

"Oh, I'm certain someone would brag or talk in their sleep. They'd be discovered. I'm sure of that." Aaron was proud of his point.

Zoe watched Aaron's face. Smug. Secure in his rightness.

"Really? I have a feeling a group could plan a perfect murder— witnesses and all—and never get caught," Anthony said.

"Well, we better hope so, or Christie never could have written that awful book and gotten away with it, could she?" Aaron turned to laugh with the others. No one laughed back.

In the quiet that followed, Aaron chuckled to himself from time to time. "Group murder." He laughed again. "Another Christie screw-up. No such thing."

After minutes more of quiet, Betty asked, her pointed eyebrows going up, "By the way, Aaron, I read in your bio that you've worked in other universities around the country. Always a Christie expert?"

"Two or three. Only two or three." He spread his hands. "If one wants to get ahead, you know, you have to take new positions offered. And yes. Always a Christie expert, though I'm moving on now."

"Was it hard to leave your old universities?" Anna asked.

"No. Not really." He frowned at her. "Why do you ask?"

"Not even the University of Michigan? I'd stay if I could get a job teaching there. I'd stay for life."

"Anyway, we were talking about *Murder on the Orient Express*," Gewel tried her best to tame her audience.

Anthony stood up. "Hey, it stinks in here. Who hid the sausage?"

Gewel pinched her nose. "Is that really sausage?" she asked those around her. "Smells like blood to me."

Chapter 52

Zoe hurried out to the damp woods and tried to dig a hole for the sausages with a spoon she'd filched from the table. When she couldn't dig far into the hard-packed wet sand, she spread the sausages over the ground, where she didn't think Emily or Bella would find them.

Before returning to the house, she stood at the edge of the forest, watching the lighted windows of the lodge. On the second floor, in a room facing the woods, Anthony and Gewel were seated on something she couldn't see. Their heads were together once again in serious and intense conversation.

Through another window she saw Anna sitting at a desk, the lamp on the desk penning shadows across her face. She didn't move or seem to write. She stared at the wall in front of her.

Only one other room at the front of the lodge was occupied. Aaron stood at that window, looking out at the sky, cloudy though the moon showed through from time to time—long beams of light fell around him. He lifted his fists and shook them at the sky. He held them there, then held his head and and rocked it back and forth. His face was grotesque.

She stepped back in among the trees when he looked down to where she stood.

He saw her. He watched her, then turned away from the window, going back into the room, where she couldn't see him.

She packed her suitcase, then took out clothes for the morning, laying them carefully on the bed, spreading her hands across them, ironing out the wrinkles.

They would gather downstairs at ten. One last event to be gotten through before they could leave. By now they all detested each other. Gewel and Anthony were traitors. The others had shown their nastier sides. Probably she had too.

She pulled out the notebook of letters and names she'd worked on before

There were the first initials: *L L A M B A G A N B E.*

The word jumped out at her: *LAMB.*

Mary had a little Lamb. She liked the way the syllables bounced in her mouth. Of course—Angela Lamb. Who else could this monstrous thing be about?

Ding-ding, ding, ding ding-ding ding.

She crossed those initials off the list. That left *A N G E L A.* And a leftover *B.*

Last initials: *A J G R B K S T P W B.*

One vowel to work with, but nothing. The message of the names was Angela Lamb. The message was the murder of a young woman who was dearly loved.

Mary and Harley Lamb's child.

Ding-ding, ding, ding ding-ding ding.

Chapter 53

At ten, Zoe sat alone in the reception room, waiting for something to happen as she got madder. She was tired of all of them and their haphazard plans. She wanted to go to bed, get up in the morning, give an amazingly short talk, and bust out of there.

At ten minutes after ten, she slid from the sofa to the floor and went to knock on the kitchen door.

Emily sat alone at the table, hands clasped in front of her. She looked up, her face a sick gray color.

Zoe opened her mouth to ask a question. But couldn't.

Emily's eyes were red and tired, as if she'd been crying. For the first time, Emily Brent looked old.

"The games are beginning, Miss Zoe. You mustn't miss them."

"It's after ten, There's no one anywhere. They must have changed plans. I'm going to bed. I have a long drive tomorrow and—"

"If you go to bed, they'll only come get you." Emily almost smiled. "You can't miss the games."

Zoe saw the shoulders trying to push against the chair and the smile that didn't make it. She looked into Emily's eyes and took a step backward, away from her, into the hall. She let the door swing shut.

She went back to sit near the fireplace until, one by one, the others appeared, headed toward the room at the end of that hall. No one acknowledged her as they went by. They didn't acknowledge each other.

She followed them to the Michigan Room. The chairs had been gathered away from the oval table where they sat for the webinar.

Anthony and Gewel stood together at the head of the room. They looked up as she took a seat but seemed to see through her.

Betty Bertram was in a front seat, a stack of papers in her lap. She turned each time someone walked in, as if noting them in her head, then looked at Gewel and back down to her papers that she straightened in her lap, then straightened again until the next person came in and found a seat.

No one sat near anyone else, not even when a chair had to be pulled away from the others. The last to enter were Aaron and Nigel, together, then Anna and Bella.

With people in place, Gewel gave a nod to Anthony.

He began. "My dear wife, Gewel—as you all may have guessed by now from our riotous ribaldry in my room—will take up murder. Though first I'd like to tell you we've been married eight years. A seven-year-old and a five-year-old at home. Many surprises here at Netherworld. But now, old, new, maybe solved, maybe not, I bring you murder. You are to solve it—if you can, with enough proof for the police to look into. You win by solving a murder. You win by being the first."

He looked from Gewel to Betty, sitting with her thin shoulders up to her ears. "So, let us begin."

Zoe waved her hand in the air, "I have one," she called out, though she was lying. "In case you need another. All of you knowing so much about murder, and all—I have an old case for you."

Gewel's eyebrows rose. "Really? A case you know of? Based on a real murder?"

She had no idea about what she'd make up, so Zoe had to think fast. "One I've been thinking about since I've been channeling Agatha Christie."

"But I have a list." Gewel held a list in the air. "I didn't hear anything from you."

"Let her give hers." Anna turned to give Zoe one of her taut smiles. "She gets to grade some of us tomorrow. I say let's not piss her off."

There was laughter and agreement.

Gewel added Zoe's name to her list. "Would you wait until we've done the—"

"Of course. I know how to wait my turn."

Anthony nodded but didn't smile. "Let's see how we do with ours first, all right? What we have may be enough."

She nodded, happy that she was irritating him.

"This is a very odd case." Gewel looked from face to face. "A murder in Toledo, Ohio, that so far hasn't been solved. Please tell us what you think about the case—any clues you can find. Solve it, if you can. And then guess whether it's a real case and whether we have enough to place a call to the Toledo Police Department.

"Nineteen-ninety," she read. "What I have is a woman with two children, married. Lived in Toledo, Ohio, but her husband lived in Flint, Michigan . . . er . . ."

She frowned, then looked back at her notes. "That's because he had to take a job in Flint during some bad times. The woman in Toledo was found dead in bed one morning. Nine AM. Her eldest son Ronald, age sixteen, found her after calling through the bedroom door and getting no answer from his mother.

"Er . . . yes . . . then he called his younger sister, Joannie, thirteen, and then his baby brother, Todd, eight. Ronald called the police. No one went in the room, and nothing in there was touched. Her husband was contacted while he was at work in Flint. He drove right home.

"At first they thought it was a natural death. But the autopsy showed she'd been poisoned. Arsenic was found in her system. A good deal of arsenic."

"How about her hair? Any sign of arsenic in the hair shaft, showing different times and amounts of the poison given?" Zoe called out. "And is there a reason we aren't told her name?"

Emily answered for Gewel. "There were traces in the hair shaft, but nothing steady that should have killed her. And her name was Evelyn. Evelyn Bowlder."

"That's significant," Zoe said.

Gewel nodded. "I guess so."

"Was she a gardener?" Nigel asked. "Gardeners get arsenic in their systems from those sprays they use. Arsenic comes from drinking water or living near a smelting plant—even living at the site of an old gun range or living downhill from a cemetery."

"Then the rest of the family would've been poisoned," Anna said. "I'd look at those children. Bet they did it together. A little poison at a time. Were the children charged?"

Gewel shook her head. "No reason to. Nothing found in the house."

"Humph. Should've been. They're the ones who killed their mother, all right."

"Any traces of arsenic found in the house or garage?" Zoe asked.

Gewel shook her head. "Nothing. And police couldn't find any fingerprints that shouldn't have been there. Had to have been someone inside the house, but who?"

"The husband, I'll bet," Betty piped up. "He didn't have to be there to kill her. Could have left a drink for one of the kids to give her. Maybe he used poison at that job in Flint. What was it?"

Gewel read over her notes then shrugged. "I don't know."

"You should," Aaron spoke up. "We can't make decisions on such slim information."

Gewel made a face and ignored him. She looked around to her audience. "Any other ideas?"

"Hmm. I say suicide." Anna was firm.

Gewel shook her head. "No glass beside her bed. Nor anywhere in the room."

Anna raised her hand but didn't wait to be called on. "The glass could have been put in the dishwasher. Was it filled with dirty or clean dishes? And the kids might have wanted to cover up what she did. Can't blame them."

Gewel shook her head. "No dishwasher in the house. The thirteen-year-old girl did the dishes by hand at night. No dirty dishes on the counter. Of course, any of them could have washed an extra glass."

"I'll bet anything the older brother and sister did it together." Anna now said. "Sixteen and thirteen. Sounds as if they had a lot of responsibility around that place. There are cruel mothers, you know."

"What?' Pileser raised his voice. "And so, they forced the woman to drink arsenic? God! What an idea!"

"Maybe ya need more information," Bella, quiet until now, suggested.

Zoe asked, "What did she do for a living, our dead lady?"

"Er . . . let me see." Gewel ran her finger down the page. "She worked for a taxidermist."

"Hmm . . ." Zoe thought hard. "Did she ever take her work home with her?" she asked.

"Once in a while. She wanted to learn the trade. Maybe have her own shop one day. The shop owner she worked for let her remount old heads for experience."

"Had she worked on any recently?" Zoe asked.

"Yes. A few were found in a workroom in her house. She redid the heads to learn, not with any idea of saving them."

"What about the man she worked for? He have any reason to kill her?" Aaron Kennedy called out.

Gewel shook her head. "An elderly man who was happy to teach her how to stuff and mount specimens.'

"That's it." Zoe sat back and crossed her arms over her breasts. "I win. Real case. Clear as the nose on your face. I say the case was never solved because it was an accidental death."

Gewel held up a hand. "Well, Zoe, we might have known. I have to give it to you. This is certainly a real case. Happened right up in Copper Harbor, not Toledo. Police never found the murderer."

"Of course not. Nobody killed her.'

"Suicide was ruled out."

"Good thing." Zoe slid off her chair to stand with her butt against it.

"What does that mean?" Aaron demanded, frowning hard around at Zoe.

"Accident. Accidental death. Nobody's fault. Ignorance is all. Ignorance kills a lot of people."

Pileser laughed out loud. "Ah, dear Miss Zola. Arsenic isn't something people play with, you know. She would have to go out and actually buy some, which she couldn't do anyway. Today it's used in very few products, and then not enough to poison anyone. I see you're tying the death to taxidermy, but the elderly man she works for was still alive. Apparently, there isn't a great threat there."

"Ah, Dr. Pileser," Zoe began, her voice showing how much she was enjoying herself, "if she was learning taxidermy and working with old mounts, she was taking her life in her hands. Arsenic was used in taxidermy up until the last twenty or thirty years. It kept the mounted animals free of insects. Did a good job and killed a number of people. Thing is, taxidermists have now learned—some from bad experience—that you don't fool with old mounts. Better to leave them alone than to redo, for fear of arsenic poisoning. Killed more than one thrifty trophy owner who tried to do a remount himself."

Zoe looked from face to face, all turned her way. "Accident. Very sad for her."

"How old is this case?" she asked Betty.

"Twenty-nine years."

There was an intake of breath.

"Anyone else in that family die from arsenic poisoning?"

"I don't know."

"I hope you call the Copper Harbor Police and tell them the death was an accident."

"I will. I certainly . . . will."

Zoe, satisfied, leaned back, and relaxed.

Gewel, clearly thrown by Zoe's easy solve, looked down at the next sheets of paper Betty handed to her. "We have more, but we could stop here. Seems too easy."

Anna harrumphed and shook her head. "No, you don't. Give us our turn at this game. What else do you have?" She turned to face Anthony. "Don't you agree, Anthony? That one was too easy."

He spread his hands wide and shook his head. "That was pretty spectacular. I don't know if I can beat . . ."

Anna waved at him and turned back to demand Gewel give them another try.

"There's one here . . ." She read over the case. "Okay. Here we go: a man was murdered in his own house. Attacked while sleeping. Killed with a hatchet. Quite vicious."

Gewel looked up.

"So? That's it?" someone asked.

Anna fired off the usual questions. "What was he like? What did he do for a living? Married? Where was his wife at the time? Did he have children? What was their relationship like?"

"Who were his friends? Anyone dislike him? And if so, why?" Nigel jumped in.

"Rather stiff man. Not warm and friendly. What did he do? Hmm, I don't really know." Gewel looked to Anthony for help.

"I think he was a businessman. And friends?" Anthony thought. "No, I don't think so. Wife was there, but also dead. Two children, both daughters."

"Was one daughter much older?" Pileser asked.

Gewel nodded.

"Has the possibility of incest being the underlying cause for his death been suggested?" Zoe asked.

Gewel seemed confused. "I have no idea."

Aaron Kennedy threw his head back and laughed. "No matter. I'd like to suggest, for everyone's consideration:

> Lizzie Borden took an axe
> And gave her mother forty whacks.
> When she saw what she had done,
> She gave her father forty-one.

There was laughter.

Aaron Kennedy stood, bowing in all directions.

Anna booed down into her collar.

"Therefore the case is the murder of Mr. Borden by his daughter Lizzie, and though she was acquitted, the evidence of the dress she burned afterward; the fact that no door was open to an intruder; that dear Lizzie bought a hatchet the day before the murder; and then, of course, Lizzie's hatred for her stepmother—I think this case has long been solved and the right person charged." He sat back, pleased with himself.

"And the real killer let off by an all-male jury," Aaron added.

"That's a pile of . . . bunk." Zoe spoke up. "Today the charge would be temporary insanity due to the extreme stress of childhood incest. I think incest was long ago suspected in this case. Therefore—solved. Yet again. Real crime."

"I guessed that one!" an indignant Aaron barked out.

"Now," Gewel said, raising her hand and ignoring him, "we have one more."

Aaron groused, "Why bother? We're all much too smart for your silly games."

Gewel ignored him and went through the papers in her lap.

"Now." She looked over at Bella. "It seems to be the murder of a young girl."

Zoe sat up. "How was she murdered? What time of year? Where was her body found? What about her friends? Did she have a boyfriend? Did she ever say she was afraid of anybody? Anybody seen with her that she shouldn't have been with? How about DNA?"

Anthony answered the questions one by one. "Throat cut. Early spring. Body not found for three years, and then found in the woods, miles away. Friends were the ones who reported her missing. The police called her parents, who were already worrying about her. Hmm. No indication she was in fear of anything or anybody. Too late to get DNA or hairs or anything from her body when they found her."

Nigel asked, "What year was she killed then? I think I remember hearing about a case like this. Right here in Michigan, was it? In all the newspapers for a while. I didn't know she'd been found."

"2015."

Gewel spoke up. "She was popular with her professors and other students alike. There was no reason to be gone, but she was."

She went on without stopping. "A friend was under suspicion until he was cleared. not even in town the day she came up missing."

Everyone turned to Gewel, watching as facts about the murder rolled out of her.

When she stopped for breath, Zoe asked. "What college was it?"

Gewel looked at the sheet of paper in her hand. "University of Michigan."

Zoe went on, "Any trouble with anyone? Was anyone known to be hanging around her? Did she report anyone to the police?"

"First question is no. Second is no. Third is no." Gewel answered. "A friend told the police Angela had been upset lately, but that didn't go anywhere because Angela didn't tell her friend anything else. The police stayed in close touch with her parents, but nothing turned up. Nothing for the next three years. Until they found her."

Zoë asked Gewel. "This girl—did you know her?"

She nodded.

"And that lead they had, what was it?"

Anthony leaned forward and handed another paper to Gewel, who read it aloud. "She told a friend just before she disappeared that she was pregnant. Very upset. She was going to see the department chair. There was someone she wanted to file a complaint against. Rape. But didn't want to destroy her reputation."

"Department chair!" Zoe couldn't help herself. "Why not the police? What do you complain to a department chair about?"

She turned to Gewel and then to Betty.

"I'd never take any complaint to the department chair. I'd take it to the dean." Gewel shook her head. "Let me see. Maybe to the Associated Students Organization office. I'd talk to a counselor. If I had trouble with a professor, or with another student—maybe the counselor first. Then I'd go to the dean of the department. But no, since it was rape, I'd go right to the police."

"I'd like to say a couple of things . . ." Zoe said. "Well, you see, I would take it as a given that it had to be an on-campus murder because a campus is a small town. Many people know each other, live together, study together, eat together, yet there's a bigger glue that holds them—the fact that they are students at an institution of higher learning. There's a mystique about such a place that intimidates outsiders. If it had been an outsider, she would have gone to the police since it wasn't a university matter. A threat. An assault. Stalking. And there is an air of secrecy to the way this girl handled what was going on."

"And, poor thing. Pregnant. A moral development. Girls tend to keep that secret as long as they can," Nigel said.

Zoe ignored him. "Therefore, I would tend to suspect another student or someone the girl came in contact with almost every day."

Anna waved her hand. "Yes, a student. Better to take it to a place where secrecy would be mandatory. That's what I think." She nodded hard twice. "Even one of her professors."

"Hmm." Aaron Kennedy leaned back and stretched. "Personally, I'd say a loner, trolling the campus. Like that John Norman Collins, who killed girls in Ypsilanti and Ann Arbor back in the sixties."

"That's crazy. Whoever it was, she knew him. She didn't run to call the police," Anthony said, jumping in.

Gewel said. "A professor. Don't you agree, Aaron?"

Betty and Anna were quiet.

Zoe was uneasy. Something real was going on.

Aaron spoke up, "Let's just move on. I'm getting bored with this nonsense. We can't stay focused on one death, you know."

"Murder," Zoe corrected him.

"Whatever." He waved a hand. "We came here to do our talks, not solve old crimes. This is above and beyond what we were asked to do—and not paid extra for, may I remind you."

"Not too old a crime, professor," Anthony said.

"I've had enough of games for tonight. I can't speak for anyone else, but I am bored out of my mind."

"I have to agree with Aaron." Nigel held up one finger. "No new evidence to look at. No one to interview. Nothing of the forensics. I say we give it up."

"I disagree." Anna's voice was quiet. She stood and bowed her head.

One by one, the others, except Zoe and Aaron Kennedy, quietly stood too. They bowed their heads.

Aaron gave a nervous laugh and rose clumsily from his chair. "I don't know what your game is, Gliese. But, personally, I've had enough of this amateur operation. I'm going upstairs to pack."

He moved through the chairs, between the standing people, heading for the door.

As he reached for the handle, the door opened. Mary Reid, Leon Armstrong, and Louise Trainer stood on the other side, faces haunted. Mary and Louise came into the room and stood among the others, with their heads bowed, hands formed into prayer, Leon filled the doorway, blocking Aaron's exit.

No one said a word. Not a head lifted.

Aaron pushed at Leon Armstrong's chest.

He didn't move, only kept his eyes on him as he pulled Aaron back, shut the door, and stood blocking the way out.

"What the hell is this?" Aaron demanded, turning to the backs of the others.

"Let me out of here," he ordered Leon, who looked over his head.

There was a light knock at the door. Leon checked, then let Emily in. She was pulling down the folded sleeves of her shirt, looking away from Aaron's startled face. On her head she'd clipped a black veil.

Chapter 54

Anthony looked down at his hands and not at anyone else. Gewel stood beside him with her eyes closed. Nigel stood where he was, never turning back to Aaron. The others were silent and motionless as Emily walked to the front, to face them.

Aaron retreated to a corner, where he spread out his arms, his fingers splayed against the walls around him.

"What's this about?" he demanded, his voice high. "I'm not interested in any more of your games."

Zoë looked at him; there was nothing to see but an aging man, his hair thinning, his face distorted.

"Let's begin." Emily said.

To Anna she said, "You keep the tally."

She looked around at Gewel. "Gewel. It's time."

Gewel took a deep breath before opening her eyes. She moved away from Anthony, not looking at him.

Zoe knew why she was here. They'd said *witness*.

She crossed her hands in front of her and bowed her head, like the others.

If she'd only ignored the invitation, she'd be home with Fida, working on her new book.

Ding-ding, ding, ding ding-ding ding.
Hubris and hatred.

She looked sideways toward Aaron, to the corner of the room where he cowered. The man's face was dark. "What are we doing, if I might ask?" he called to the others. "Agatha's laughing at us right now. You've gone overboard, you know." He smiled, but it was an awful smile. "I'd like to leave." He nodded to Emily.

He sighed, even chuckled deep in his throat. "I imagine I'll be forced to sue every one of you very soon."

He shook his head three times, and reached out to a chair, where he sat down, head in his hands.

"Anyone else have anything to say before we begin?" It was Emily asking.

Ding-ding, ding, ding ding-ding ding. The little rhyme skipped through Zoe's head.

"Then let's begin." Bella joined Emily. She called out to Gewel. "Gewel, dear, it's time."

Gewel took a deep breath and turned to the others. She stood with her head bowed. They waited, eyes on her, until she collapsed into the chair behind her.

"I can't do it." She shook her head.

Zoe watched Aaron tighten his fists. His whole body stiffened. He searched from Leon Armstrong, standing at the door with his arms folded, to the others with their faces turned down, eyes staring at the floor.

The silence in the room was an echo just out of hearing.

Zoe kept her head up; eyes watching everybody.

Aaron took a deep breath and gave an abrupt hawk of a laugh.

"Another of your grand surprises, Emily Brent? The dead have risen, have they? Do you mind, dear lady, if I miss this part of your cheap theatrics? Another play is it? More bad drama by Agatha Christie."

There was something new in his eyes.

"Anyone else have anything to say before we begin?" Bella asked.

That silence that wasn't silence moved in around them.

Bella closed her eyes. Zoe could hear the woman breathing, and then heard when her breathing slowed. She was afraid she was going to hear Agatha Christie's voice again.

Aaron could be right: another game.

"You may all ask one question." Bella said in her normal voice, but devoid of her Finnish accent.

"What are we doing? Questions about what?" Zoe called out, frustrated with all of them.

"You mean questions about tomorrow?" Anna turned to Bella, ignoring Zoe.

"Yes. Tomorrow."

After a few minutes, Emily Brent said, "Can we finish the vote first?"

"What about the others?" Mary asked.

"They're on their way."

"Then we can begin. Gewel is a no." Anna pulled a small notebook from her purse, wrote a name in the book, looked up and called out: "Mary? Of course you and Leon should've voted first."

Mary threw her head back, took a deep breath, and called out, "Death."

Leon, at the back of the room, didn't move from the door. He lifted his voice. It no longer quavered. "Death," he said.

To Louise: "Death."

Bella: "Death."

Anthony voted: "Death."

When Anna got to Gewel again, the girl sat as she was, with her head down. She looked around at the others. "I don't believe in killing."

"Will you stand with us tomorrow?" Mary asked.

Gewel nodded. "Of course. I'll always stand with our family."

There was a quiet knock at the door. Leon opened it a little, then more, and let a young woman, holding a smiling baby at her chest, into the room. Behind her was an older, squat woman with a flaming scar down one cheek.

Anna called out: "Nigel?"

"Death."

She looked over at the two newcomers.

She called, "Marya?"

The girl with the baby answered, "I can't do it. I vote we take him to the police."

Anna made a mark in her book and passed on.

"Inka?"

"Death."

"And I vote death," Anna said.

"And I, too," Bella said.

"I say we announce the verdict." Nigel walked over to take Aaron by the arm. "Would you stand next to me?"

Aaron pulled away. "If this is about things that happened at my schools—I had nothing to do with a murder. Nothing to do with any of it."

Sweat ran down the side of Aaron's face, giving him an almost green sheen. He gave a nervous laugh. "All I had was one innocent dalliance, maybe. That's all. An innocent dalliance. One of those rural girls who had no real reason to be where she was" He laughed. "That one was bound to end up in some two-bit town with a dozen kids."

He expected laughter. He got none.

"I heard something happened to her—that was after I was in California. Pregnant by someone, I heard, and then dead. It happens all the time in colleges across the country. There are girls, you know, who don't deserve a college education."

"Angela Lamb was our daughter." Mary Reid went to stand beside her husband, at the door.

A collective silence.

Betty stood, lifted her head, then pointed at Aaron. "Death," she said.

Aaron leaned forward. "You bastards," he swore, then turned from face to face. "You filthy bastards."

Bella stood. "You left the University of Michigan. You left your wife, who swore you were a killer, then you ran from another university after a girl was murdered there. On to the University of California. You don't have a job anymore, Aaron Kennedy. That's gone now. Netherworld was the perfect place to hide until you had a new plan."

He yelled at her, "A place to hide? Five days? You must be crazy, old lady."

"This last girl had pictures of you, didn't she?"

"You don't know what you're talking about."

"Death," Emily said.

Aaron threw his shoulders back, turned, and ran at Leon, striking him in the face, then pushing Mary out of his way.

He was gone.

No one but Zoe leaped up or made a sound.

No one spoke. Leon stood at the back of the room, a bloody handkerchief at his chin.

"What now?" Zoe finally asked, her voice stiff. They sat as they were, backs turned to her. "What's going to happen next?"

No one answered.

"Why am I here?" Zoe whispered.

Finally, Emily Brent said, "We told you, Zoe. Witness."

"To what?"

Emily shook her head. None of the others looked at her.

"This is your chance for redemption. Do what you have to do to protect us."

'Redeem myself?" Zoe eyes lasered on to Emily's. "You're not going to kill him, are you? Of course, I'll tell. And tell. And tell."

Emily's smile was faint, almost loving. "You won't."

One by one they left the room without looking back. Only Marya and her baby stayed behind.

"Zoe?" She came to stand nearby. "I added the black edge to your invitation. I didn't want you to know. And I was the one who threw a rock at you your first day here, when Louise and Anna took you back to the lodge. And I was outside your window, with my husband. I'm sorry. It's just that . . . nothing is fair here. I wanted you to leave."

Zoe couldn't talk to her. She had no interest. There was a single strange word spinning in her head: *Witness*.

Part 7

Thursday Morning

Chapter 55

It was early morning and very dark except for the rosy glow of streetlights in town. The night was warm, but always with a thin rush of cold coming in the window next to Jenny. No mosquitoes. No sound from the town. A cat crossed in front of them and disappeared behind a deserted mine building.

At least Lisa was with her—like their old days. Good to fall back into patterns of teasing and tormenting each other, if only for a few minutes at a time. Good to see how Lisa worked. Now another one of her odd stories was developing. But this time, a contract. There'd been a call from an agent. Maybe this was Lisa's breakthrough documentary. Maybe this whole "odd" time would pay off for her.

Jenny leaned back, stretching as far as she could extend her feet under the dash. It seemed only seconds afterward that there was a hand on her shoulder and a voice near her ear, whispering, "Jenny. We're here."

Startled, Jenny sat up, ready to fight the hand on her until she saw Tony's face in her open window. She reached up to grab his face and hold on until he took her hands in his and kissed them.

Behind him, Dora bent forward over Tony's shoulder. In her arms, Fida yipped and tried to get away.

Tony opened her door for her just as Lisa woke up and jumped out to come around the other side and hug their mother.

Everything in town was closed. There was no place to go to get caught up on what was going on.

"They're going to kill somebody." Jenny could barely get the words out.

"Kill who?"

"I don't know. Two women warned us. Zoe's with them, at Netherworld. They're stranded because of the rain. Zoe said, in the last phone call we got from her, that something's going on there. I believe Zoe when she says a thing like that. She's in trouble."

"Okay, okay," Tony said again and again as he caught the whole story. "So, you don't know exactly what's going on."

Lisa said, "I just . . . just know Zoe needs us."

"It's late." Tony took Jenny's hand. He looked at his watch. "Or early. I don't know which one to hope for. Should we try the local police?"

She squeezed his rough fingers—so good and tough. A workman's hand. She closed her eyes and allowed herself to take in the fact of Tony and what it meant to have him with her.

"Let's go find a cop," he said. "I think that's the best place to start. You drive, okay, Lisa? You know your way around here, I imagine. At least better than the rest of us."

"And tell us about the flood. How bad is it? I wish I had stopped her from coming up here." Dora was angry and sad at once. "And anything you're suspicious about. Just supposed to be an academic meeting, wasn't it? How'd Zoe get into so much trouble?"

* * *

At the red brick police station, Tony ran up the steps and wrote down some numbers.

Back in the car, he called out an address on Tenth Street to Lisa. "The deputy's at home."

"You call him?" she asked.

"Nope. We'll just show up. Can't see him refusing to take this seriously at nearly four o'clock in the morning."

*   *   *

The house on Tenth Street was large and white and square, like the others in town, only not made of red stone. They all got out to climb the steep front steps and stand in a group, waiting as Tony knocked at the door.

It took awhile.

"Should've called," Dora said, leaning toward Jenny.

When the door opened, a man's shaggy black head came around the inside door and looked at them one by one. Then back to Tony. "What the hell you want, this time o' the morning?"

"We've got to talk to you," Lisa said.

Tony pulled out his old badge and held it up for the man to see.

"That Detroit?" the man asked.

Tony nodded. "Something's going on out at Netherworld lodge. We've got to get there. Maybe a boat. Don't care how we do it. Just have to get there. A friend of ours is in trouble."

The man opened the door and stepped out to the porch, closing the inside door behind him.

He stood in front of them, sighed, and scratched at the back of his head.

"You see now, I can't do a thing about that. In the morning, I'll get right over there, see what's going on, but until then . . ." He looked directly at Tony. "Doesn't matter what department you're with, nor what city—I can't do a thing until it gets light."

"How about a boat?"

"You don't know floods, do you?" he said.

"I know what a cop is supposed to do."

"Really?" He looked over the end of his nose at Tony. "Then suppose you go and do that thing a cop's supposed to do when he's got a flood going on, and he's got no men left to do anything, and the real chief of police is out a town. Rescues are first. Sick people who have to get to a hospital are second. Somewhere after that come friends stuck in a big, safe building with people around her. Sorry."

He went back in the house and closed the door behind him.

Chapter 56

During the night, with the window open, Zoe heard their voices calling his name out in the woods. The sounds were lyrical, one bird calling to another and then to another. "Aaron. Aaron."

It went on until shortly after three o'clock. And then the voices stopped.

There was nothing but the sound of wind in the trees, a few night birds calling, the howl of a wolf or coyote not far off.

She sat at the window for hours, hoping not to hear something worse—a scream, yells of discovery.

There was nothing she could do. This was her family.

Witness!

She didn't believe it.

And Aaron Kennedy, out in the woods? Or back in his room, laughing at her with the others.

There was time to fill until morning. No place to go in the dark. No one to talk to.

She got her papers from the drawer and looked again at the lineup of names she'd been playing with—back and forth. Lines of letters, then rows of names.

Emily Brent
(or Susan Jokela)   E B

Anna Tow	A T
Louise Joiner	L J
Aaron Kennedy	A K
Leon Armstrong	L A
Nigel Pileser	N P
Gewel Sharp	G S
Anthony Gliese	A G
Mary Reid	M R
Betty Bertram	B B
Bella Webb	B W

She wrote down the first initals—*E A L A L N G A M B B*—and reworked them over and over. She knew the names were all false, but maybe there was a message.

Her mother, Evelyn, had loved her sister Susan. Susan Jokela Winton was Zoe's aunt. Zoe thought hard. Had her mom mentioned another name? There had to be a connection. Or why was she brought here? To witness what?

She bent so close to her computer, her nose was almost on the screen. The word *GAMBLE* leaped out. Nothing. Only Lamb.

Angela Lamb. The dead Angela. There all the time.

And Mary Lamb.

And Harvey Lamb

And the others?

"Mairzy doats and dozy doats and liddle lamzy divey." A mixed-up mess, nothing sounding as it should sound, but all the little Lambs were gathering.

Chapter 57

"Plan B," Tony growled, skipping down the porch steps.

"What's plan B, Tony?" Dora didn't sound as if she believed in a plan B.

"What now?" Jenny asked.

"We've got to get out there," Lisa said. "We don't know what's going on. We don't know if she's in danger from a flood or people."

"Only thing is to keep trying to call, Jenny."

"Sure," she said, though she knew there was no use. Zoe's cell phone and the lodge phone were both dead.

"You mind driving?" Tony asked Lisa. "You've been there. I'll be making wrong turn after wrong turn."

"I'm just worried about the water. If it's higher than before," Lisa said.

"Not raining," Tony said. "Now, tell me everything you know. Why're you this worried? What's happened?

Lisa drove down and out the same highway they'd taken before. She could see buildings she thought she recognized—hazy lights in front. It was that first back road that was hard to find.

In places the dirt road was flooded, but not so bad Lisa couldn't drive straight through.

It was the next turn they couldn't find.

One road, and then another, and then back to the first turn they'd taken. The GPS directed them to turn around. On the way back to where they'd been, Tony suddenly yelled, "Stop!"

He threw his door open and leaped out, turning to ask Lisa if she had a hitch.

After her quick "Sure," Tony was gone, running up the lawn of a house set back so far they could only see outlines of a building.

When he came back, he was dragging something big behind him, gesturing to Lisa to back up the driveway. When Jenny jumped out to see what was happening, he motioned her to get in the car.

"What are you doing?" she called to him.

"Stealing a boat!" he yelled back.

Back in the car, Jenny could feel the car move as Lisa and Tony got the boat hitched to the back. Dora kept turning around, asking Jenny what was going on as she held Fida so close that she yipped now and then. All Jenny could do was keep herself together and look over at Tony from time to time. Now they could all end up in jail for stealing a boat, but she wasn't afraid of anything.

Looking behind them, she saw lights come on in the house and then the outline of a figure standing in the doorway. She vaguely heard someone yelling.

Dora turned and rolled her eyes at Tony, who frowned at her.

"Can't get through a flood without something," he said.

"Looks like a pretty good motorboat," Lisa said. "I could use one. They had it for sale. Might have to buy it after this, but it's for a good cause."

"How do you know it's got gas in it?' Lisa looked through the rearview mirror at Tony.

"How was he going to sell the thing if he couldn't turn on the motor?"

The GPS told them again to take the next road. It was the right one. Jenny recognized the large swamp they'd passed before.

"Right here?" she called when Lisa, going very slow to try to keep out of the worst of the puddles and actual lakes of water rushing over the road, came even with the crooked sign on the fence announcing "Netherworld Lodge."

Chapter 58

When it was a gray first light; she could hear people still calling his name. When there was a knock on her door, Zoe was ready.

Gewel came in, dressed in jeans and a black sweatshirt, a black bandana wrapped over her hair. No makeup this morning. And nothing cute about her—not a smile, not cheerful eyes.

She stood at the bottom of the bed, her head bowed, hands folded in front of her.

"You have to come, you know."

"My ankle's killing me. I don't think I can walk."

Gewel took an arm and pulled her out of bed, Zoe fighting all the way, then fighting Gewel dressing her in a pair of jeans she found, and two sweatshirts, one with a hood.

"There," Gewel said. "You should be warm enough."

Zoe wrapped her arms around herself, shivering, and said nothing. *June.* She'd opened the window an hour ago. The air was close to icy.

As she pushed her feet into sneakers, tying them very slowly, she looked up at Gewel.

"You're Angela Lamb's sister, aren't you?" she asked, wanting to peel away the layers.

Gewel nodded, her bare face without expression.

"We've got to get going." She was irritated, motioning for Zoe to hurry.

"How many will die today?" Zoe stood and reached out for a sweater she'd packed at the last minute, then wrapped it around her neck.

"Come on, Zoe." Gewel was impatient.

"Did they find him?"

Gewel nodded. "He's being herded. He won't get away."

She followed Gewel downstairs to an empty reception room. It was as if no one had ever taken a breath in this room. Nothing but chairs and sofas, lamps and tables, and rugs and dust. Dust she hadn't noticed before. A staged room already neglected.

Gewel waited for her in the doorway, frowning, breathing fast. "Please . . ."

"Why me?" Zoe asked.

There were quick tears in Gewel's eyes. She put a hand out toward Zoe but abruptly turned and ran off the porch.

Zoe closed the door quietly behind her. Sometimes it seemed sinful to make noise. She felt that now: sinful, about to take part in something she didn't want to see or hear or be near. There hadn't been many times in her life in the last few years when she'd felt helpless and fought it. Now, here she was. To watch. To witness? What was she supposed to see?

Gewel didn't take the road back toward the entrance. She took the other one, the wet path that would lead by the cottage.

She put up a hand, standing very still to listen.

It came.

"Aaron!" a voice called and then an echoing voice came from the other side of the path, down a ravine.

"Aaron?" another voice called, off in front of them.

And then farther off, toward the river: "Aaron!"

The voices stopped.

They got to the cabin clearing. Leon, Mary, and Louise stood on the porch, waiting. Their faces were fixed, not friendly or unfriendly. They glanced at Zoe but concentrated on Gewel. They fell into step behind her.

Again, from a place ahead in the woods, someone called, "Aaron!"

Another voice called, farther away: "Aaron!"

Voices echoed from other parts of the woods, moving closer together each time they called.

Zoe covered her ears and kept walking.

A little farther along the path, two people she didn't know joined their march toward the river.

Betty and Anna joined the group next. They ignored her, walking side by side.

Zoe could hear the river.

There were more calls to Aaron. The sounds were narrowing. Anthony and Nigel stepped out of the woods and joined them. The walk was slow; large drops of water dripped from the trees. The cries among the firs and the wild call of the river kept getting closer.

Chapter 59

When Tony and the women got to the bridge, there was nothing but water flowing peacefully across what had been the road and a few boards floating where the bridge had been. And then the road on the other side, rising straight and dry.

"We'll take the boat." Tony was brisk, turning to the boat and trailer, then standing in water that lapped at his shoes. Together he and Lisa got the trailer down into the creek with Jenny's help.

Dora got in the boat, with Fida tucked under her arm. Lisa crawled in, over the side. Jenny and Tony got in last, with Tony getting her leg over the side, then dumping her into the bottom of the boat and climbing in after her.

She didn't say anything as she wiped blood off her face. Didn't even think about it. She took a seat across the middle and held on. Tony was praying—or swearing—out loud.

It wasn't a small boat, and the creek water wasn't wild, but they would run over new dark places they could hardly see until Jenny pulled out her cell phone and shone the light at the water ahead of them, all the way to the other bank.

The boat bounced. Jenny held on, riding the occasional wave until Tony pulled the rope on the motor.

He smiled as the motor caught on the second pull. "I was afraid it wouldn't work because I stole it," he said, grinning around at the others.

He revved the motor, then knocked it down and turned without incident toward the other side.

The creek fought them more than expected. It splashed over the side and into the boat. Tony kept the rudder straight. The opposite side was better though they were soaking wet by the time they dragged the boat up on shore and started along the road toward the lodge, Fida running beside them.

They hadn't gone far when Jenny stopped, tapping her ear, warning them to listen.

Far off, the sound weak, they heard people in the woods calling to one another.

"Someone's lost," she said, listening harder. "They weren't calling 'Zoe' were they?"

"Don't think so. Sounded more like Alan, or maybe Aaron. Like that. Zoe's more distinctive, I think." Dora listened harder.

Jenny put a finger in the air. "There it is again. Should we head that way?"

Tony didn't think long. "First the lodge. You said that's where they all stay. More likely to be there."

"But listen to those voices."

"Lodge first. We'll hunt those people down after we get Zoe."

He started up the road, Fida barking at his side.

For some reason, it didn't seem right to Jenny. The sounds came from the woods. Different voices at different times. Why would anyone be at the lodge?

They turned at the top of the road. Netherworld Lodge lay directly in front of them.

The long building was the same as it had been when Jenny had last been there. Nobody around now. Porch empty. Front door closed. The porch light was on, but in the growing dawn it hardly shone at all.

Jenny didn't bother knocking. She opened the door, leading the others straight in and across the reception room to the stairs. They stood at the bottom, looking up and hollering for Zoe. No one answered.

"Hey! Anybody here?" Tony called from behind them. "I'm coming up."

Tony took the stairs two at a time, noisy on the bare steps. Jenny heard him knock on door after door, the sound fading and then stronger as he checked the rooms along the front of the house.

"Nobody." He called to them. "Not one damned person anywhere."

He ran down the stairs.

"Any signs the people are still here? I mean suitcases, clothes, books?" Lisa asked.

He nodded. "Like everybody got up and left together."

"Maybe the voices in the woods," Dora said as she scooped Fida up into her arms.

"That's all we've got," he said.

Outside they heard the calling voices and started down a path going straight into the woods.

Running, stopping to listen, then running again; it was when they came on an empty cabin that the voices stopped. Almost magically.

The dark trees moved a little but barely made a sound.

Silence. No rustlings. No voices.

"Which way?" He looked into the woods.

Dora pointed ahead, leading beyond the cabin. "Just stick with the path. At least we'll be able to find our way out again."

Chapter 60

Aaron Kennedy stood on the high edge of the old pier jutting out above the water. Zoe could see him only from time to time, when the people blocking him parted. His arms were out straight at his sides, balancing himself. He was trying to stand at the edge as others—men and women—walked toward him one step at a time, testing the structure to see how many it would hold before crashing down to the river. The crowd of silent people watched Aaron as he tried to push beyond the group in front of him, then cried out for them to make way. "I'm leaving this place. And to think I came to add luster to your Agatha Christie event."

The pier moved a little, pilings creaking beneath. All the people held their breath until the pier settled into place.

Kennedy's eyes rounded with fear, but still he argued with the group. No one argued back or said a word. They advanced, only a step at a time, moving as if made of one body.

"This thing could go at any minute. If you'll just make way," he pleaded now, head to one side, hands out, begging for help, for the forgiveness it would take to get him off the high edge.

Someone's finger prodded his chest so that he leaned forward, arms cartwheeling, then reaching out to grab a handful of Anthony's shirt and having his hand forcefully knocked away.

"Zoe!" he screamed when he saw her through the crowd for just a minute. "Zoe Zola! Do you see what's going on here? These people are insane. Would you tell them—"

Nigel pushed Aaron again, but not too far. He stumbled, caught himself, and yelled. "Zoe—I think they want to kill me. Can you see what they're doing? You've got to do something about this. It's up to you. We need police. We need a sheriff. You've got to see the law is called." His voice broke with fear as the crowd moved forward another step, blocking him from her sight.

The sound of the river was muted by the bodies packed around her. She wanted to help him, but she was too small to push through. And if she did, would she go off the edge with him? Protecting what?

There was a sea of legs around her. She thought she might get through—an opening here and there—but they quickly tightened the spaces between them. They pushed her back until she couldn't see him anymore.

There was murmuring ahead. All the legs and bottoms surrounded her so she kicked as hard as she could, then bit until she heard Aaron calling out, his voice almost gone. "You're nothing but a pack of murderers." The voice cracked. "You think you're better than I am? Your girl was a tramp. Blaming me for someone else's bastard child! What did you expect a man to do?"

The people stopped moving, and then came a chant of "Angela. Angela. Angela."

Zoe got caught in the middle of a surge, people moving left and right. Her feet were trampled. She was in tears. The crowd of people dragged her along with them until they stopped.

The pier wasn't shaking.

Zoe could see Aaron again, tears running down his face. A hand out toward her.

The people closed in. There was a descending scream.

A splash and the screaming stopped.

There was only the sound of the water, growing as if it came alive.

Ding, ding, ding, ding, ding, ding, ding burst in her ears.

She watched as women and men formed a line down the center of the pier; one by one they walked forward until the pier began to shake again. Each person pulled a blue vial from a pocket and held it high. They waited their turn to stand above the river, to open their blue vial, and throw ashes into the wind.

"*Angela Evelyn Lamb, my child,*" Mary Lamb called out, swinging her arm around, the words flying off with the ashes.

Behind her: "*Angela, my daughter.*" Harley Lamb lifted his blue vial high and shook the ashes over the water.

Susan Jokela Winton. "*My beloved granddaughter.*"
Gewel Sharp. "*My beloved sister.*"
Anthony Gliese. "*My treasured sister-in-law.*"
Nigel Pileser. "*My dearest grandchild.*"
Bella Jokela. "*My beloved grandniece.*"
Anna Tow. "*My cousin.*"
Betty Bertram. "*My friend.*"
Louise Joiner. "*My student.*"

The ashes joined and flew into a spiral, then down to the water, where they floated and spread wider and wider until the river carried them around the bend, out to Lake Superior.

Soon there was nothing of the man, or the ashes, left behind.

Chapter 61

Tony, Jenny, Dora, and Lisa stood in the trees, with Fida at their feet. They saw some of what happened. They heard the words of a frantic man screaming at the group of people moving up the pier until there was nowhere left to go. They'd heard a chant, a scream, and then a splash into the water.

The retreating group parted around them. No one seemed surprise that they were there. No one did more than glance up as they passed.

Zoe almost walked on by until Fida went wild and jumped on her, knocking her over so that she got up with pain back in her ankle and Fida in her arms. She shook her head but had trouble getting words to come out.

Sensing the terrible thing that lay around all of them, Jenny took Zoe's hand and, with Tony walking in back, led the way toward the lodge to get Zoe's belongings and get away from there.

* * *

Jenny hastily stuffed things into the suitcase while Zoe stood outside the door, with Tony protecting her. They could hear voices of the others downstairs.

Jenny dragged the suitcase into the hall for Tony to carry. She went back for Zoe's stinky briefcase, her useless phone, and anything else she found that belonged to Zoe.

When they heard familiar voices in the reception room, Zoe pulled back.

"It's okay," Tony said. "They won't touch you."

She looked up at him, round blue eyes huge. "But I know what they did—everybody from this lodge, the women—their husbands.

"Does it matter, Zoe?"

She said nothing more until Jenny asked, "What was it, Zoe? That thing on the pier. We couldn't see."

"And didn't hear?"

"I heard a scream. And then a splash in the river."

Zoe held on to the stair rail and closed her eyes, only to hear the woman who called herself Emily Brent say her name from below.

"Are you all right, Zoe?" The woman's plain, upturned face twisted with concern. "It was terribly windy out there. For a moment, I thought we'd be blown down into the water. Our closing ceremony." She looked beyond Zoe, up at Tony and Jenny and Lisa.

"I have your check." She forced an envelope into Zoe's hand at the bottom of the stairs, but it dropped, falling where she stood, and stayed there as Zoe and the others walked toward the door.

Everybody but one from the event was there, gathered in the reception room. Aaron Kennedy was absent.

Gewel was dressed in her colorful clothes again, her curly blonde hair puffed up, with a blue ribbon tied through it. Beside her, her husband, Anthony—or whatever his real name was—smiled and said, "I'll be looking for your Agatha Christie book, Zoe. Can't wait to read it."

The others avoided her.

"Why was I here?" Zoe asked when she turned back to Emily.

"A witness. That's all, Zoe. Did any of us hurt Aaron?" she asked.

"You all did."

"No, Zoe." She smiled and shook her head. "Which one of us?"

"I saw. It was all of you."

"But which one? Who do you blame for what happened at the river?"

"No one."

"Yes. So, what can you tell the police?"

"Nothing."

Zoe breathed normally, almost smiled as she asked Emily a last question. "We weren't replaying *And Then There Were None*, were we? All along, not the Agatha Christie novel I thought. The disappearances were just a distraction."

Emily shook her head. Her face was sad.

"Murder on the Orient Express," Zoe said. "You're all killers."

"Or no one is." Emily smiled and turned away, motioning for the others to follow her out the door.

"What would you have done if it hadn't rained?" Zoe asked Emily Brent's back.

She turned. "We had a plan, but the storms were better."

"Why me?" Zoe called after her. "You don't even know me."

"Ask Mary," she called over her shoulder. 'She's gone to the cabin. You were her idea. Something you owed your mother."

Chapter 62

Mary Lamb stood on the porch of the cabin, waiting for Zoe.

"I'm glad you came," she said, motioning her into the house.

Zoe shook her head. She wasn't going in, nor staying long.

"You know we're related."

Zoe nodded, seeking anything in that face related to her. Maybe a bit of Evelyn. Maybe something of their grandmother. She couldn't know.

"This ends everything." Mary put her hand on Zoe's shoulder, only to have it shrugged off. "Our mothers family was a very strict one, Zoe. Our grandmother was a harridan. A harridan. She ruled the family. No indiscretion was overlooked. Except hers.

"There were whispers about our grandmother . . . a child born alive but soon found dead, a pillow over her face. I've heard many different stories . . ."

"Deformed?" A drawf?"

Mary took a deep breath. She shook her head. "My mother once told me the child had no limbs at all."

Zoe said nothing. She watched Mary's mouth, waiting for a single word that would make them sisters, or at least loving relatives. In the deep blue, down-turned eyes, in the lines carved from forehead to chin, Zoe saw the agony of suffering people. Three generations of her family.

"You did this for all of us and I'm grateful. Mostly for my Angela. The next generation, Zoe. You have to know the police couldn't prove it was Aaron, though everybody knew. He left Ann Arbor right after she went missing. They found things in Angela's room:. letters from a man signed with a large *A*. And a positive pregnancy test. Everybody knew who killed her, but the police wouldn't arrest him.

She clapped her hands. "Now we're even, Zoe. You've paid your mother's debt to the family. You'll be our witness, should the police come asking. We all, together, have avenged Angela. I'll make sure that the rest of the family gets the news. A healing has begun." She looked so happy.

"What debt?"

"Why," Mary said, rolling her eyes and rubbing her hands together, "I suppose you. The child."

"She didn't murder me."

"But back in my grandmother's day, what else could she do?"

"Love her baby."

"Aw, Zoe. You don't understand . . ."

'You're right," Zoe nodded. "Your mother—Susan—she never wrote or called Evelyn."

"Well, she couldn't, could she? The family would have done the same thing to her. That's why I left Cheboygan and came up here. I've made wonderful friends. Harley's Finnish too, believe it or not. Lamb's a Finnish name. When we began our plan, so many were excited to help. Like Marya, until she soured. I knew you were in Bear Falls. I knew that was where you lived. I knew a lot about you. It got me thinking. That we could be friends."

Zoe turned away and started up the path to where her real friends waited.

"Zoe!" Mary called after her from the porch. "We'll be in touch, won't we?"

Zoe walked on.

"We can be loving relatives now."

Zoe lifted her hand and waved without turning.

Chapter 63

They heard the voices before they reached the creek. The National Guard lined the banks, standing where trees were fallen to turn into logs and then into a bridge spanning just above the water. Men in uniform leaned on axes and roaring gas saws.

People behind the Guards waited for a rope railing to be attached to wooden blocks affixed to standing trees. Others waited on the shore, calling encouragement to the men.

Behind everyone else waiting to cross, Marya stood alone, holding Johnny close.

Finally, they were helped, one by one, across the makeshift bridge to where the cars waited. A boat trailer was pulled down into the river. No sign of the boat anywhere.

Zoe and Fida had their own Guardsman to take Zoe's arm and hold on during the walk across to stand with Tony and Jenny, Lisa, and Dora, all stopped by an officer talking seriously and pointing down the river.

The Guardsman turned to Zoe, with Fida growling. "You know anything about a boat and trailer found over here?" He watched Zoe's face. "Stolen not far away. Trailer left on this side of the creek, so someone must've headed to the other side. Boat's gone."

Zoe shook her head, frowning as if she were thinking hard about it.

"I saw the trailer when we got here." Lisa shook her head at the man. "Didn't see a boat though."

"I see you got a hitch on your truck," the man said. "State police are looking for a boat thief."

"I live up here. We're always needing to tow something or somebody, aren't we?" Lisa smiled.

The man nodded. "Right about that, ma'am. Must be somebody still over there. We'll get him. Any of you know anything about a drowned man found at the end of Dead Man's River, right where the river feeds into the lake? All hell seems to be breaking loose around this place."

No one answered him. He shrugged and walked away.

The five of them went together, Tony at one end, carrying Zoe's suitcase, Jenny beside him; Lisa at the other end, carrying the smelly briefcase, Dora beside her; with Zoe in the middle, carrying Fida.

Dora leaned down to Zoe's ear. "You'll always be our family, Zoe."

At the two cars, there was a time of decision.

"You know," Dora said. "I just might stay up here with Lisa for a while." She turned to Jenny. "You take care of the Little Libraries, okay? I just got designated Bear Falls' official librarian. Nobody can shut me down now."

Lisa hugged her. "Congratulations, Mom. I'd love to have you stay. For a minute I thought I was going to give up on the documentary. Too much high drama." She shrugged and toed the ground. "Now I see what I've been after all along. These are the truths about women's lives, beyond good and evil. It's not only about the outside. There's a different kind of justice hidden here. Stay. Help me find out what that is."

Dora took Zoe's hand in hers. "You stay too. You might find people you like among these women."

"Marya, for sure," Zoe agreed.

"Anyway, unlike Jenny, you're small." Lisa laughed. "You'll fit in the linen closet."

It was agreed: Zoe would stay in case she still had to speak to the police.

She was the witness.

She would tell them she saw nothing.

Later, she and Dora could drive Jenny's car home.

Before Jenny and Tony left, Dora hugged her child, then slipped a handkerchief into her hand.

Jenny didn't need to be told what Dora gave her. She opened the lacy handkerchief and slipped the ring back on her finger.

She stared down at it, wondering what she could say to Tony. He put his hand on hers, folding his fingers, one by one, over hers. "Don't worry," he said, leaning toward her, his scarred face warm. "When you're ready, Jenny. Only when you're ready. There'll be mums other autumns."

"Or roses," she said. "I think I'd like roses."

* * *

In the backseat of Lisa's Jeep, safe with Dora and Fida, Zoe fixed in her mind what she would do when she got back home. There was a trip to a cemetery in Detroit to make, to Evelyn's grave. She would kneel beside Evelyn's stone and whisper that Anas Jokela's sin, the murder of her baby, was open to the light. Then she would whisper to Evelyn that the last sin against the women of their family had been washed away in a raging river.

The slate was clean.

She would whisper to Evelyn: *Justice for us, Mom.*